Love Along the Esplanade

By Sarah E Stewart

Copyright © 2019 Sarah E Stewart
All rights reserved.

ISBN: 9781091278752

To Tricia, thank you for being such an amazing friend for nearly forty years!

Special thanks to Cate Hogan!

Cover Design by Chris Whiton/ White Mountain Images

Thank you Tracey, Jess, Sarah, Delphine, Diana and my husband Brian for reading drafts!

Table of Contents

Part 1: Much Ado
1. Ty Kent is Trending — 2
2. Interviews, Lectures, and a Handsome Stranger — 17
3. A Fellow Runner — 30
4. It's All About the Scoop — 36
5. Is It a Date? — 42
6. Drinks and a Dinner: Together yet Separate — 46
7. Sunday Fun Day — 53
8. Everyday Challenges — 62
9. Back to Reality — 68
10. Party Planning — 74
11. Assumptions and Corrections — 79

Part 2: Never a Dull Lull
12: And So It Begins — 86
13: A True First Date — 95
14: Brunch and a Blog — 98
15: A Mid-Week Rendezvous — 104
16: The Gender Discovery — 111
17: Cooking for Two — 116
18: Blogs and Spies — 127
19: A Dessert Bake Off — 138
20: A Relationship Exposed — 147
21: Flowers and a Thank You — 156

Part 3: A Word from Ty Kent
22: Everyone is Scheming — 164
23: The Power Shift — 175
24: One Step Closer — 184
25: Surprises — 191
26: Fair Warning — 202
27: A Picture Does Not Lie — 216
28: A Quest for Redemption — 220

29: A Book Launch Party 235

Part 1:
Much Ado

1
Ty Kent is Trending

"Can you believe this?" Sydney says as she throws the Boston Globe across the table at her friends. "This is all anyone is talking about, it's all over the morning news, and it's on the front cover of the Sunday Globe. This is absurd."

"Well, it's clearly a slow news cycle." Michelle responds.

"Who is Ty Kent?" Jordan reads the headline of the Boston Globe.

Neither Sydney nor Michelle respond.

"No, really, who is Ty Kent?" Jordan asks again.

"That's the point. No one knows." Michelle says.

"But, why would anyone care?" Jordan presses deeper.

"Seriously?" Sydney asks.

"Seriously."

Michelle grabs the front page of the Boston Globe. "Ty Kent is the pen name of an author who writes romance novels. He has written a lot of books. He's like the James Bond of romance novelists. Well, assuming he is a he. But everyone thinks he's a man, mostly because everyone wants him to be a man. Everyone wants to believe there is a man out there who could write this."

"Um, wow, should I be worried?"

Michelle rolls her eyes.

"I believe the correct term is fairy tales." Sydney interjects. "He writes fairy tales about romance that no one and no relationship can ever live up to."

Michelle gives Sydney a sideways glance. "Ironic, those

words coming from a relationship coach." She turns her head back to Jordan. "Anyway, this person, no one knows who he or she may be, but Kent has written tons of books and has a huge following."

"Huh, so if he has been writing for a long time, why is everyone so curious now?" Jordan asks.

"Well, again, this Kent person has a huge following especially among women. His books are all over the most popular blogs. Finally, someone just wanted to know who this Kent person is and set up a challenge. The first person to reveal the true identity of Kent will get $50,000." Michelle explains.

"$50,000!" Jordan's eyes nearly pop out of his head.

"Yes, $50,000." Sydney responds in disgust. "But, it's not just any one, it's Harris."

"Harris? As in the owner of the Insightful Blogger and your boyfriend's boss?" Jordan asks.

"The one and only." Sydney quips.

"So what does Ben have to say about all of this?" Michelle inquires.

"Honestly, he thinks it's just another one of Harris's publicity stunts that will blow over in no time."

"I don't think $50,000, is just going to blow over." Jordan says shaking his head.

"How are you and Ben doing?" Michelle asks.

"Fine."

"Fine?" Michelle repeats while shooting Jordan a smirk.

"Yes." Sydney states boldly. "Fine is good. We are grounded. We communicate. What?" She asks responding to the curious looks on her friends' faces.

Jordan shrugs his shoulders. "Nothing, you're the relationship coach and blogger."

"YouTube star and novelist." Michelle chimes in.

"I'm not a novelist. I'm an author of a self-help book. Which by the way, is based on real life. I'm teaching people to have real expectations about love and what it really takes to be in a relationship."

Neither Jordan nor Michelle responds to her. They quietly focus on the plates of food in front of them.

"What?" Sydney demands.

"Well, I mean come on Sydney. You're a relationship coach and expert, but your romance with Ben, well…" Michelle hesitates.

"Well what?"

"It's just, how do I say it." Michelle struggles to articulate her thoughts.

"Boring." Jordan chimes in.

"That's it." Michelle snaps her fingers at Jordan's response.

"That's reality. Relationships are not all rainbows and unicorns." Sydney defends.

"You are my rainbow." Jordan says as he looks at Michelle.

"And you're my unicorn." Michelle says while smiling back at Jordan.

Sydney rolls her eyes. "Enough. Okay, you two are the anomaly. I admit. But most of us feel fortunate enough to enjoy dinners and great conversations with someone who shares our common interests. As a matter of fact, Ben and I will be doing just that this evening, and I can't wait. Now, moving on. I have to run. I have clients this afternoon and the next two weeks are packed full with interviews. Oh and please, please do not forget the book release party Thursday, October 18th, a mere five weeks away. I need both of you there."

"We wouldn't miss it." Michelle reassures Sydney.

"It's Sunday. Why do you have clients on Sunday?" Jordan asks perplexed.

"Because Sunday is a big day after a weekend of dating."

"Ah, good point."

"Jordan, after ten years of knowing Sydney and having

brunch together almost every week, how do you not know she has clients on Sunday?"

"Well, because while you two are talking, I'm reading the sports section. Don't hate on me Michelle, just manage your expectations of me." Jordan says proudly. "See, I pay attention sometimes!"

Sydney laughs at his comments as she stands up. She gives both Jordan and Michelle cheek kisses as she leaves. She steps out onto a bustling Newbury Street. As she inhales the fresh September air she reaches for her sunglasses to temper the mid morning sun. She saunters up the street trying to physically slow down the thoughts racing through her head. *Why does Ty Kent have to be a big deal now? Why when my book is about to come out, does this have to take center stage? Why can't people just let him remain anonymous?*

Sydney keeps walking. She decides to postpone her duties, writing her daily blog post and prepping for her afternoon clients; instead, she heads to the Common to clear her mind.

Sydney strolls through Boston's Public Garden admiring the trees. She notices a smattering of red and orange leaves. Even though it's nearing the end of September, it has been warm so the vibrant autumn colors that New England is famous for, have yet to pop. She exits the Garden and stops at the crosswalk on Charles Street focusing on the light that lets her know it is okay to cross. The light signals her to walk but she still looks before she crosses, it is Boston after all. As she passes by the stand selling all things Boston, she notices all of the dogs racing across the Common catching balls and frisbees. She would love to have a dog, if only she had the time to devote to one. She continues to stroll up the walkway mesmerized by the leaping fur balls fetching and catching.

"Hey, look out!"

Sydney hears this and turns quickly to see an out of control skateboarder coming right at her. She leaps to the side and falls flat on her back, as she hears the balls of the skateboard speeding along the pavement. She sits up on the grass thankful to be in one piece.

"Are you alright?"

Sydney looks up. The sun is glaring into her eyes. Even with her sunglasses all she can see is a very tall shadow reaching out a hand.

"Hey," he says, "are you okay?"

Sydney reaches up and grabs the very tanned hand extended to her.

"Yes, I am. Thank you." She replies as she brushes off grass and dirt.

"That guy was out of control!"

Sydney still struggles to see the face of this tall stranger. By his outfit, she can see he's obviously a runner. He seems to have pulled one ear bud out of his ear and she notices an IPod strapped to his muscular arm. She tries to see his face but all she can see is a thick head of dark hair and a jawline that resembles Superman.

"So, you're good?"

"Thank you again. Yes, I'm fine." Sydney feels herself shrink as she says the word "fine".

"Good. Well, watch out for crazy skateboarders. Enjoy your day."

And he was off. Sydney watches as his tall, broad-shouldered body ran away. *Okay, that's enough of the Common for one day.* Sydney thinks to herself as she turns around to head back home.

After arriving home, Sydney changes out of her dirt and grass stained clothes. She grabs some lemon water and her laptop and heads up to her top floor terrace. She steps out and takes in the tranquil view; she can just barely see the Charles River. She plops down on her chaise and begins to read through her email looking for any topics her readers would like her to blog about. After reading her fifteenth email Sydney leans back in defeat. All anyone seems to want are her thoughts on the mysterious Ty Kent.

Sydney ponders her topic for some time. Fall is Sydney's favorite time of the year. It has always reminded her of fresh starts. When she was a kid she always looked forward to the new school year starting, which also meant some new clothes and untouched notebooks.
Sydney smiles as her blog starts to come together in her mind.

Blog Post #520: September is My Tabula Rasa

Up until five minutes ago, I had no idea what tabula rasa meant. Tabula rasa is a Latin term for scraped tablet. According to dictionary.com it also means: *1. A mind not yet affected by experiences, impressions, etc. 2. Anything existing undisturbed in its original pure state.*

Tabula rasa sounds much sexier than clean slate! Am I right?

To me, September has always felt like a month of new beginnings. The combination of the air feeling a little cooler and drier, all of those years of school beginning in September, and my birthday being in September probably accounts for that fresh start feeling. Now after 30-something years, I'm not sure I could ever bring my mind or body to its original pure state. (College parties, baby oil and a tar roof, the damage is done).

Honestly, I don't want a perfectly clean slate. Life is about experiences and those experiences, although not all favorable and some regrettable, have certainly brought me to right here, right now, right where I'm supposed to be. So how do I get my tabula rasa?

I envision it to be just like when I was a kid and got my brand new school notebook. So that's what I do. I get a brand new notebook, my tabula rasa, and it's empty and clean. I like to keep things simple so mine is a two subject, one side for personal and one side for professional. I look at this empty notebook and think, I can do anything. What is it going to be?

I write down my professional and personal goals and ideas. Some are crazy and lofty, but that's okay. That's what a clean slate is all about, possibilities.

I look at last year's notebook and take things that I want to keep doing or enhance and add those items to my lists. Everything else, well, that stuff just stays in the old notebook. Why would I want to mess up my tabula rasa with crap from the past?

When do you begin your tabula rasa? At the beginning of a new season? New Year? On a birthday? Even if you've had a difficult year, looking at a blank piece of paper, imagining that anything is possible and writing it down can do wonders.

Okay my wonderful readers! Grab your notebooks and start writing down your goals. The sky is the limit and anything is possible!

To your success in love and life,
Sydney

. . .

Insightful Blog Headquarters

Ben sits at his desk, flipping page after page of Ty Kent's latest novel, <u>Paper Cuts.</u>

"Come in." Ben responds to the knock on his door without lifting his head from the book.

"Hey, Benjamin, what are you doing here on a Sunday?"

"Hey Harris." Ben says as he stands up to shake the hand of his twenty-two year old boss. "My roommate has family in town this weekend and I needed a little peace and quiet."

"Got it. And doing a little reading I see."

"Yes. This Kent person is actually a great writer."

"Indeed. Did you see the front page of The Globe this morning?"

"I did Harris. Quite the buzz you have started."

"Thank you Benjamin. So I was thinking, your girlfriend, she is a relationship expert right?"

"Yeah," Ben responds hesitantly. "She's a relationship coach and blogger."

"She has a very popular YouTube channel and she has a new book out right?"

"Yes, well it debuts in about five weeks."

"Do you think you could interview her on her thoughts about Ty Kent? I mean, that seems like it would be one interesting read as she is the complete opposite of this Kent person."

"I'll see what I can do."

"Great! Thank you Benjamin." Harris says as he excitedly exits Ben's office.

Ben puts his head down on his desk and wonders what he's doing. He is thirty-four and works for a blog company started by a twenty-two year old rich kid who is only interested in getting the scoop and printing it first regardless of consequences.

Twelve years ago, when Ben graduated from college with his degree in journalism, working for a gossipy blog was not at all on his radar. Yet, here he is. And now it gets worse. His boss wants him to get thoughts from Sydney, the pragmatic relationship coach, who is also Ben's girlfriend. The last thing Sydney will want is to be quoted on the Insightful Blogger.

Ben picks up the book that is resting on his desk. He is so enthralled by the stories that Ty Kent tells. He wonders about he and Sydney's relationship. It's solid and predictable. It's dependable. It's passionless. Ben sighs. He wants passion. He wants energy and adventure. He wants what Ty Kent describes in his books. He wonders if he and Syd could ever turn their bland relationship into one full of zest and romance.

A Realistic Dinner

Sydney takes one last look in the mirror before heading out to meet Ben for dinner. Her hair is pulled back in a sleek ponytail. She admires her recently purchased new dress. It's a vibrant red sleeveless dress that is snug at the top and flares out a bit below the waist. She does a quick twirl, as she loves seeing the skirt puff out. *This dress is certainly not boring.* She grabs her jacket, purse, and keys and heads out the door.

As she walks up to Newbury Street, Sydney is plagued by comments made earlier in the day by Michelle and Jordan that her relationship with Ben is boring. She wonders if maybe they're right.

Perhaps they are too regimented, too stuck in their ways. However, they're both very busy people and are practical with the time that they have. She thinks about suggesting a trip together at the end of October, when things slow down. Maybe a nice romantic cabin in the mountains, but then she remembers that Ben is not a fan of the woods. Perhaps a trip to Vermont would be a better idea. She could find a cute town with a harvest festival or something.

Sydney was so lost in her thoughts about a romantic get away she walks right passed the restaurant. She quickly turns and walks by all of the outdoor tables without a glance. Sydney knows there is no way Ben would sit at an outside table. He finds it odd to have people walking by you as you enjoy a meal. He doesn't like the idea of being on display and having people stare at what he's eating. And sure enough, as Sydney walks into the restaurant she spots Ben at their usual back table for two. She smiles at the hostess as she heads to the table.

"Sydney." Ben stands up as he sees her approach and gives her a kiss on the cheek as he pulls out her chair.

Not boring at all. Sydney thinks to herself. *This is called lovely and respectful.*

"I went ahead and ordered us a few appetizers."

"Great thank you."

"May I get you something to drink Miss?" The server asks Sydney.

"I will have a glass of cabernet please."

Sydney turns to Ben. "How was your week?"

"Well, it was interesting. I'm sure you have heard about all of the hubbub Harris started."

"Yes." She says while rolling her eyes.

"Well, I've actually been reading his books."

"You have?" She replies unsure of whether she is shocked, offended, or interested.

"Yes, well, I mean I have to know who and what I'm writing about."

"Did you say books? How many have you read?"

"Well," Ben starts sheepishly, "I'm on my third, <u>Paper Cuts</u>."

"That hasn't even been released yet."

"Well, Harris has his ways of getting things early."

The server brings over Sydney's wine. She thanks the server, picks up her glass and raises it to Ben and says, "cheers". She takes a big sip before Ben can even respond.

"So, what do you think of Ty Kent's books?"

"Honestly, I really like them."

Sydney is trying to contain her shock. "You do?"

"Yes, sorry, I guess I'm a romantic."

"Well, Ben, I think there's a difference between being romantic and actually believing the fairy tales that are being told in these books. I mean you can be romantic and still have your feet on the ground."

"I don't know. Being romantic, having a nice dinner by candlelight or something, there's more to it than that. I'm not sure how to say this."

"What are you talking about?"

"I'm talking about the energy you feel when you get

swept off your feet. I'm talking about a wonderful love story not just a romantic gesture here and there."

"But, I thought you and I were based in reality. Those novels are just stories."

"Sydney, I'm not sure what to say. I'm sorry, but that's what I want."

Sydney tilts her head confused. "What do you mean?"

"I'm saying I want to be swept off my feet. I want to feel that exhilaration, the passion. I want to experience what is being described in the novels."

Sydney sits back in her chair. "Are you breaking up with me?"

"Yeah, Sydney, I guess I am. I'm sorry I want the romantic fairy tale." He says as he shrugs his shoulders.

Sydney takes a deep breath and nods her head. "Okay. Well, I wish you luck. And um, I'm going to go now."

Ben stands up as Sydney does. She waves her hand at him signaling him to take his seat. She picks up her purse and walks out the door.

Stunned, she walks down Dartmouth Street trying to reconcile the fact that Ben just broke up with her because he started reading romance novels. That is more ridiculous than the romance novels themselves. And she was the one who was going to ask for a romantic get away. She is all about romance. But a relationship is not always romantic. *Why do people buy into this?* She wonders. Sydney pulls out her phone and calls Michelle.

"Hey Sydney, what's going on?"

"You're not going to believe this but Ben just broke up with me."

"What? He broke up with you?" Michelle screeches through the phone.

"Yep. He says he wants the whole romantic package."

"Oh my gosh. I can't believe he wants romance. And he broke up with you! Sydney, Jordan and I are just hanging out watching a movie. Come over."

"No, thank you. I don't think I would be very good company tonight and definitely not in the mood for a romantic comedy."

"Are you sure? It's not! It's a mystery and we have ice cream."

Sydney chuckles. "No, thank you though. I'm just going to go home and lick my wounds. I think I have enough mystery in my life right now."

"Okay, well we are here if you need us. Call me tomorrow and good luck with everything."

"Thanks Michelle. I will."

Sydney walks into her apartment, heads up one flight of stairs and flops on the couch. She wonders how all of this can be happening. She is the relationship coach who focuses on centering all of her clients in reality. Her book is about to come out and yet she just got dumped.

The funny thing is she's not even that sad. She's shocked, but also relieved. Michelle and Jordan were right their relationship was boring; so utterly boring. Sydney is most concerned with facing her upcoming events alone. And now she doesn't even have a date for her own book launch party. Sydney lets out a moan.

. . .

Michelle hangs up the phone and looks at Jordan with a sad face. "I can't believe Ben broke up with Syd."

"I know!" Jordan responds.

"And he wants more romance!"

"Well, that part I get."

"True, but poor Syd."

"There's nothing poor about Syd, Michelle."

"What?" Michelle asks as she watches Jordan cock his head and wave his finger in the air like he's on to something.

Jordan stands up and starts pacing around the living room. "How many clients does Syd have each week?"

Michelle shrugs her shoulders, "I don't know. She says she never likes to have more than eight clients at a time."

"Eight clients at a time, that's it?"

"Well, she has everything else going on, her blog, her YouTube channel and she did just write a book."

"Okay." He pulls his phone out of his pocket. "Eight clients at… wait what does she charge?"

"She charges monthly, $2000 per month." Michelle says. She sits up on the couch, as she begins to get excited by Jordan's antics.

"So eight clients at $2000 per month that is $16,000 per month. Now we both know how much she likes to travel and she is gone about eight weeks a year?" Jordan looks to Michelle for confirmation.

She nods excitedly.

"So that puts her annual gross income at about $160,000.00."

"Well, plus she has the advertisers on her blog and YouTube channel."

"Oh right, what do you think that is?"

"Well, she said once that she makes as much from advertisers as she does coaching."

"Wow, really? Go Syd. Okay, so she makes 160,000 from advertisements. That puts her at a gross of $320,000.00 per year."

"Damn, she makes a fortune!"

"Not really Michelle. She has her own business. She has to pay both sides of payroll tax up to $133,000. So that is $22,000 plus another $10,000 for Medicare. She now is down to $288,000. If she puts in the full allowable amount into her 401K, we subtract $56,000. And let's say she has about another $50,000 for business expenses and health insurance, that puts her gross at $182,000.00 per year, minus federal and state tax, I estimate she nets about $134,000 per year."

Michelle looks at her husband in awe. "You're so sexy when you start speaking in numbers!"

Jordan gives her a smile, raises his eyebrows, leans over and gives her a kiss. "Stay with me baby, I'm just getting to the good part."

Jordan backs away from Michelle, closes his eyes, and raises his hands in the air for his grand announcement. "How does someone who earns $11,083 per month even afford the taxes on her property, that was just assessed for seven million dollars? I mean, think about it, her property taxes are probably $70,000 per year!"

Michelle just stares at Jordan.

"Michelle!" He yells trying to get her excited about his soon to be revealed hypothesis. "She has to have another source of income. There is no way she could afford to live where she does making what she makes."

Michelle continues to just stare blankly at Jordan.

"Another source of income. What if she, Sydney, our Sydney, is Ty Kent?" Jordan takes a bow as he waits for his wife's reaction.

"Baby, well done." She says as she claps her hands for his performance.

Jordan looks up from his bow and asks, "So you agree with me?"

"No."

"What? Why not, baby you have to look at the evidence I just presented, she has to have another source of income."

"Jordan, I love you. You're an amazing accountant, but a lousy sleuth. First of all, we've known Syd for ten years. Have you ever seen one romantic bone in her body?"

"No, but this is about the numbers babe, they don't add up."

"Right. However, she bought that place ten years ago for a steal when the market crashed; and she has done a lot of work over time."

"Yes, but I'm saying she can't even afford the taxes on it now." Jordan says as he desperately tries to defend his fading hypothesis.

"Jordan, when her parents died, they left to her a huge trust fund."

He flops on the couch next to Michelle. "Darn it. I forgot about the trust fund."

Michelle rubs her husbands head and gives him a kiss. "It was a great performance babe. A plus hot."

Jordan looks up at Michelle, "really, how hot?"

Michelle smiles. "Super hot!" She whispers as she clicks the remote and turns the movie back on.

2
Interviews, Lectures, and a Handsome Stranger

Sydney steps into the crowded coffee shop on Newbury Street and quickly begins to scan the room.

"Syd!"

Sydney hears her name and looks to her left to see her publicist Maryann sitting at a table with two coffees in front of her.

"Good morning Maryann."

"Hey Sydney, great to see you." Maryann says as she stands to give Sydney a hug.

"I grabbed you a coffee, I wasn't sure about food."

"No, this is all I need thanks."

"You look fabulous! Are you ready for these crazy weeks?"

"Thank you. Well, ready or not here they are."

"True. Now let's go over the schedule. We need to be at the Boston Harbor Hotel by nine-thirty this morning. We are doing a live spot on Good Morning Boston at ten o'clock. Next we head down the hall and are having a private meet and greet with some key local book club members who are also loyal readers of your blog and YouTube subscribers. At one in the afternoon, we have a question and answer session with local press and bloggers at The Book Bag, everyone's favorite bookstore. Lastly, we have one hundred people attending your lecture, *Managing Your Love Expectations.*" Maryann pauses and looks up at Sydney. "Do you want to hear the rest of the week?"

"No, thank you, let's take it one crazy day at a time."

"Okay, now before we jump into the car, we need to discuss your responses to a few things."

"Like what?"

"Well, more than likely you will be asked your thoughts on the Ty Kent issue. All of the authors are getting asked about that right now."

Sydney rolls her eyes. "I don't have any thoughts Maryann. For all I know Ty Kent isn't just one person, maybe it's a group of people with some great imaginations."

"Sydney, that's brilliant."

"What?"

"No, that's perfect. No one has even hinted at the angle. That's exactly what you need to say; of course we need to work on softening the delivery. Perhaps a little less sarcasm in your voice and a little more, I don't know, a more sinister tone that will lead people to believe you may be on to something. I can see the headlines now, 'Best- selling author Sydney Graham suggests Ty Kent may be a group of people not just an individual.'"

"Whoa, slow down Maryann. First of all, I'm not a best- selling author. Second, I'm not buying into this. I don't want to be tied to this circus."

"You'll be a best-selling author and why not?"

"Because it's crazy. Maryann, there are real things going on in this world. This Kent thing is just a bunch of nonsense. And obviously this person uses a pen name for a reason. We need to respect the privacy of this individual or group of individuals."

"You're right, there are many important things going on. That's exactly why this is taking on a life of its' own. It's a wanted, fluffy distraction. It's the reason why people read fiction. They need an escape. They need fun. What's the harm in joining in on the fun? And quite frankly, you could use a little." Maryann says as she pulls out her laptop.

"What are you doing?"

"Selling out your book tour! Now start giving me some good quotes."

Sydney sips her coffee. This whole situation has been annoying her so much and now she is about to put herself smack dab in the middle of it. Sydney is torn. She knows Maryann is right. This will bring larger crowds to her book events. And moreover she does need some fun in her life. She always over-thinks things. Maybe she should just go with the flow and enjoy the ride. But she has an uneasy feeling about it. Sydney knows this could all go very wrong.

"Earth to Syd." Maryann says as she snaps her fingers in front of Sydney. "What's the problem?"

"I don't know Maryann, something just makes me uncomfortable about this whole thing. It just doesn't feel right."

"They're called stunts for a reason. This is public relations, plain and simple. You didn't cause this ruckus, but you may as well get some benefit from it."

"Okay, I'm in." She says hesitantly.

"That's my girl."

Boston Harbor Hotel

Sydney is a bit nervous for the first book signing with the book club members. Even though these are invited guests she has a nagging fear of walking into a room and having it be empty. She enters the conference room and is relieved to see fifty or so women who are chatting, drinking coffee, and noshing on the various calorie-laden treats. The chairs are set up in rows facing a podium at the front of the room. Maryann is already in the room ushering people to their seats.

Maryann gives Sydney a lovely introduction and Sydney is greeted with applause as she walks up to the podium. She begins by thanking everyone for taking time out of their busy lives to come and be here with her.
"Book clubs are the new book stores. It used to be that

authors could release their books and rely on the bookstore foot traffic to help with sales. Now, with so many people being able to buy just about anything from the comfort of their living rooms, book clubs are vital to authors. And I can't thank you all enough for being such loyal readers of my blog and subscribers to my YouTube channel. I appreciate each and every one of you and I do hope you enjoy this self-help book."

    Knowing she was on a tight timetable before her next event, Sydney reads a brief yet powerful excerpt from her book. Upon finishing she is met with a round of applause and an almost instant line of women waiting to have their book signed. This is what makes everything worth it for Sydney, meeting the real people who read what she writes.

    Sydney sits back in her chair and rubs her tired hand as she watches the last of the attendees exit the conference room. Maryann suddenly appears with two plates of food and plops down next to Sydney.

    "We have twenty minutes before we leave for The Book Bag, so eat quickly."

    "Thank you. I'm starving."

    "So that press release I sent out." Maryann starts.

    "Yes."

    "Well, just so you are prepared, there is a moderately sized crowd outside of The Book Bag."

    "Why are they outside?"

    "Because the inside is sold out."

    "What?"

    "Yep. I'm loving me some Ty Kent."

    Sydney sinks into her chair as dread washes over her.

. . .

    Her eyes widen as their car pulls up in front of The Book Bag. "Is this what you call moderate, Maryann?" She asks as she slides down the car seat to shield herself from the mass of people and cameras that swarm around the car.

"Just stay in the car until I come around, but be ready to push. This is good Syd. This is press for your book, just remember that."

Maryann steps out of the car and fights off the swarm of cameras and people shoving microphones in her face. The response is even more than she expected. She pushes her way through the crowd to get to the other side of the car. In one fell swoop, Maryann opens the car door, yanks Syd out, and rushes her inside. Once inside an employee quickly leads them to a back room. The room is small but has two leather chairs, and a coffee table hosting some waters, coffee, flowers, and a fruit and cheese platter. The employee informs Syd and Maryann that the venue is packed and that someone will come to get them in about fifteen minutes. She asks if there is anything else they may need before leaving the room.

"My goodness!" Sydney proclaims once they are safely alone. "That's crazy. Do you think they will be out there when we leave?"

"Probably." Maryann replies rather nonchalantly as she scrolls through the emails on her phone.

"This is all because of a press release you sent out like, what, three hours ago?"

"It is. Look Syd, this is huge and we are just jumping on some media buzz. Plus, these days, every other person is trying to start a blog or podcast. So half of the people out there are amateurs trying to get some momentum behind their stuff. I know this is about your book but there are also real reporters inside. You are going to be asked questions about your thoughts that Ty Kent is perhaps a pen name for a group of people. Are you ready to answer those questions?"

Sydney rolls her eyes. "Do I have to?"

"Yes, Syd, you do. To be honest, this venue had fifteen people signed up as of seven this morning. It's now sold out, as in 150 people are in that room."

"Gosh, Maryann."

"It is a different age. People do everything on line. Your dedicated followers were there this morning and we have some of those along the way, but what we need are more readers, more people to know who you are. It's hard to create buzz about yet another self-help relationship book, but we can create buzz about you. They start reading your blog, watching your videos, and then make a purchase."

"But it's not about me it is about some other person."

"Well, technically, according to you it might be about a group of people, remember, that's your spin on things. Now can you do this? Can you come up with some legit, believable, not sarcastic comments about what leads you to believe this?"

"Maryann, I'm a relationship coach who just wrote a self help book. Reality is the whole basis of my work, my blog, videos, and my book. I can't just make stuff up."

"I know. But today I really need you to try. Shall we role play?"

Sydney pauses for a moment. "No, I just need to sit with this in silence."

Although the room is quiet, Sydney's head is filled with noisy thoughts, as if she was live-streaming six movies at once. She understands she needs this publicity to sell more books. Yet, she feels like a fake for jumping on the coattails of Harris's publicity stunt. She is now in the center of a mystery that she did not create. How does she do this and maintain her personal and professional integrity? How does she do this and prevent it from blowing up in her face, or worse, how does she prevent herself from blowing up in the face of someone else?

Should she be honest? Should she just say how she feels or what she knows to be true? If she does, so early on in the book tour, will the rest of the rooms she is about to face over the next few weeks be empty? She knows that Maryann is correct, she needs more people to sell her book. *But this could go so very wrong.* Syd buries her face in her hands as she tries to sort through what to do in five minutes and counting.

The door swings open, "they're ready for you!" Announces some person Sydney will probably never see again.

"Thank you, we will be right out." Maryann calmly replies. She turns to Syd and just nods.

Sydney's eyes scan the room as Maryann takes the stage and gives Sydney the brilliant and wonderful introduction. She actually doesn't hear a word Maryann is saying she just assumes what it is. She's too caught up in her own thoughts. And even though Sydney is not paying attention, on cue, she hears her name, applause, and walks on the stage.

She gets up to the microphone; she's still on autopilot. She smiles brightly and begins her program. She thanks everyone for coming, she throws out some interesting angles that the book presents to its readers and goes on to read a brief excerpt. When she's finished she is rewarded with a round of applause. Maryann then comes onto the stage and asks the audience if there are any questions pertaining to Sydney's new book. Sydney's waits patiently. Not one hand is raised. Her eyes drift from one side of the room to the other. She notices a tall man standing in the back of the room. He is leaning against the wall. He's wearing a grayish colored tee shirt and his hands are shoved into the pockets of his jeans. He's both strikingly handsome and oddly familiar. Sydney wonders if she's attracted to his appearance or his seemingly lack of interest.

"Other questions?" Maryann's voice snaps Sydney's attention away from the mystery man.

And it begins. "Sydney, have you read Ty Kent's books?"

"I have."

"Sydney, how many have you read?"

"A few."

"Sydney do you like his books?"

"I didn't realize Ty Kent was a man."

The room chuckles at Sydney's quip. She begins to relax a bit, as she gets more comfortable volleying with the press.

"Sydney do you think Ty Kent should reveal, his or her identity?"

"I think that is for Ty Kent to decide."

"Sydney, why do you think there is so much energy surrounding this mystery?"

"I think that is a question I would like to ask all of you."

"Sydney how do you feel about pen names in general?"

"After experiencing all of this chaos, a pen name is starting to sound like a brilliant idea." The room once again laughs at her response.

"Sydney, what makes you think that Ty Kent is a group of people?"

Sydney pauses for a moment. Things have been going so well she doesn't want to blow it now. *Keep it light Sydney, keep it light.* "Well, honestly, the question is why do you all think Ty Kent is just one person. Maybe Ty Kent represents two people or three, or four. I mean I'm just a writer suggesting a different angle. All of you are the reporters, the investigators. You tell me."

The room becomes silent. Maryann quickly stands up and jumps to the microphone. "That's all for today folks. Thank you all for coming."

Sydney is anxious to get out of there as soon as possible as she feels she may have just blown it. She gives the room a wave goodbye and to her and Maryann's surprise, the room stands up and gives her a round of applause and shouts of "Thank you Sydney." Sydney smiles as she gives the room once last look. She remembers the man in the corner, who has since vacated his spot. She looks around the room again to see if she can find him, to no avail. Maryann grabs her arm and leads her off the stage.

Sydney follows Maryann out a side entrance of The

24

Book Bag and is incredibly grateful to see their car waiting for them. Once safely in the car they both let out huge sighs of relief.

"Sydney you were fantastic." Maryann says as she pulls out her cell phone. "Wow, Twitter is blowing up."

"Blowing up good or blowing up bad?" Sydney asks unsure if she really wants the answer.

Maryann scrolls through her Twitter feed. She puts down her phone and looks over to Sydney. "Blowing up great. They love you. And they love this dynamic. You the pragmatic love realist and Ty Kent the dreamy romance novelist. This is so great Sydney."

"I don't know Maryann." Sydney says as she leans her head back into the seat.

"What don't you know? This means book sales."

"It just feels wrong. I don't want to sell my books based off of this. I mean, clearly this person wants to stay anonymous. We, or at least I should respect that."

"You are Sydney. You're not outing him or her, or them. You're simply riding a wave. Now your lecture is in one hour. What do you need?"

"Coffee. A big one." Sydney says as she turns and stares out the window. She wants to focus on the positive but she has a bad feeling about all of this.

"Ladies and Gentlemen, please join me in welcoming Ms. Sydney Graham!"

Sydney walks on to the stage. She smiles and thanks her host for a lovely introduction. She looks out at the ballroom, which is filled with about 800 people clapping their hands as she waves to them from the stage. Although her audience instantly grew from 100 people to 800 people all due to the antics of the day, Sydney is feeling the best she has all day. This is her element. This is one of her favorite things to do. She is a coach and she loves to energize people and move them to want to take control of their own lives.

"Thank you all." Sydney pauses to let the room settle.

"Wow, what a crowd. I want to thank each and every one of you for coming out here this evening. I'm really excited about the topic tonight and it's one that is near and dear to my heart. 'Managing your Love Expectations.' As a coach, I have been working with people and their relationships for over a decade. I work with people during many different stages in life. I work with people who are dating, people who are engaged or married. I work with those who are dating after the end of a marriage or a long relationship. At every stage there is one common topic that needs to be addressed and sorted through, and that is managing your expectations about love, relationships, your partner or potential partner, and most importantly your expectations of yourself.

We live in an age of instant gratification. We are bombarded with information and choices. And we can get just about anything we want delivered to our doorstep. Now when I start working with a client I ask them what they are looking for, expect or "want" in a relationship and in a partner. As you can imagine that list can get rather long." Sydney pauses as the crowd giggles.

"I also ask people what they bring to a relationship or what they have to offer a potential partner. This question is not answered as easily. I then ask a harder question, what is it that they can't bring to a relationship or offer to a partner. We sort through this information and we begin to look at not only what you expect of others but also what you expect of yourself. Not only what you are looking for from someone else, but also what you have to offer someone. That is where the hard work begins. Are you expecting more than you are actually willing to give? Do you want more from someone than you have to offer him or her? Or, are you expecting too little?"

Sydney continues with her lecture saving fifteen minutes for questions from the audience. She lets everyone know that they can find expectation exercises among other things in her new book. She thanks everyone and leaves the stage to a standing ovation.

Upon exiting the ballroom, Sydney is met by Maryann who is smiling ear to ear. "You were fabulous Sydney! Amazing! Now let's get you out of here before everyone starts wanting a private session." Maryann says as she grabs Sydney's hand and leads her down the stairs and out the door to their awaiting car.

"Maryann, thank you for setting all of this up. I know I was extremely reluctant at first but tonight was incredible."

"You were incredible. They love you. Gosh, you just do such a great job with those audiences. Your book will be flying off the shelves."

"I hope so."

"No hope needed Sydney. Your pre-orders jumped by 10,000 today."

"What?"

"Yep. Of course Ty Kent's books are also seeing a huge jump in sales, but that is to be expected."

"How do you know that?"

"You and Ty Kent have the same publisher."

"Right. I knew that. So obviously someone at Green Publishing knows who Ty Kent is. How has it not been leaked?" Sydney asks feeling a bit uneasy.

"Apparently only one person who works for the publisher knows the real identity of Ty Kent and was made to sign a strict confidentiality agreement. But believe me everyone at Green Publishing is over the moon about all of this free press. And of course we all owe it to Harris at the Insightful Blogger for creating such a buzz. Speaking of which, Harris reached out to me asking for an exclusive interview with you. Why wouldn't Ben just do it?"

Sydney lets out a groan. "Ben and I broke up."

"Oh my gosh, Sydney, I'm so sorry."

"It's fine, really. But I don't want to do any exclusives Maryann. I don't have anything to say. I'm hoping this just fizzles out."

"We don't want it to fizzle out just yet! We have five more weeks of this Sydney, and I'm telling you your book launch party is going to be a real celebration! Now, tomorrow you have one interview at ten in the morning with a radio show in Chicago and one at eleven with a radio show in Los Angeles. They will call you. Wednesday, I will pick you up at nine thirty in the morning. We will head to Portland, Maine where we will have a book club meet and greet and a lecture that evening. We will stay in Portland on Wednesday night and then head to Portsmouth, New Hampshire, where you are doing a live radio show and another book club meet and greet. I have sent all of this to you in an email. And, not to worry, I will not schedule any exclusive interviews with the Insightful Blogger. Got it."

"Okay. And Maryann, thank you for working so hard to make this book a success."

Maryann gives Sydney a wink as the car pulls up in front of Sydney's building. "Go get some rest! Perhaps make a batch of your famous mulled cider! See you Wednesday."

The Best Fall Drink: Mulled Cider

Ingredients:
1 quart of apple cider
1 orange
1 lemon
About 5 cinnamon sticks
Organic honey

Peel the orange and lemon and toss the rinds into a deep, medium-sized saucepan.
(Use the lemon and orange for pitchers of flavored water, or just eat the orange.)
Add cinnamon sticks and apple cider to the pot. Heat until it just begins to boil. Reduce heat and simmer for about 25 minutes.
Serve warm, in mugs, with a cinnamon stick (optional) and stir in one teaspoon of organic honey.

3
A Fellow Runner

Sydney wakes up at seven in the morning. She feels refreshed and excited. She's so pleased with how yesterday's craziness ended on such a high note. She hopes this positivity continues. She walks through her kitchen and turns on her coffee maker. She heads up a set of stairs to her meditation room. Sydney starts off every day with meditation. It clears her head and helps her focus on her clients and being the best coach she can be. The room is a small area on the top floor of her condo. She had it built specifically for the purpose of meditation and centering. The ceiling of the room is all glass, like a pointed pyramid. This allows her to get the most natural sunlight, which is not easy in the northeast.

She sits on some large pillows and crosses her legs. She rests her hands gently on her knees and begins to breathe deeply. She let's her thoughts flow in and out and then she begins to focus on only the positive thoughts. After ten minutes, she stretches her legs out in front of her and looks up at the morning sun. Some of her friends think her morning ritual is "flakey" but she finds it centering and she starts each day with gratitude. Even if later in the day the gratitude is stomped out by anxiety and chaos, at least she starts out strong.

Sydney walks downstairs and pours herself some coffee. She grabs her laptop from her office and sinks into her couch to read through her email.

"Oh my gosh!" Sydney screeches as she opens up her email and sees 2500 new emails. She let's out a big sigh. She has two and a half hours before her first phone interview. "Let's see how much I can get through."

After four and a half hours, responding to eight hundred emails and completing two radio interviews, Sydney feels like she needs a nap. She has communicated with so many people, yet she has seen no one and has not left her couch. Since napping is not an option during this whirlwind of activity, a run seems like the next best thing to boost her energy and at least visually see other human beings.

Sydney tightens up her shoelaces on a bench next to the Charles River. The Esplanade is bustling with lunchtime runners, walkers, and some tourists sprinkled about taking in the sites and the fall sunshine. As she begins her run, she intentionally ignores any of the chatter in her head and focuses on the sights, sounds, and people around her. She tries to be as present as possible. As she approaches the first dock on the Charles River she takes notice of the people on it and what they are doing. Mostly college aged kids studying or just hanging out. She smiles as she sees a chocolate Labrador launch himself from the dock and snatch a ball out of mid air before crashing into the water. She continues on and focuses on her steps and her breathing. She rounds a corner and dodges walkers and groups of school children visiting the Museum of Science. She tries to ignore the noise of the snarled traffic. She crosses the bridge into Cambridge and then follows the path back down to the river. Sydney slows her pace.

She is suddenly startled by a yell, "look out" and she leaps out of the way as a group of bicyclists whiz by her. She stands on the side of the path trying to catch her breath. She wonders what the universe is trying to tell her.

"Are you okay?"

Sydney turns her head to see a tall, dark haired man jogging towards her.

"They almost ran me over too. They need to be on the road, not this path."

"Yeah." Is all Sydney can manage to say. She's quite taken with how handsome this man is and he seems somewhat familiar.

"Wait, aren't you the girl who almost got plowed over by the skateboarder the other day?"

"I am. How do you know that?"

"I helped you up."

"Oh, wow. Thank you. I'm Sydney." She says as she extends her hand.

"Thomas, nice to meet you Sydney. And well, in full disclosure, I know who you are."

"You do?" She feels a bit of anxiety come over her.

"Yeah, I was at The Book Bag the other day. Congratulations on your new book. You handled all of those reporters remarkably well."

"Ah yes, the event at The Book Bag, well, that was different. Why were you there, if I may ask?"

"I like books."

"Of course." She responds as she wishes she had never asked the question in the first place.

"Okay, well, I'm glad you survived the bicyclist gang. I'm going to continue on my run. Would you care to join me?"

"I actually have a client in forty-five minutes so I'm just going to run back. But, you enjoy your run Thomas and it was a pleasure to meet you. Thanks for helping me out the other day."

"All right, well, you're welcome, and enjoy the jog home."

With that comment Thomas heads in the other direction. Sydney begins to jog home very disappointed in herself. She lied to Thomas. She doesn't have a client for another two hours. She wonders why she was so afraid to take his invitation. It's certainly not the relationship coaching advice she would give to others. As a matter of fact, if one of her clients did what she just did, Sydney would absolutely start to explore their fears.

"Sydney!"

Hearing her name shouted startles her out of her self-pity. She turns to see Thomas running back toward her. She feels something funny in the pit of her stomach, nothing bad, just funny.

"Hey." Sydney says as she waves. "Wrong direction?"

"No." Thomas says as he finally reaches her. "I was just wondering, and, no pressure, as I'm sure your schedule is insane. However, I have two tickets to see this great author at The Book Bag on Saturday morning. Would you like to join me?"

"Tell me it's not Ty Kent."

"No, it's not; however, I should warn you, he is a man who writes about Shakespeare."

"Shakespeare? The greatest romance novelist who ever lived." Sydney quips.

"The one and only."

"I'd love to go."

"Great! How about we meet in front of the store at nine thirty? The event is at ten in the morning but it's sold out."

"I'll be there."

"Looking forward to it Sydney. You better start hustling to make it back for your client."

She looks at her watch and raises her eyebrows to appear more convincing as she perpetuates her little lie. "Good point. Got to run. See you Saturday."

She sprints back to her condo. Once inside and still half out of breath, her first and most important call is to her friend Michelle.

"Hey Syd, what's up?" Michelle says as she answers her call.

"I think I'm in love!"

"I'm sorry, is this Sydney or did you steal her phone? Whom am I speaking with?"

"Ha ha. I know I deserve that. However, that butterfly

thing you, Jordan and everyone else I know, keep talking about…"

"Yes," Michelle interrupts, as she is eager to hear the rest of this sentence.

"I think I finally get it."

"Oh my gosh! My practical relationship coach, slash BFF is finally experiencing unicorns and rainbows?"

"Slow down there, Lucky Charms, no rainbows, no unicorns, just a flutter of butterflies."

"Details now!" Michelle demands.

Sydney laughs. "Well, I will say he's very handsome."

"How handsome?" Michelle asks as she lowers her voice.

"Stupid handsome. And, I just happen to have a date with stupid handsome this Saturday."

"Wait, what? I think you're skipping an entire monologue that describes, I don't know, everything who, what, where, when, why and the often forgotten how?" Michelle screeches through the phone.

Sydney goes on to answer each and every question Michelle asks. She gives her the entire summary of their little run-ins and details of how she took note of Thomas at The Book Bag.

"Well, well Miss Sydney, it looks like you have found yourself caught up in a real life romance novel."

Sydney grins. "Let's not get carried away."

"No Syd, that's exactly what you need. You need to be swept up in romance. This is good."

"I'll think about it. Talk to you later." Sydney says as she hangs up the phone.

As her afternoon progresses she realizes that Thomas is all she seems to be thinking about and that's a problem. Her thoughts flit between each and every encounter with Thomas. She thinks about the running encounter. Her mind remembers dark hair, tanned skinned, and full lips. How she would love to kiss those lips. Her favorite thought is of him

34

leaning against the back wall at The Book Bag. There is something about his casual, seemingly uninterested vibe that Sydney finds irresistible. Her warm sensations quickly dwindle when she thinks about going on a date with Thomas. She has not been on a first date with a stranger in years. She tries to coach herself through her fears by reminding herself that it's not a date it's just a meeting. It's a meeting between two people who don't know anything about each other. A simple discovery session with a man she finds incredibly attractive. *Ugh, Sydney stop it!* She screams in her head.

Sydney picks up her phone to look at the time. She has thirty minutes before four back-to-back coaching sessions. She tells herself she has five minutes to think about Thomas and then she has to get to work. She sets the timer on her phone and dreams away.

4
It's All About the Scoop

Insightful Blogger Headquarters

Ben walks down the hall with his messenger bag slung over his shoulder and a metal coffee cup in one hand. He raises his cup and nods at fellow workers as he passes all of the cubicles. The place is buzzing at nine in the morning. Every one seems a bit frantic and most are on the phone appearing to be deeply involved in serious conversations. Ben walks into his office and is quickly followed by Harris.

"Benjamin, Good morning."

"Good morning Harris. Things seem busy this morning."

Harris' eyes widen. "It is busy Benjamin. This Ty Kent thing has really taken off. Everyone out there is following up on some sort of lead. We're going to get this guy Benjamin!"

"Whoa, Harris, 'get this guy', he is not a criminal, he or she, is an author. Let's remember that."

"Of course. But you know me, I love a good mystery and it looks like we may be able to solve this one. Speaking of which Benjamin, did you speak with Sydney? It appears as though she is catching quite a wave off this thing."

"No, I haven't spoken with Sydney."

"Why not? I mean Benjamin, she has thoughts and you could do a great side story you know. The pragmatic relationship expert versus the elusive romance novelist: our readers would love that."

Ben closes his eyes and shakes his head. "It's not going to happen Harris. We broke up."

"What? Why?"

"It just wasn't working for me."

"Oh, okay." Harris says as he backs out of Ben's office.

Ben is grateful that Harris didn't probe any further. Although he anticipates his reprieve will be short lived. He knows Harris all too well and expects that Harris will be back in Ben's office within the hour with a new angle on the Ty Kent story for Ben to pursue.

Even though it has only been a few days, Ben does find himself missing Sydney. He misses their texting banter, their dinners out, and their conversations. He adores Sydney. What's not to adore? She's smart, funny, determined, caring, and beautiful. Ben can come up with a long list of great words to describe her, as she is a lot of wonderful things. The issue is more with what she isn't. The levelheaded Sydney is not whimsical, romantic, or spontaneous. Ben is well aware that he isn't any of those things either, but he wants to be. He desperately wants to be and dare he say, needs to be, with someone who can help him loosen up and be more adventurous.

Ben runs his hand across the cover of <u>Paper Cuts</u>. He's curious about this person who writes these intriguing love stories. What's this person like? Has this person experienced all of the adventures and romantic interludes so eloquently described in the books? He would like to meet the person who clearly is having a major impact on Ben's life. Ben broke up with Sydney after reading Ty Kent's books. That's a big deal. Yet, as a journalist, Ben can understand the want for anonymity. If this author does experience life to its fullest and then writes about it, would exposing who they are ruin his or her ability to freely experience life?

Ben sits back in his chair and considers his own questions. He purses his lips as he considers the ethics of revealing Ty Kent's identity. This is a question that has been bothering him for days. How does he keep his job and his ethical integrity?

"I've got it!" Ben says confidently as he springs out of his chair and heads to Harris's office.

Portland, Maine

Sydney and Maryann exit the Portland, Maine book club meet and greet and step out onto Middle Street. They are in the center of Portland's Old Port area that is filled with shops and restaurants. Sydney inhales the crisp midday air.

"I always forget how great this town is." Sydney says as she continues to inhale and exhale.

"It is adorable and so much to see. Shall we shop or grab lunch?"

"I say let's do a little of both, but definitely food first."

"Great." Maryann responds. "I'm starving too. Let's walk and see what looks good."

Maryann and Sydney settled on a place called Central Provisions. It was a perfect lunch spot with a nice Maine feel to it and the menu looked great. They place their orders and both women immediately begin to scroll through emails to catch up on things and make sure they haven't missed anything important.

"Oh my goodness!" Maryann slowly says as she continues to read something on her phone.

"What? Is it bad news?" Sydney asks concerned.

"Listen to this. Today the Insightful Blogger announces part two of their Ty Kent contest."

"Part two? How can there be a part two?"

Maryann holds up a finger as she reads quickly. "Interesting. Okay. It has come to the attention of the Insightful Blogger that not all team members believe that Ty Kent's identity should be revealed. There does seem to be quite a bit of interest in finding out Ty Kent's real name as our phones have been ringing off the hook and our team members are busy investigating every lead. However an exceptional argument was presented by our esteemed team member Benjamin Whitney." Maryann pauses and looks at Sydney to gauge her response.

"Go on!"

"Benjamin suggests that perhaps Ty Kent keeps his or her identity as a secret so that he can truly experience all of the adventures and romantic trysts he or she lays out in each book. Furthermore, Benjamin believes that revealing the identity of Ty Kent could possibly end his or her career, as he or she would no longer be able to truly engage in such activities on the level that he or she currently is engaging in them.

We believe that this argument is absolutely worth looking at. However, since the Insightful Blogger is already offering the $50,000 reward for Ty Kent's true identity, we cannot be the ones to offer a reward to continue to conceal his or her identity.

If anyone out there would like to put up the money to keep Ty Kent's identity concealed. Please contact us we would love to chat. Oh and neither Ty Kent nor any relatives of Ty Kent may put up the money for this. We have a safety net in place so if we have a valid taker we will connect them with Ty Kent's publisher to be sure that this person is indeed not Ty Kent or a relative of Ty Kent. Stay tuned our friends."

"I'm so confused. When was that posted?"

"About an hour ago. And it has already been shared a ton and has five thousand comments. If someone wanted to be smart another blog or newspaper should jump in on the action." Maryann stated.

"I can't believe Ben is the one trying to keep Ty's identity concealed. I mean I am and I'm not. Ben is an ethical journalist so of course he would consider this stance."

"I feel like there is a big 'but' coming."

Sydney stares out the window. "You know Maryann,

Ty Kent is the reason Ben broke up with me."

"What?"

"Yep. Ben started reading Ty Kent's novels and that's what he decided he wanted and was missing in our relationship."

"Wow." Maryann says shocked. "Ty Kent must be a really convincing writer. I'm going to have to start reading the books."

Sydney laughs. "Go right ahead but don't forget I need my hard-nosed publicist, at least for the foreseeable future."

Maryann puts her hands in the air as if to surrender. "I won't even pick one up until you have sold your first million."

Insightful Blogger Headquarters

"Benjamin you are brilliant." Harris shouts as he walks into Ben's office. "Did you see all of the action we are getting on the last post?"

"I did Harris and we have a problem."

"A problem? What problem?"

"I just got off the phone with Green Publishing. Apparently, someone circumvented us and went right to Green Publishing with an offer."

"Well, that's okay. Who is it? Wait, let me guess, a newspaper or another blog?"

"Neither. It is an individual. And, this individual wants to remain anonymous but Green Publishing has guaranteed me that they are not related to Ty Kent."

Harris considers what Ben is saying. "That's clever. This individual wants to remain anonymous because they are defending Ty Kent's anonymity. I like it."

"There's more. This person also upped the stakes. They are offering $150,000.00 to keep Ty Kent's identity sealed."

"$150,000.00 geez, what rich guy did we tick off?" Harris says as he flops down on a chair in front of Ben's desk.

"First of all, with this site it would probably be easier to figure out who we haven't ticked off. Second of all, why are you assuming this person is a guy?"

Harris nods. "Like a fan, a rich super fan of Ty Kent's. That's a good point Benjamin. Okay, we are in. Go ahead and let Green Publishing know."

"Seriously Harris? $150,000."

"Yep!"

"But how is this going to work?"

"Well, it will be a good race. If any of our team members or fans of the Insightful Blogger find out Ty Kent's real identity, then we reveal it and someone gets $150,000, from us. If someone on the other side finds out Ty Kent's identity and decides not to reveal it then super fan wins and shells out $150,000." Harris says as he stands up and begins to walk out of Ben's office. Harris quickly stops at the office doorway and turns to Ben. "Oh and Benjamin, I want to win. I want to know who this Ty Kent is. And that is now your only focus."

Ben just stares at Harris with a grimace on his face.

"Benjamin, I'm a curious guy. I need to know things."

"Curiosity killed the cat Harris!" Ben shouts to Harris as he walks down the hall away from Ben's office.

"And satisfaction brought it back!" Harris shouts his retort.

5
Is It a Date?

Well if it's not a date, my closet sure says otherwise. Sydney thinks to herself as she looks at the heap of clothes on the floor of her walk-in closet. Sydney silently repeats her new mantra; *this is a morning meeting between two strangers.* She picks up three dresses off the floor and hangs them up. *It's not a big deal, he likes books and she wrote one. They are meeting at The Book Bag at nine thirty in the morning on a Saturday. This is definitely not a date.* Sydney continues to debate herself in her head. She hangs up two blouses and two skirts.

Geez, Sydney, grow up! She picks a pair of jeans off the floor and puts them on. *It's a date!* Sydney pulls a light sweater over her head and zips up her tall black boots. *Stop freaking out and make the most of it.* She silently reprimands herself as she checks out her outfit in the full-length mirror.

Sydney arrives at The Book Bag and was surprised by the amount of people waiting to get inside. She snakes her way through the crowd searching for Thomas to no avail. She checks the time on her phone, nine twenty-five.

"Better three hours too soon than a minute too late." Thomas quotes William Shakespeare into Sydney's ear.

Sydney smiles and turns around to see Thomas dressed in jeans and a long sleeved tee shirt and holding two cups in his hand.

"Warm cider?" Thomas asks as he hands her a cup.

"Thank you."

"I was going to grab us coffees; but I wasn't sure how you took yours and since I don't have your phone number, I figured warm cider was a safe bet."

She slightly opens the lid on her cup; she inhales the sweet steam and feels a rush of warmth run through her body. "Perfect choice!"

Thomas smiles. "Shall we?"

Thomas and Sydney follow the crowd shuffling in to the storefront. The room fills up quickly so they grab two seats in the back row.

"Are you going to be able to see from back here?" Thomas asks.

"I don't need to see, I just need to listen."

Sydney is pleasantly surprised by how much she is enjoying the lecture. The author demonstrates a comical view of what Shakespeare's plays would be like had he been born in this century. It was as if Shakespeare was writing all of his plays as a Saturday Night Live skit. What she finds even more impressive was how well he engages with his audience. Sydney listens intently. However, the majority of her focus is the audience. She watches the interactions. She notices the woman in front of her, who was once stiff in her seat, and is now laughing and conversing with the couple beside her. This is his brilliance. Not only is this man engaging the audience, he is engaging them with each other. Sydney knows she can engage an audience, but she has yet to be able to ignite this kind of interaction. She watches the interactions of random strangers, who at first barely gave up their personal space, now, leaning in, laughing, and lightly touching. This is what a relationship coach needs to achieve. Sydney leans forward, placing her arms on her knees; she listens and she watches.

Thomas feels a bit smitten as he glances over at Sydney and sees her intently listening. He was unsure if coming to this lecture was going to be of interest to someone who seemingly takes a pragmatic view of relationships. Sydney turns her head, looks back at Thomas and smiles. *She does have an amazing smile.*

Thomas and Sydney decide to grab a coffee after the lecture. The Book Bag is still overrun with Shakespeare fans; so they opt to head to a trendy pastry and coffee shop a few blocks away.

Thomas and Sydney set down their coffees at a small table in front of a window overlooking the street.

"I must say Sydney, I didn't peg you as a black coffee drinker."

"I wasn't always. I had to train myself. As my speaking engagements had me on the road more frequently, I found it easier to drink black coffee. There was always too much cream or not nearly enough sugar."

Thomas laughs. "I get that. Now what kind of speaking engagements are you doing? Is this something other than your book promotions?"

"Yes. I have an active blog as well. A lot of people write comments and questions on the blog. I take the 'hot topics' and turn them into lectures."

Thomas listens intently as Sydney describes her events and blunders. She is so passionate and yet laughs at her missteps so freely.

"Enough about me. What do you do, when not running or going to lectures?"

"Well, I lecture. I'm an English Professor."

Sydney's eyes widen, she never would have guessed that he was a professor. "Wow, where do you teach?"

"Harvard."

"Oh so you are like a genius English professor."

Thomas smiles.

Two coffees and one apple turnover later, Sydney looks at the time. "Oh shoot, I have to go." She felt a wave of disappointment come over her as the words came out of her mouth. The last thing she wants to do is leave this incredibly handsome man. She can't believe how the time just flew by.

"Is everything okay?"

"Yes, I have clients this afternoon. I'm so sorry to have

to rush off like this."

"On a Saturday?"

"Yeah, Saturday and Sunday afternoons are a bit busy for a relationship coach. The pre date night, post date night sessions can be intense."

"Ah, I see. " Thomas says as he and Sydney stand up and exit the pastry shop.

"I had a really nice time, Thomas, thank you."

Thomas stands in front of Sydney with his hands in his pockets. "As did I."

After thirty seconds that felt like thirty minutes, Sydney breaks the awkward silence. "Well, thank you again."

Thomas nods. "Enjoy your afternoon and I hope your sessions go well."

Sydney turns and begins her walk back home. She is perplexed by how things ended. *What just happened there?* They had a great time. They each had two coffees and split a pastry. There wasn't one second of silence until the end. She really thought there was going to be a next time but he didn't even ask for her number. As she continues her journey, she ponders every detail of the last few hours; Sydney realizes this was the first conversation she has had in a long time that didn't include the Ty Kent saga. This fact just adds to Sydney's disappointment. *Ugh, why didn't I get a second date?* She wonders.

6
Drinks and a Dinner: Together yet Separate

"So let me get this straight." Michelle states as she and Sydney sip the pink martinis sitting in front of them and Jordan sips his beer. "Every thing was great and you really feel like you both hit it off."

"Yes. I was funny and I flirted a little. I mean, come on Michelle we shared food from the same plate."

"And then when you left he just stood there with his hands in his pockets?"

"Yes."

"Maybe he's just really shy and not good at asking people out."

Sydney cocks her head to one side. "He chased me down on the Esplanade to ask me out. I don't think shy is an adjective for this man."

"Pensive? Maybe he likes to sit with things before he asks again. The second date is a bigger deal." Jordan pipes in.

"Or maybe he's just not interested. I need to face that fact and move on."

"Sydney, if by moving on, you mean burying yourself in your work and not going on another date for six months, that's not going to be acceptable. Jordan has someone at work that he thinks would be great for you."

"Oh no. No way you two, no blind dates."

"But he's really nice Syd." Jordan protests.

"Is he now? Well that's what you said about Doug. Remember, Jordan, the really nice guy Doug that you two set me up with? He made the waitress cry!"

Michelle shrugs.

"Good point. I misread that guy."

"No blind dates!"

"Okay, okay." Michelle says as she puts her hands up to shield her face.

"Can I add a guys perspective here?"

Michelle shoots Jordan a *think twice* look.

"Absolutely." Syd is eager to hear a man's point of view.

"Okay, look just last Sunday Syd, I was surprised you had client's on Sunday. What if this guy thought you were blowing him off? You said you lost track of time and had to rush off."

Sydney considers Jordan's point and thinks he may actually have one.

"Jordan, the guy is on a date with Sydney Graham. One Google search and you can see how busy she is." Michelle defends.

"Yeah, but Michelle, I've known Syd for ten years, I know how busy she is. I was surprised she had clients on Sunday.

"Oh my God!" Sydney says as she slides down into the booth.

"What?"

"Switch sides with me."

Michelle obliges and slides out of one side of the round high top booth, walks to the other side of the table and slides back in so Sydney is now crouched down in the booth between she and Jordan. "Are you going to tell us what is going on and why you are hiding behind the menu?"

"Thomas is at the hostess desk with a woman."

Michelle inhales quickly and tries to see over the crowd of people at the bar to get a look at the hostess desk. "Wow!"

"What?"

"Umm nothing. He's attractive."

"I know what he looks like, what about her?"

Michelle pauses. "They are both very good looking."

"I need to go."

"Well, you can't just yet they're still at the door."

"This is humiliating."

"Hold on. Okay they're being seated."

"How do I leave though, half the dining room faces the door?"

"Sydney sit up!"

Like a child, Sydney slowly raises her head from behind the menu and sits up straight in the booth.

"Here's what is going to happen. We are going to finish our very expensive drinks. I will then go upstairs to the restroom and on my return I will scan the dining room to see where they're sitting."

"Wait you are going to leave me here alone, you can't do that Michelle."

"I'm right here Syd." Jordan grumbles as takes a gulp of his beer.

"Sorry Jordan."

"Sydney, not only are you a grown up, you are a relationship coach who went on one date. Don't give this guy any more power."

"Wow, that was impressive Michelle."

"Thanks, I've learned from the best."

Michelle makes her way up a flight of stairs towards the restroom; she reaches the top and scans the dining room for Thomas and his date.

That took forever." Jordan says when Michelle returns to the table.

"The bar is crowded. Getting from the stairs to this table is what took the longest."

Sydney, Michelle, and Jordan decide to veer from the original plan. They finish their drinks and order another round. This is their Saturday night too. Eventually, upon finishing their second round of drinks, they make a quick and undetected exit. Their walk home is silent until they arrive at

Sydney's place.

"Are you going to be okay?"

"I am." Sydney says with a grateful smile. "You know, you were right. It was just one daytime date. And Jordan thanks for the male perspective. You were right too, until…"

"Until we saw him on a date. Yeah, sorry Syd." Jordan interrupts.

"I can learn from this. I've been out of the dating scene for a while and this is good. I've gained some much-needed empathy to use with my clients. I love you guys!"

"Night Syd." Michelle and Jordan simultaneously say as they walk away and wave.

. . .

"Well New York seems to agree with you, little sister, you look great."

"Thanks Thomas. I do really enjoy New York, never a dull moment."

"And how is your dissertation coming along?"

"Slowly, I'm spending a great deal of time in the lab these days."

"I bet you are. I would offer to help but organic chemistry was never really my forte."

Kim laughs at her brother's honest joke.

"Are you sure you want to be a professor after all of this work. I mean Kim, you can make some great money with your degree."

Kim shrugs her shoulders. She has heard that line from everyone she knows. "I'm sure. I'm surprised to hear that coming from you, Professor Peters."

"Kim, I have a PhD in literature. There are not many career paths to choose from."

"Sure there are. You could become an author."

Thomas smiles over his glass as he takes a sip of his water.

"What? Thomas, Grandpa Kent always said you are a gifted writer."

"Yes, well writing essays and writing books are two very different things. And point taken. I will not question your career choice again."

"Thank you. So, any new love interests?"

Thomas takes a sip of his drink and shakes his head.

"Hmm, no eye contact and a strategic sip of the drink. Who is she?"

"No one. Well, she is someone. She's a rather big deal around here, but she's not interested."

"Really? Who is she?"

Thomas rolls his eyes.

"Spill."

"She's a relationship coach and blogger who just wrote a book."

"Wait, are you talking about Sydney Graham?"

"Yes." Thomas says surprised that his sister knows Sydney.

"Thomas, she's a big deal every where. I can't believe you are dating Sydney Graham. This is the best news ever." Kim screeches with excitement.

"Shh. Kim, I'm not dating Sydney. We went on one date. And how exactly do you know her?"

"Thomas every woman who is in her twenties, thirties and forties knows Sydney. Her blog and YouTube channel are huge and I've already pre-ordered her book."

"You have?" Thomas is shocked that his brilliant sister who lives in New York City would know of a relationship coach from Boston.

"Yes. Now, what happened?"

"Nothing really."

"How did you meet her?"

"I just ran into her. Well, technically, I helped her a few times after other people almost ran into her. We went to a lecture this morning and had coffee. But she is not interested."

"Did she tell you that? She's really direct. She's always giving that advice on her site; to be direct and not lead anyone on."

"No. She didn't tell me that."

Kim frowns.

"Things seemed to be going great. She's funny and interesting. We had coffee and the conversation flowed really well. But then she suddenly looked at the clock and said she had to go because she had clients this afternoon and tomorrow afternoon."

"Seriously?"

"Right, who works on a Saturday or Sunday afternoon? Clearly she was blowing me off."

"First of all, who works on Saturday or Sunday? Try anyone in healthcare, police, fire, um everyone in this restaurant."

"And second of all?"

"You're an idiot. She wasn't blowing you off Thomas. She does see clients on the weekends."

"How do you know?"

"She talks about it all of the time in her blog. I've seen clients post comments on her blog about how the advice she gave them earlier in the day really helped for the date they had that night, that Saturday night. And, she posts to her blog every Sunday."

Thomas leans back in his chair. He did not get that right at all.

"How did you even come up with that?"

"I don't know it just seemed like a classic blow off."

"Wow, you really are bad at dating."

"I prefer rusty."

"Well, may I suggest that you read Sydney's blog and get some dating tips before your next date with Sydney."

"You think she will go out with me. I mean now that I think about it, I was a jerk."

"You were. However, you misunderstood. If you are honest with her, you may be lucky enough to get a second shot."

Thomas inhales and exhales slowly. "I need to use the restroom, I'll be right back."

Thomas makes his way through the restaurant and heads up the stairs to the restrooms. Once he reaches the top he turns around to take in the view of the contrasting rooms, the quiet and intimate restaurant that backs up against a bustling bar. His eyes scan the bar and then stop. He focuses and then turns away toward the restroom.

"Well, you are very wrong." Thomas says as he takes his seat back at the table.

"About?" Kim responds, confused.

"Well, I was buying what you were saying, but now, I know I'm right."

"How's that?"

"I just saw Miss Sydney cozied up with a guy."

"What? Sydney Graham is in this restaurant!"

"Kim!"

"Sorry. I mean, you're kidding?"

"Yeah, you can see the bar from the top of the stairs and she was in a booth with a guy."

"Really. That doesn't seem like Sydney."

"Well, you know internet Sydney. I know the Sydney who blew me off and now is wearing the same clothes and with another guy. Are we done with this topic?" Thomas asks firmly.

"Yes." Kim responds quietly. However, Kim isn't done. She knows there must be more to the story. Or, maybe there isn't and her brother is right. Sydney is a fraud.

7
Sunday Fun Day

Blog Post #521: The Challenge: Let it Go!

Hello to all of my wonderful readers. Can you believe it? This is my 521st blog post. I'm so grateful to all of you for reading, commenting, and being so wonderful. I thought for this blog post I would do something a little different. Today I would offer a challenge, if you are willing to accept, and one that is of great benefit to all of us.

First, write in the comment section about the one date you can't get out of your head, for whatever reason. It was a great date, it was a bad date, it was a date that you thought was wonderful and then you were ghosted. The circumstances do not matter. It's just the date you can't seem to forget. Now, here is the challenge. If you write about this date on this blog, you can never mention it again. You have to let it go. If you're not truly ready to let it go, then don't write about it.

So how am I going to hold you to this? I'm not, you are. In your comment, you also have to name your accountability partner; that person you honestly know will hold you to never speaking of this event again. Are we ready to let some stuff go, wonderful readers?

One last incentive, the first one hundred people who post will get a free, signed copy of my new book! Don't forget to leave me your email!

I will kick us off!

I had a fabulous first date, or so I thought. We hit it off!

We had great conversation. He was smart, witty, and incredibly handsome! As I was leaving, everything changed. He suddenly became very aloof and just said good-bye. I mean he stood there with his hands in his pockets and told me to have a great afternoon. I would like to over analyze this date for days. But the date only lasted a few hours and so I'm only going to analyze it for a few hours. I have done that; and now I'm done with the first date, that I thought was great, but wasn't. Poof and that is the last you will hear of that date. My accountability coaches are my dear friends Michelle and Jordan who heard all about it last night!

To your success in love and life, (And for today, this challenge)!
     Sydney

     Sydney hits publish and leans back in her chair. *Hopefully the flurry of responses will keep me busy for most of the day.* She thinks. Sydney grabs her coat, keys, and some cash out of her wallet. She steps outside onto the top step of her brownstone and feels her head push back as she is greeted by a gust of cold air. It's a particularly cold morning; thankfully she is just going up one block to grab the Sunday paper.
     Sydney waits in a line four deep to pay for her paper. The Comm Ave Mall is quiet this morning, just a handful of runners and a few people walking their fury friends. Sydney forcefully squeezes her eyes together and clenches her fists when she realizes that she will have to change her running route so as to not run into Thomas. *That's a bummer.* She thinks. At least it will only be for a day as she leaves for another whirlwind of events on Tuesday. Sydney pays for her paper and begins to scan the headlines as she walks away.
     "The Ty Kent Mystery Just Became More Mysterious." Reads a headline in the middle of the front page. Sydney shakes her head. She wonders what Harris and Ben could be up to now as she reads the article while slowly walking back

to her condo.

"One hundred and fifty thousand dollars." Sydney quickly looks around as she realizes she said that aloud. Who would offer so much money to keep Ty Kent's identity a secret? That is someone Sydney would like to meet. She keeps reading while simultaneously unlocking the brownstone door and walking up another flight of stairs. Once in her apartment she flips on the coffee, and tosses the paper on to her dining table. She stands by the table holding on to the back of a chair and stares into her living room. She didn't think this could get any crazier but it just did. The upcoming events for her book tour this week are certainly going to be interesting.

Sydney reaches for her phone and sees six new text messages and ninety-eight new emails. It isn't even eight in the morning. Apparently her blog post has got her readers up early. The texts are all from Maryann her publicist, talking about the Ty Kent update, wanting to know how she is going to spin things for this week, giving Syd a jab about the book give away without telling her and finally: *I will pick you up at eight thirty in the morning on Tuesday. We have a full day in Providence, Rhode Island.*

Sydney pours herself a cup of coffee. She opens up her laptop and begins to tackle all of her emails and responses to her blog post. She begins to read stories of fabulous first dates, humorous mishaps and the woes of no shows. The majority of posts were actually similar to Sydney's experience; a date that seemed to go really well, only to end with never hearing from the other person again. *Well, I'm certainly not alone in this experience.* Sydney thinks to herself.

Sydney keeps at her work, reading and replying to comments on her blog. She comes across a comment from Sunshine865:

Dear Sydney,
This happens to me only in reverse. I'm generally a

nice person and avoid conflict. When I date, I will do everything I can to make the experience fun and pleasant even if I know I don't have any interest in seeing the person again. If the person reaches out and asks for another date I used to say thank you but no thank you. Unfortunately, this was often met with anger or wanting further explanation. Now, I admit, I just ghost the person. Sometimes feelings aren't reciprocated. That is life. Perhaps you should re-read your blog post #422. I love all of your work! Keep being real! Sunshine865.

Sydney leans back in her chair, puts her arms over her head and exhales. She just got coached. She searches through her blog to find post #422.

Blog Post #422: Date Night: Don't Forget to Leave Your "Crazy" at the Door!

Hello my wonderful readers and welcome to my blog post #422!

In a previous blog I discussed divorce and "divorce brain." Shifting gears a bit I would like to bring up a topic that haunts so many singletons, "crazy dating brain".

Let's take the example of "Alice" (obviously not her real name). Alice is in her late thirties; she has been divorced for many years and does not have children. Alice lives a happy life; she has a great career and excels in this area. She has good friends and a nice place in a hip area of a major metropolitan city.

Alice, like many adults, has turned to online dating to meet eligible men. She is attractive and smart; she does not have any problem getting a first, second, and even third date.

Over the last 5 years or so Alice has had a myriad of short relationships and a lot of dates. She is getting older and she really wants to be in a committed relationship. Alice is frustrated and cannot understand why she can be so successful in so many areas of her life and so unsuccessful in the one she feels she really wants, a loving, committed, healthy relationship. Sound familiar? If you can't identify with Alice's situation, I bet you know someone who can.

To move forward, Alice had to look at and change some of her own behaviors that got in the way of dating. Sometimes these behaviors kept her dating men that she really should have cut loose.
It is time to check your own crazy if:

1. You start planning your life together after dates one through ten.
2. You and you alone are the only one talking about the future.
3. You spend more time trying to interpret their texts messages than actually conversing with them or spending time with them.
4. You are looking past things you really do not like just because you want a relationship.
5. He/she is not treating you the way they should. But you hope it will get better.
6. He/she only reaches out to you late at night, and you engage.
7. You have only communicated via email, text, or phone and you consider this an actual relationship.
8. You change all of your plans just because they suddenly have time to hang out.
9. You are the one making most if not all of the effort.

It's great to get excited about a new person or potential new relationship. However, when one date or a month of dating ends and you are just crushed or angry; it's time to take a look at your patterns and perhaps make some changes. Here are some things that maybe helpful:

1. Keep your fist date simple, one drink, one cup of coffee, one hour that is it. Besides, if you do not like them, that

would be one long dinner to get through.
2. Have something really fun and exciting planned for later that day, night or the next day. (With yourself or anyone but said date). It is a chemical thing! When you like someone and your brain starts firing off all those chemicals that make you feel fabulous, and they do, you need to recognize it. Having something equally fabulous to do will help ground you.
3. Keep your thoughts in check. Try to curtail planning your future with this person you just met! Admit it, we have all done it.
4. Know that if they want to see you again, they will reach out. Period. There will not be any guessing, you will know.
5. If they do not treat you the way you deserve to be treated, it will not get any better. Move on.
6. If you do get caught up in a whirlwind. If you do let yourself get way ahead of the relationship, and then it ends. Remember to compare how many days or weeks you have spent with this person versus how many years have you lived without them. You will be okay, just move forward.
7. Let the past stay there. Remember to clear your mind and embrace your current moment. Forget about what has happened, don't bother with what could happen, and enjoy the present. If your mind is occupied and full of thoughts about all of the relationships that didn't work out, how will there ever be room for the one that may work out?

To your success in love and life,

Sydney

Sydney thinks about Ben and their predictable relationship. Things were safe with Ben. Their relationship was easy, scheduled, and totally boring. Although she doesn't like the feeling of not knowing why Thomas didn't want to go out again, and despises the fact that she saw him with another woman last night, she has to admit she enjoyed everything else. She liked trying to figure out what to wear. Thinking about how she felt nervous and excited about meeting someone new and doing something completely different, makes her smile. Her thoughts go to Thomas standing in front of her with his hands in his pockets and then they quickly flash over to seeing Thomas walking into the Eastern Standard with a woman. Sydney lets out a moan as she rests her head on the table in front of her. She thinks about climbing back into bed. "No." Sydney says out loud as she picks her head up and reaches for her phone. She sends a text to Michelle and Jordan inviting them over for an early Sunday dinner. Fall comfort food with friends is a much better solution.

Chicken, Apple, Broccoli and Stuffing Casserole with Apple Cider Gravy

Preheat oven to 350 degrees.

The Stuffing
1 14oz package of Pepperidge Farm herb stuffing mix (you can use any brand)
1 Medium Onion chopped
3 large Macintosh apples (peeled and chopped)
4 Celery stalks chopped
5 Tbsp. of butter
2 Cups of Chicken Stock (I use unsalted)

    In a medium sauce pan over medium heat, sauté the chopped onions and celery. About 5 minutes. Add the apples cook another 3 minutes. Add chicken stock and bring to a boil. Remove from heat and add stuffing mix. Stir, cover and let stand.

Casserole Ingredients:
4 Cups of cooked shredded chicken
1 Medium onion chopped
4 Large Macintosh apples (peeled and chopped)
3 Cups of chopped broccoli
½ cup of Apple Cider
1-¼ cups of Water

    Saute the chopped onion in olive oil in a skillet over medium heat. About 5 minutes. Stirring often. Add apples and broccoli and ¼ cup of water and continue to cook about 3 to 5 minutes until broccoli and apples are tender.
    In a 9x13-baking dish, place the chicken on the bottom. Then add the onion, apple, and broccoli as the next layer. Pour 1 cup of water and ½ cup of apple cider over the layers.

Add the stuffing as the top layer.
Bake uncovered for about 25 minutes.

Apple Cider Gravy

3 tablespoons of butter
3 tablespoons of flour
1 cup of apple cider
1.5 cups of chicken stock (again I use unsalted)
2-3 dashes of Cinnamon

In a saucepan over medium/high heat melt butter and stir in flour. Cook until light brown. About 1 minute. Whisk in the apple cider and chicken stalk. Add two to three dashes of cinnamon. Continue to whisk and cook until gravy thickens, about 5 minutes.
Serve casserole warm with gravy!

8
Everyday Challenges

Thomas picks up his phone and reads a text from his sister, Kim. *You have to read this!* Attached was a link to something but Thomas had to put his phone in his bag as his American Literature students started to file into the lecture hall. On the white board in the front of the room Thomas has written: The Sun Also Rises: Analysis and Discussion.

Before Thomas is able to begin his discussion, a young woman in the front row raises her hand. Slightly perplexed, he asks what she may need.

"Professor Peters, um, before we begin today, is there anyway we can have a conversation about the Ty Kent issue? I mean I would love your thoughts about anonymity as a writer."

"Well, this is American Literature, I think that conversations is better suited for a law class."

A hand is raised in the third row and Thomas gives the young man a nod to speak.

"Professor, I agree this is a legal issue. However, the majority of us in this room are English or Journalism majors, and this is a very current event that could effect all of our future careers." This comment is met with positive nods throughout the room.

Thomas narrows his eyes as he considers the students' questions and commentaries. "Why are you all so curious about a romance novelist?"

"Well sir, the idea is brought up by a recent Harvard drop out who has a very successful business."

62

"Harris." Thomas responds blandly.

"Yes. And we don't necessarily all want to be Harris and have a gossip blog, but we admire his success. And he is cutting edge."

Cutting edge is the last phrase Thomas would use to describe Harris. Harris took about six classes with Thomas over the years. He would rather describe Harris as annoying, disengaged and yet, challenging and tenacious.

"How many of you are declared English or Journalism majors? Raise your hands." Thomas asks. Seventy-five percent of the people in the room raise their hands.

"How many of you aspire to be a journalist or a professional writer?" Raise your hands." Ninety percent of the people in the room raise their hands.

"Okay then. I have a challenge for you. If you win, we may have this conversation. If you lose, then we will go on with the lecture I have planned."

The entire classroom agrees. Thomas asks that everyone leave their phones, watches, and anything else that may give them access to the Internet at their seats. They oblige and the entire room walks down to the front with Thomas.

"Okay, here is your challenge question. In what year did Ernest Hemingway win his Nobel Prize for Literature?"

Thomas watches as his students collaborate and debate. He likes seeing them working as a team. This inadvertent exercise will make them a stronger class to work with. They will collaborate more and learn more. Thomas is actually grateful for the challenge.

"Professor, we have an answer."

"Do you? And does everyone agree with this answer?" The class nods in agreement.

"So, absolutely no protests? No dissidents?"

"No sir."

"And your answer is?"

"1953."

"Okay, you may all go back to your seats now. However, do not touch your devices just yet." Thomas instructs. "That was a valiant effort; but you are all wrong. Ernest Hemingway did earn a prize in 1953 but it was the Pulitzer. His Nobel Prize was won in 1954. Okay, challenge over. I win. Now let's move on to the book of the day, <u>The Sun Also Rises</u>, by Ernest Hemingway."

Insightful Blogger Headquarters

"Good, magnificent Monday morning team!" Harris gleefully shouts as he enters the conference room clapping his hands. "Let me have the run down of where things are with Ty Kent."

The room remains silent.

"Anything?" Harris asks with less enthusiasm.

"We've followed up on all of the leads Harris and they're dead ends." Ben states.

"Hmm." Harris rapidly taps his pen on the conference room table. He stands up and paces around the room five times. The team members have their eyes glued to Harris as he paces. He sits down and starts tapping. Ben grabs the pen out of Harris's hand and places it in front of him.

"Benjamin, this is how I think."

"It's annoying and no one else can think."

"I have a thought."

"Lisa, share it." Harris spouts.

"Well, I have read most of Ty Kent's books. However, I haven't read them looking for clues as to who he is. We keep looking to the outside for clues maybe there are some clues in his books." Lisa responds.

"Like what kind of clues Lisa? I've been reading his books and they all seem to be different." Ben adds.

"Well yes the locations and settings are always different. However, if we really read the books looking for clues as to whom this person is, any hints or even the style of writing. Is the style similar to any other authors? Can we garner any information about this person's age or interests from the books?"

"It would be like looking for a needle in a haystack." Ben groans.

"Isn't that what we are doing." Lisa quips.

"I like it!" Harris says. "Maybe start by comparing the first and last couple of books. Lisa, Benjamin, Samantha, and Alex, I want this to be your sole focus. Everyone else, we still have a blog to run so pitch me your stories. Go."

"Harris, before we start burying ourselves in romance novels, I would like to suggest another angle. What about Green Publishing? Ty Kent has been with them for at least ten years." Benjamin suggests.

"Great idea. Benjamin you start digging up everything you can on Green Publishing. Lisa, Samantha and Alex, start reading. I'm going to give the four of you this conference room for the week. All thoughts, hints, ideas put it up on the board. Everyone else, let's go to my office and go over pitches."

Harris and the rest of the team leave the room. Lisa, Samantha, and Alex are already on their devices downloading Ty Kent's first three novels and the most recent novels. Ben is excited. For the first time in a long time he feels some energy around his work and like an actual investigative journalist. Of course what he's researching is completely ludicrous, but exciting nonetheless.

A Quest for Butterflies

Sydney wakes up feeling sluggish. She can't quite figure out if she's tired from all of the stuffing she ate the night before or if she's still down about Thomas. She thinks about the comments made by Sunshine865. She wonders if it's possible for someone to fake having such a good time. None of it matters. Thomas was with another woman. Why would Sydney want to waste any more time on a man who was on another date just hours after theirs? She really liked the butterflies. There is only one solution. She needs to find a way to get those butterflies. That is her self-imposed challenge.

Knowing that she will not meet anyone sitting in her apartment. Sydney begins her quest with a run. If it worked once it could work again. She thinks about where to run and decides to head to the Esplanade. Thomas doesn't own the Esplanade and he's certainly not going to keep her away from her favorite route.

Sydney fails to find butterflies on her run. She takes a shower, gets dressed, packs up her things and meanders up to the Starbucks on Newbury Street. Even if she doesn't find butterflies at least the people watching will entertain her. She thinks about something Michelle asked at their dinner last night. She asked if Sydney had ever been in love. She knew she wasn't in love with Ben, but thought perhaps it could grow into love. She tries to remember a time when she felt so excited about someone and can't.

Sydney orders a coffee, sits down at a table near the window, and flips open her laptop. She doesn't have an interest in writing right now. Her laptop is nothing more than a prop. A book probably would have been a better choice. She continues to try and think of a time when she was in love. She can't. She is thirty-six years old and has never been in love. That is of course if she defines love as having both butterflies and a solid relationship that can be boring at times. Michelle and Jordan have that.

If she has never been in love, how can she be a relationship coach? That would be similar to having a ski coach who has never skied. How could that work? These questions swirl about in Sydney's head. However, Sydney reminds herself, she has had tremendous success as a relationship coach. She thinks back to Sunshine865. Sydney had lots of questions about why things went the way they did. Sunshine865 gave her a dose of reality when she needed it. And that is exactly what Sydney does. Even though we all like to feel the butterflies. When they disappear quickly, we all need help facing reality.

Sydney smiles and shuts her laptop. *Time to get back to reality Syd, no more butterfly fantasies.* She sips her coffee and starts watching the real life people flutter in and out of the Starbucks.

Harvard Campus

Thomas unlocks his office door and throws his bag on the desk. He flips open his laptop and powers it on. He grabs his phone and sees the text message his sister had sent that morning. *You MUST read this.* He clicks the link and begins to read Sydney's blog post. He shakes his head after reading. He is unsure as to why his sister sent him the post. They established last night that he was wrong in assuming that Sydney was lying about seeing clients. However, it doesn't change that fact that he saw her with another guy. He sends a text to his sister saying as much. He puts down his phone and it immediately buzzes. *The guy was her best friend Jordan, the husband of her other best friend, Michelle. Did you read the last line of the blog??*

He considers what Kim is saying. He responds to her text. *Okay. One date and two big misunderstandings. It already seems like too much work.*

Stop being such a dude Thomas! You like her. Fix it. Xo K.

Thomas chuckles at his sister's text. He puts his phone down and pulls out a stack of papers he needs to grade.

9
Back to Reality

Tuesday Morning

Sydney walks out of her brownstone promptly at eight-thirty in the morning. As promised, Maryann is waiting in a car. Sydney hops in the back seat and Maryann hands her a coffee.

"Thank you."

"My pleasure. Now just as a review, we have a small book club of about thirty people at ten this morning. We have a second book club meet and greet at one in the afternoon. Your lecture begins promptly at five this evening."

"Great. How many for the lecture?"

"One hundred and sixty-eight."

"Not bad. Oh and I have the list of the first one hundred people who responded to my blog. I will email that over to you."

"Great. Now what the heck happened this weekend to prompt that blog post?"

"Nothing happened Maryann. It was just a lousy date."

"Then why do you seem so melancholy?"

Sydney shrugs. "Because I spent all day yesterday chasing butterflies."

"Oh." Maryann has no idea what Sydney is talking about but decides not to push any further as Sydney doesn't seem to want to discuss anything. Maryann is a bit concerned though. She hopes Sydney sheds this layer of gloom before the events.

Maryann was more than pleasantly surprised by how well Sydney did at both book club meetings. And now she is absolutely killing her lecture. *Just get through the questions Sydney and we are home free.* Maryann thinks to herself.

A roar of applause comes from the crowd as Sydney wraps up her lecture. Sydney smiles and thanks the crowd. As the applause begins to fade Sydney asks for questions. A line begins to form in front of the microphone that has been placed in the center aisle.

Sydney gracefully answered questions about Ty Kent and shared her thoughts about re-kindling old flames. "Okay, we have time for one last question." Sydney stated.

"Sydney, I'm an avid reader of your blog, what prompted you to write Sunday's blog post. I'm not sure I've ever read a post like that from you."

Sydney smiles as she is prepared for this question. "You mean because I sounded more like a reader than a coach?" Giggles come from the audience.

"Well, yeah." The questioner replies.

"Look, I had an experience. I felt the butterflies. I was fired-up and a little nervous. I was caught up in the moment and the excitement and perhaps made it out to be more than it was. Which by the way, was really fun, until it wasn't." The crowd lets out an empathetic group laugh.

Sydney continues. "We are all human and we can all get tripped up by our emotions from time to time. I actually got so tripped up that I spent all day yesterday chasing butterflies. I was determined to have a run-in with another handsome stranger and experience the rush. I was unsuccessful, exhausted and in bed by eight o'clock last night.

More importantly I learned a few things. I hadn't felt those butterflies in a really long time. I had forgotten what it's like to get ahead of myself and/or the relationship. And, I had to experience the process of not letting this one failed date have more power over me than it should. What kind of coach would I be if I didn't pass on what I learned? I want to thank you all so much for coming out and spending the evening with me. To your success in love and life."

The crowd stands with applause for Sydney. She gives them a wave, a smile, and a bow before heading off the stage.

Tuesday Evening, Insightful Blogger Headquarters

The conference room at the Insightful Blogger looks less like a conference room and more like a fraternity living room on a Sunday afternoon. The trash can and recycle bin are overflowing with takeout containers, coffee cups, and water bottles. Notebooks, pizza boxes and Ty Kent novels cover the conference table. Ben and his discovery team, which includes Lisa, Samantha, and Alex, have managed to read eight of Ty Kent's novels in two days.

Ben stands at the front of the room with a dry-erase marker in his hand. "Here is what I'm thinking. Before we get started on leads or ideas about who Ty Kent is, I think we should list our biases about who we want him to be."

"I'm not sure I understand what you mean." Alex says.

"Let's use me as an example." Ben puts his name on the white board and writes the word *male* underneath. "I honestly hope that Ty Kent is a guy. I have to acknowledge this so that I'm not ignoring clues that may indicate Ty Kent is a woman. I also hope that Ty Kent has in someway, fully or partially experienced most of the trysts in his books."

"So you hope he's a serial dater." Lisa chimes in and everyone laughs.

Ben smiles. "Exactly! Does anyone else have hopes as to who Ty Kent really is?"

Lisa groans and puts her head down on the conference table while simultaneously raising her hand.

Ben cocks his head to the side. "Um, Lisa, you okay?"

She picks her head up and let's out a big sigh. "If we are being honest, and you can't laugh at me." Lisa protests as she looks at her colleagues.

"No laughing or judging Lisa." Ben pauses. "Well, maybe just a little snickering."

"I really hope Ty Kent is a guy about twenty-eight years old, and single." Lisa blurts out.

"So you want to date Ty Kent?" Samantha jests.

"Don't you?" Lisa asks Samantha.

"Totally."

"I'm guessing you two would like him to be good-looking as well?" Ben asks as he begins to write Lisa and Samantha's biases on the board.

"And tall!" Lisa replies.

"I don't read romance." Alex starts. "I'm more of a science fiction reader. I'm assuming based on the genre and number of books Ty Kent has written, we are going to discover that Ty Kent is a woman in her forties or fifties."

"Wow, stereotype much?" Lisa quips.

"Moving forward." Ben says trying to prevent any further verbal jabs among the team. "Now that our hopes and biases are out in the open we should be better able to analyze any leads we garner from the books."

"I have a thought."

"Yeah, Alex, what is it?"

"As we are reading all of these books it may be helpful to take note of the point of view. Are there any trends? Do all of the books tend to be from a female perspective versus a male and how accurate is it?"

"Excellent idea Alex. Everyone, be sure to list the point of view in your notes about each book and whether you find it to be believable. And let's not forget Sydney Graham's suggestion that Ty Kent may be more than one person. Do we have any hints or leads based on what has been read thus far?"

"Ben, I think we can rule out the group idea based on what I've read." Lisa says.

"Why?"

"Well, the style of writing is so consistent. Although the content has matured and the stories have matured, I feel as though if it was a group of writers we would see obvious variations in the style or the writer's voice." Lisa looks around the room at her teammates and they nod in agreement.

"Okay, so we are ruling out a group of writer's. Good." Ben says.

"I believe that Ty Kent has actually traveled to and spent time in every location that his, or her, stories take place versus just doing research on the internet."

"Interesting why do you say that Alex?"

"I would like to know what others have experienced. I read Love Petals in Paris, which was Ty Kent's tenth novel. Now it didn't take place in any commonly thought of romantic spots in Paris. The characters didn't meet at the Louvre or on the Champs-Elysees. They meet in non-tourist parts of the city and their love affair blossoms in this out of the way neighborhood. The writer's descriptions give the vibe that the writer was there."

"I noticed that same thing in My London Love." Samantha chimes in. "I also saw it in Celebrity Crush. That book takes place in and around Beverly Hills, California but in lesser-known areas. I lived there. Ty Kent definitely spent time on location to get the detailed descriptions that are in that book."

"Okay, for the sake of argument, could it be that Ty Kent interviewed people who lived in those areas? And perhaps just combined the interviews with Internet research?" Ben asks.

"I don't think so." Samantha says. "Ty Kent really captured the energy and nuances of the area not just random street and restaurant names."

"It's getting late. Let's pick this up tomorrow. I will get the rest of Ty Kent's books here by ten in the morning. Thank you all, have a good night, and rest up."

10
Party Planning

Sydney waits in front of the Boston Public Library. She is a bit early for her two o'clock meeting with Maryann and her caterer, Linda. Sydney is excited and nervous for her book launch party. Her pre-orders have been great but her worry is that sales will just die off after the launch.

"Syd!"

Sydney turns as she hears her name called and sees Maryann and Linda walking towards her.

"Are you excited?" Maryann asks as she gives Sydney a hug hello.

Sydney shakes Linda's hand. "I am. A little nervous as well."

"Nothing to worry about Syd. Linda and I have got everything under control. Shall we."

The ladies enter the Guastavino Room in the Boston Public Library. The room is breathtaking even without anything in it.

"I can't believe you were able to secure this venue, Maryann."

"It's perfect. Okay, let's get down to the details shall we."

Maryann guides Linda and Sydney through the vision for the event. The event is small, only seventy-five invited guests consisting of friends, fans, local reporters, and bloggers.

Because the event is only two hours in length, Maryann has ordered small, round, high-top tables and chairs that will be draped in white linen. They will be passing hors d'oeuvres and will set up a buffet table in the middle of the room so guests can easily access it from all sides and avoid lines. The bar will be simple serving beer, wine, and champagne.

"Now for my favorite part, the center pieces. They are small, round silver vases with pink tea roses."

"Elegant." Linda responds. "Do we want a signature cocktail to match the fall hors d'oeuvres menu? I could do something that is champagne or wine based."

"I love that idea!" Sydney responds.

"Great. Sydney I will send over some drink options when I send over the menu. Is there anything you would love to have or absolutely don't want served?"

Sydney thinks about it for a moment. "You know Linda, one of my favorite things are apples and cheddar slices wrapped in phyllo dough."

"Yes, brushed with butter and baked?" Linda asks.

"Exactly!"

"How would you feel if I put a bit of a twist on that by adding just a tad of my signature cranberry puree?"

"What I feel is my mouth watering." Sydney jokes. "Ladies, this is going to be incredible. It's my first book launch and I'm so grateful for all of the work you are both putting into it."

"You worked hard on that book, Sydney. It's a big accomplishment that deserves a party. I have to run. I've got a four o'clock appointment back in my office. Sydney, I will call you tomorrow to go over the meetings we have on Friday."

"I'll head out with you Maryann. And I will get the menus over to both of you this evening."

Maryann and Linda head out together leaving Sydney alone in the empty Guastavino Room. The room no longer feels empty to her. Maryann did such a great job describing the details and flow that now all Sydney sees is a room full of people enjoying the evening. Her anxiety has since waned. Maryann is right. Sydney has put a lot of work into the book and the promotion of it. She deserves this.

. . .

Thomas sits down on a bench on the Commonwealth Avenue Mall. He is exhausted. He ran the entire loop from Cambridge. He crossed over the Charles River Damn Bridge, passing the Museum of Science over to Boston. He ran along the Esplanade to the Mass Avenue Bridge, crossed back into Cambridge and ran back towards where he started. Once back to the Charles River Damn Bridge he ran across it and headed up to the Boston Common. He then came back down, through the Garden to where he is now, half way down the Commonwealth Avenue Mall.

Thomas is aware that it would have been much easier if he had just emailed or called Sydney versus running all over the Back Bay. He wanted the romantic gesture. He envisioned haphazardly running into her and being able to deliver a poetic apology that she couldn't turn down. She can delete an email or ignore a phone call. But, if he could have the opportunity to look her in the eyes, she may see and feel just how truly sorry he is.

Sydney races to the corner of Exeter Street and Commonwealth Avenue, yet misses the light and her opportunity to cross. She lets out a frustrated sigh. She turns her head to the left and watches the stream of cars speed by. She looks across the street and sees a man sitting on the bench with his head down.

She focuses her eyes and realizes it's Thomas. Sydney panics. She could run down the sidewalk to Fairfield Street and hope that he doesn't pick up his head and see her. She decides that is too risky and turns around and briskly walks back up Exeter Street towards Newbury Street.

Her pace is fast and her thoughts even quicker. She wonders what he's doing. It looked as though he was running, why would he be sitting down. She hopes he's okay.

Maybe it wasn't Thomas. She thinks. She quickly dismisses that thought, as she knows it was Thomas. Sydney slows her pace. She questions why she was so abrupt to turn and run. Sydney stops halfway up Exeter Street. She scolds herself for running away from the opportunity to have complete closure.

Sydney hustles back to Commonwealth Avenue. She reaches the corner and looks over to see an empty bench where Thomas was previously sitting. She scans up and down the Mall and the sidewalks. Nothing. Disappointment washes over her as she crosses the street and heads home.

Apple, Cheddar, & Cranberry Phyllo Dough Wraps

Ingredients:
One box of Phyllo Dough defrosted
3 Medium McIntosh Apples peeled and sliced
Sliced Cheddar Cheese
Butter
1 small can of Whole Cranberry Sauce

Preheat oven to 400 degrees.
Lightly spray a 9X13 inch-baking pan with cooking spray.
Cut the Phyllo dough sheets in half.

Take one apple slice and an equal sized slice of cheddar cheese and place ¼ of an inch in from a corner of the Phyllo dough. Add one small drop (about a quarter teaspoon) of cranberry sauce. Starting with the corner tip of the Phyllo dough begin to wrap the apple, cheddar and cranberry by rolling and continually folding in the sides of the dough as you go.

Once your baking dish is full. Melt about 2 tablespoons of butter and brush over the top of the Phyllo dough. Bake about 20 to 25 minutes.

Let cool about 10 minutes before serving.

11
Assumptions and Corrections

Sydney wakes up at six Thursday morning and heads straight upstairs to her meditation room. She tossed and turned all night long. A long meditation is exactly what she needs. She sits on her floor, crosses her legs, and rests her hands on her knees. She begins the process of slow and deep breaths. All she can think about is Thomas. She tries not to fight with her thoughts and just lets them pass through. There is no need to force other thoughts, as that would be counter productive. She is there to let her mind drift, and not to think.

She sees a flash of Thomas leaning against the wall at The Book Bag. She exhales as she lets the thought go. She squeezes her eyes a bit and then relaxes them. She sees a vision of Thomas and a beautiful woman. She listens to the sound of her breath. Her thoughts drift to Ty Kent. Her stomach makes an awful noise. Finally Sydney opens her eyes and lies back on her mat. She thinks she may need to journal her way through her issues before trying to meditate tomorrow.

Sydney grabs a seat at the crowded Book Bag Café. Her thoughts about Thomas and her concerns about the Ty Kent saga have been so troublesome she thought real life distractions would do her some good. She pulls out her journal to do some writing the old fashioned way, an actual pen and paper. She sips her chai tea and breaks off a piece of her blueberry scone. She flicks her pen against the journal struggling to write. She begins to aimlessly doodle between nibbles of her scone.

"Something on your mind?"

Sydney jumps. "Ben. What are you doing here?"

"May I?" Ben asks as he points to the chair across from Sydney.

"Of course. Please."

"Ty Kent, huh?" Ben grimaces as he points to Sydney's doodling.

Sydney looks at her notebook and has apparently written Ty Kent's name six times. She wrote his name in puffy letters, and then in what looks to be stick figures. She has his name surrounded by geometric shapes, in a cloud, teetering off a mountain and the worst, a big broken heart in the middle of the page with Ty on one side and Kent on the other. *Oh boy.* She thinks to herself.

"Sydney just the other day, I was thinking about how much I miss you. I miss our conversations and our dinners. I miss not being able to text you and joke about the craziness that is The Insightful Blogger."

Sydney just stares blankly at Ben.

"Syd, I care deeply for you and it pains me to think that our breaking up has caused you this much heart-ache." He says as he points to the doodles.

"Ben, this is not…"

He puts his hand up to stop her from continuing. "Please, let me finish. You are an incredible woman. You're smart, driven, and funny. You light up rooms, not just any rooms, Sydney, you light up rooms filled with frustrated, single women. Who else can do that?"

Sydney begins to silently list the names of hot celebrities who could quite easily light up a room of frustrated single women. They wouldn't even have to speak; they'd just have to show up.

"Syd. I'm sorry. I truly am. You're perfect. I'm not. This has nothing to do with you and everything to do with something I'm searching for. I know I'm being selfish, but it's something I need to do. I hope you can understand that."

Sydney can't believe what she is hearing. Her frustrations with Ty Kent run deep and have nothing to do with Ben. They may have for a second, when he initially broke up with her, but not now. And she completely agrees with Ben, they were fine but not a forever match. Sydney then finds herself doing something she rarely does; she just went with the flow. "Ben, thank you. And really I'm okay. I truly appreciate you checking in, we all handle things differently. I hope you find all that you're looking for."

Ben puts his hand on Sydney's, smiles at her for a bit too long, and then leaves.

Sydney presses her lips together to contain her laughter. She finds the whole situation quite humorous. She closes her notebook and wonders if she was being mean by not telling Ben the truth and letting him believe she was heartbroken over their breakup. In her defense she did try to interrupt him. After he kept going on and seemed so serious, she didn't want to embarrass him by telling him how completely wrong he is. Sydney tells herself to not overthink this situation. She has enough on her plate and clearly as quite a bit of inner turmoil surrounding Ty Kent.

Sydney's phone vibrates on the table. She picks it up and sees a text from one of her clients. *Sydney, any time for an emergency session? I just saw my fiancé having coffee with a very attractive woman. I have no idea who she is and I'm freaking out! Emily*

Sydney looks at her schedule and texts Emily that she can speak with her at three o'clock this afternoon. Technically she could speak with Emily sooner; however, Emily has a tendency to overreact. Sydney is hoping by delaying the call the situation will resolve itself. Sydney will then use the coaching session more productively and focus on the work Emily really needs to do which is to stop jumping to conclusions.

Sydney taps her pen on her journal and stares out the window. She is grateful that she now has more empathy for

Emily. After her rush of emotions for Thomas, she has a better understanding of Emily's frequent and rash judgments that spin her into an emotional web of despair. Sydney did the same thing when she saw Thomas having dinner with a woman. That was after one date, she can't imagine if she was engaged. Although she hopes, that if engaged, her level of trust would be high and she could maintain a more rational mind.

"I hope you're lost in positive thought."

"Thomas!" Sydney says a bit too loudly. "Um, hi."

Thomas hesitates feeling a little sheepish. "May I sit?"

"Ah, sure, I was going to be leaving soon anyway. The table is all yours." Sydney says as she nervously begins to put her journal into her bag.

"Oh, you have a client?"

"No. Well, yes, but not right now."

"May we chat for a moment?"

"About?"

"I want to apologize for my behavior on Saturday."

"I don't understand you were perfectly friendly."

Thomas nods. "I was. I had a great time. However, I blew you off." Thomas pauses to look up at Sydney.

She doesn't say anything but the little voice in her head says, *well, clearly you had a date to get to.*

"I jumped to an incorrect conclusion. I thought you were blowing me off by rushing off and saying you had clients."

"I do have clients on Saturdays and Sundays." Sydney protests.

Thomas nods apologetically. "I know. And then I made another miscalculated judgment. I saw you at Eastern Standard Saturday night. I saw you with a man and assumed you were on a date, not knowing that he was your friend Jordan."

Sydney can't believe what she is hearing. She closes her eyes and puts her fingers to her forehead. "Okay, wait, this whole time you thought I was blowing you off?"

"Yeah."

"But, how do you know Jordan?"

"I don't. My sister, as it turns out, is a big fan of yours and an avid reader of your blog. She's the one who informed me that you actually do have clients on Saturdays. It was more like a scolding over dinner. And she sent me the link to your Sunday blog post."

"Wait, what do you mean a scolding over dinner?"

"Well, that's why I was at Eastern Standard. I was having dinner with my sister."

Sydney puts her head down and starts to giggle.

"What's funny?"

"Wow, Thomas all of it. I too have a confession to make. I assumed you were blowing me off. And then when I saw you walk into the Eastern Standard with a woman, I assumed you were on a date."

"Hence the blog post on Sunday."

Sydney nods. "Your sister is beautiful by the way."

Thomas smiles. "Thank you. Kim will be over the moon when she finds out her idol, Sydney Graham, thinks she's beautiful."

"As long as we are confessing, I might as well keep going."

"There's more?" Thomas asks surprised.

"I saw you yesterday, sitting on a bench, on the Comm Ave Mall. I was across the street and freaked out and ran back towards Newbury. Then I realized I was acting like a teenager, but by the time I got back to Comm Ave, you were gone."

"Sydney, I ran all over the Back Bay yesterday hoping I would run into you. My legs still hurt." He says as he leans forward in his chair.

"Well, we got that all wrong."

Thomas laughs. "We sure did. Any chance we could have a do-over?"

"You have tickets to another book reading?"

"No, I don't. I was thinking more along the lines of dinner tomorrow night?"

Sydney smiles as she feels the flutter in her stomach. "That would be perfect."

Part 2:
The Never Dull, Lull

12
And So It Begins

Insightful Blogger Headquarters

"Benjamin! Happy Friday!" Harris says as he walks into Ben's office and plops down in a chair in front of Ben's desk. "So, how are we progressing with the Ty Kent discovery?"

"Actually Harris, we are doing well. We are currently trying to narrow down Ty Kent's age and gender."

"Really." Harris says, intrigued. "How?"

"Well, we have noticed some patterns as we read the first novels compared with the latest novels. The romances and characters mature. We are still in the discovery stage; however, we feel as though once we finish all of the books we can narrow down the age."

"So your saying the characters may be maturing at the same rate as Ty Kent?"

"Exactly."

"Interesting."

"Now as far as gender is concerned. That is a bit trickier. We are taking about ten books to start and having both a male and a female read the same book. We are trying to ascertain the point of view of the writer. Is Ty Kent leaning more towards a male perspective or that of a female? By having both genders read the same book we will have stronger evidence."

"That is fantastic Benjamin. Now am I hearing that you and your team are narrowing in on one person? So that tells me you have ruled out Sydney Graham's suggestion that Ty Kent maybe a group of people?"

"We have ruled that out Harris."

"How so?"

"Well, even though characters and situations are maturing from book to book the style of writing doesn't change. It has been, thus far, incredibly consistent and dare I say, predictable."

"Are you sure?"

Ben looks at Harris with a frown. "What do you mean, am I sure?"

Harris sits up on his seat and puts his elbows on Ben's desk. "I need you to be 100% sure Benjamin."

"Why?" Ben asks still totally confused.

"Look, I know finding out Ty Kent's identity is not an overnight project. However, I'm hoping to glean some leading stories along the way. I, we, need to keep this game alive. So if you and your team have absolute evidence that can denounce someone who's getting quite a bit of media attention right now, then we need to jump on that gravy train. How great to declare Sydney wrong in the middle of her pre-launch. It's just like taking a big arm and sweeping all of her attention right in our direction."

"Harris, why do you want to destroy Sydney's progress?" Ben protests.

"I don't care about Sydney's progress Benjamin. I care about our progress. And me caring about our progress is how everyone gets paid. I want the absolute answer and a blog post disputing Sydney by end of day Monday." Harris then reaches into his jacket pocket and pulls out a Starbucks gift card. He tosses it on to Ben's desk. "Here's a one hundred dollar gift card. You and your team are going to need it."

Ben waits for Harris to walk down the hall before he leans back in his chair and lets out a heavy sigh. *As if Sydney doesn't hate me enough.*

Ben drags himself into the conference room and his

team can instantly see that something is up. "Okay gang, we have a slight change in focus. We need to comb through all of these novels with the focus on proving that Ty Kent is one person, not a group."

"I thought we already agreed that's the case." Alex says confused.

"We're fairly certain. Now, we need to be absolutely certain with evidence to support it. Harris wants a fifteen hundred-word blog post for Monday disproving Sydney Graham's theory."

The team members give each other side glances. No one says anything. They put their heads down and get to work.

. . .

Sydney pops into the car with a big grin on her face. "You know Maryann, I love it when we travel in these black SUV's. I always feel like we are FBI or Secret Service. It's so cool."

"Well aren't you chipper this morning. Do tell." Maryann says as she hands Sydney a coffee.

"Thank you. I'm always chipper."

"Not lately."

"Yeah, I'll give you that. It's Friday. The venue for the book launch party is absolutely perfect. And after today we have the two-week lull. Only one lecture, four book clubs, and five interviews, that means I can get some much needed rest." Sydney pauses for a few seconds. "Oh, and I have a date with Thomas tonight."

Maryann spins around in her seat in disbelief. "What? The hot runner guy?"

"Yes, the one and only. Oh and he is also a Professor at Harvard."

"I was just with you thirty-six hours ago. Wow, your life moves quickly. We have a long ride to Northampton, so start spilling."

"Paul, how much longer before we arrive?" Maryann asks the driver.

"About thirty minutes, ma'am."

"Thank you."

Maryann turns to Sydney. "Okay. Do you have your Sydney Graham, the ever tough and honest relationship coach hat on or Sydney Graham, I can't stop thinking about my date tonight, hat on?"

"What are you talking about?" Sydney asks a bit miffed by Maryann's tone.

"Look Sydney, I'm so excited for you, for tonight. However, as your publicist, we still have three weeks to go before your book launches in stores and on line. We need you to be the ever-clever and realistic Sydney, no matter what. That's what we are selling."

Sydney turns and looks out the window. As much as Maryann's words sting a bit, she's right.

"Sydney, I'm just looking out for your best interests."

"I know. And you're absolutely right. I'm going to get into my email and start responding. Honestly, I've been putting it off as I've had my head in the clouds. This should help me get my focus to where it needs to be."

Maryann smiles with relief.

Sydney steps out of the car in front of the Hotel Northampton and twirls around. "Oh my Goodness, it's so great to be here."

"At the hotel?" Maryann asks confused.

Sydney inhales deeply. "Just here. I mean of course, yes the Northampton Hotel, the Grand Dame of Northampton. But here, this is where it all started."

"Where what all started?" Maryann is suddenly feeling as if she doesn't know her best client as well as she thinks.

"Everything. This was my sanctuary, this is where I came to write."

"Write? I'm not following Sydney."

Sydney gives her a smirk. "I was a psychology major, Maryann, I wrote a great deal. I would do my research on campus and then write all of my papers here. I felt like being here, a mere nine miles away from campus, brought my research to life. Obviously, most of my work in psychology was about research and data, however it was also all about people. So when I wrote my papers, I wanted to be around people."

"That makes sense. And it clearly brings you to life."

Sydney smiles. "You have no idea."

The women walk into the grand lobby of the Hotel Northampton and are greeted by their event planner, Erin.

"Oh my gosh, Ms. Graham, it's such a pleasure to meet you, I'm a huge fan." Erin says as she eagerly shakes Sydney's hand.

"A pleasure to meet you Erin, are you still in school?"

"I am. A hotel administration major at UMass."

"Well, my Alma Marta. Erin, let's make this a big success for both of us. Lead the way."

Erin leads Sydney and Maryann to the Northampton Room. The room is set up with five round tables seating ten people each. At the front of the room is a podium with a wireless headset and next to it a small table with a pitcher of water. The back of the room hosts a buffet table set with coffee, tea, water, and light refreshments. The sun's natural light streams through the room's three walls of windows. It's breathtaking.

Maryann slowly walks around the room carefully inspecting each table setting. "This is perfect Erin. Thank you. Is there a place for Sydney to work before the event?"

"Absolutely we have a room right across the hall set up for the two of you. The book club organizer, Louise should be here shortly and she's all set to greet the members."

Sydney stands outside of the Northampton Room, listening to Maryann introduce her. She slips inside the room when she hears the applause and gives the audience a grateful smile and positive nods.

"Thank you everyone. I'm so thrilled to be here with all of you today. Thank you Louise for all of your hard work in organizing this event. A big thank you to my publicist Maryann for that wonderful introduction and well, everything she does for me. And thanks to all of you for coming out on this spectacular fall day. Now, I must share something with you before we get started. If I seem at all soft today, please don't be alarmed, I have a soft spot in my heart for this place as it is where I spent most of my time as an undergraduate."

Maryann is pleased with the thundering applause given to Sydney at the end of her lecture. Sydney's cautionary announcement prior to her speech gave Maryann some cause for concern. Now they just have to get through the audience questions unscathed.

"Okay, I have time for one more question." Sydney says as she scans the audience for raised hands. "Yes." Sydney says as she points to a young women sitting on the left side of the room.

"Sydney, many of us who belong to this book club are huge fans of you and all of your work. We are also big fans to Ty Kent." She says sheepishly.

Sydney smiles. "I would assume you are all fans of many writers."

"Yes, of course. I'm curious as to why you think that Ty Kent maybe more than one person?"

"Well, to be honest, I don't have anything to back that up. It was just something I said amongst an onslaught of questions from reporters. I was simply suggesting a different point of view. Ty Kent and I write about the same topic, we just approach it from a different angle. Ty Kent writes about all of the good stuff and there is always a happy ending. That's wonderful. I focus on real life. I help those when they struggle or argue. I help when there isn't a happy ending. My ultimate goal is to help everyone be better prepared and more grounded in real life."

Maryann smiles to herself. Sydney is presenting a bit softer than normal; yet, she's perfect.

After the second book club, meet and greet, is successfully finished, Maryann and Sydney settle into the car for the long ride home. "So," Maryann begins as she turns toward Sydney, "you did a great job today. More importantly, what are you wearing tonight?"

"What?" Sydney asks surprised.

"For your date, silly."

"Oh my gosh, Maryann, don't do that to me. I thought for sure I had forgotten something. I can't switch gears that quickly. So, you were pleased with today?"

"I am pleased, Sydney. You did a great job. Are you pleased?"

"I am actually. It was a lot of fun. I felt more relaxed, you know, more myself. Even with the Ty Kent question, I didn't feel the pressure to have a perfect answer. I felt like I could answer it, without second guessing myself."

"You did a very good job answering that question Sydney. And you're right; both you and Ty Kent are focusing on the same subject just from different points of view."

"I just hope I didn't give Harris and the Insightful Blogger more ammunition."

"Who cares? If you did, that just means you're a part of the story and more free press for you." Maryann says excitedly.

Sydney feels her gut twist, but tries not to show any worry on her face.

"Again, what are you wearing tonight?"

"Right. I don't even know where we are going. He said he would call." Sydney says as she searches through her bag for her phone. She finds her phone and scrolls through her voicemails. She smiles when she sees the name Thomas Peters.

"Well, I have a voicemail."

"Put it on Speaker."

"What? No Maryann."

"Come on Syd, I've been married for fifteen years, let me have a little vicarious romance through you."

Sydney rolls her eyes and reluctantly puts her phone on speaker while hitting the play button.

"Hey Sydney, this is Thomas. I hope your events are a smashing success today. I was thinking I would pick you up around seven-thirty this evening. I made a reservation at Mistral. I know you will have had a long day so I don't want to be too late. Just text me and let me know if that's okay. Oh, and I need your address. Looking forward to seeing you."

"Oh my!" Maryann gushes as she leans back in the seat.

"What?"

"What? Where do I start?" Maryann asks as she quickly sits back up. "His voice. That's the sexiest voice I've ever heard. I mean seriously, the guy could make a killing in voice-over work. And Mistral! That place exudes romance."

"Maryann, stop, you're freaking me out."

"Sorry. Um, but, does the face match the voice?"

Sydney pulls up Thomas's picture from the Harvard website and hands her phone to Maryann.

"Oh!" Maryann says as she puts her hand to her cheek. "So, that's a solid yes."

"Stop! Maryann. I'm really struggling. I'm one of my clients. I have butterflies and I can't think straight. He is, yes, really good-looking and has an amazing voice. He's kind and super smart. He's a Harvard professor. I'm none of those things. I'm a plain Jane relationship coach. Ugh."

"Sydney, you're one of the most successful people I know. You're a relationship coach, a blogger, a YouTube star, and an author. You have millions of people following you on all of your sites. You got here not only because you're brilliant; but also, because you're diligent and charismatic. And you are no plain Jane!"

"I don't even know what to wear. Maybe this was a

bad idea after such a long day."

"Now you stop, Sydney. When we get to your place, I'm coming in and picking out the perfect date night attire. Now text him your address."

13
A True First Date

Thomas pulls up to the corner of Marlborough Street and Exeter Street at exactly seven twenty-nine in the evening. He puts on his hazard lights, jumps out of his car and walks up the steps of the brownstone and has a look at the buzzers on the side of the building. He finds it odd that the apartments are not labeled with names, not even last names. He checks his phone to look for Sydney's text to be sure he has the right address and apartment. He presses the button next to the label, 2.

"Hi this is Sydney."

"Hey Sydney, your chariot awaits."

Sydney laughs. "Right on time. I'll be right down."

Sydney walks out of her brownstone to see Thomas looking quite handsome, standing on the sidewalk. He's wearing dark jeans, a button down shirt and blazer.

"You look amazing." Thomas says as she walks down the stairs.

"Thank you. You're looking rather dapper yourself."

Thomas takes Sydney's hand and leads her around the car. He opens the door and waits to be sure she is all in before shutting it. He walks around to the driver's side and takes his seat. "I hope you're hungry."

"Starving." Sydney says with a large grin.

The hostess at Mistral leads Thomas and Sydney to one of the more private tables for two. Thomas pulls out Sydney's chair and smiles. She feels a flash of warmth come over her. She notices a bottle of Silver Oak on the table. She looks at

Thomas as he sits down.

"Rumor has it this is one of your favorite cabernets. I hope you don't mind that I called ahead."

Sydney smiles. "How thoughtful of you. Thank you. I love this restaurant, the food is fantastic and the atmosphere is comfortably elegant."

"Well said."

The waiter comes over with fresh water for both of them. And after letting both Thomas and Sydney taste the wine, pours each of them a glass and let's them know about the specials for the evening.

Thomas raises his glass of wine. "I would like to thank you, the beautiful Miss Sydney Graham for joining me on a second, first date."

Sydney smiles as she clinks Thomas's glass and takes a sip of the wine. She feels herself blushing a bit. She can't remember the last time someone called her beautiful.

"So, what is your favorite dish on the menu?'

"Well, being that this is our first meal together I should probably say it's one of the more sophisticated dishes. However, if I'm honest, it's the beef tenderloin, mashed potato flat bread." Sydney says as she shrugs her shoulders.

Thomas bows his head and chuckles. "That's a perfect choice. How about this, we order the beef and potato flatbread, the fig and prosciutto flatbread and you meet me tomorrow morning for a long run?"

"Throw in the Mistral fries and you've got yourself a deal."

"Done. And I must say, I think I just set a record."

"How's that?"

"Thirty minutes into the date and I already have another date." Thomas says as he gives Sydney a playful wink.

Sydney nods her head smirking a bit. "Well played."

Sydney is amazed by how smoothly their date is going. The conversation flows effortlessly. This shouldn't come as a surprise as their first date was also comfortable and easy. She's happy that their communication mishaps didn't pose any problems this evening. She is a bit in awe of him. He has so many great qualities that are topped off by him being genuinely nice. That may be one of her favorite parts about him, she has witnessed him interact with a number of people and every time he is truly kind. Of course he is the man that checked in on her after she was almost run over by a skateboarder and a pack of bicyclists.

Thomas parks in front of Sydney's brownstone. He pops out of the car and around to her side to open the door. He walks her to the steps of her brownstone.

"Thomas, thank you so much for this evening. I had a great time."

"As did I. Are you still good for a run tomorrow?"

"Of course!"

"Great, you want to meet me on this side of the Mass Ave Bridge, say nine in the morning?"

"Perfect. I will see you then."

"Go get some rest. I'm not leaving this spot until you're safely behind those double doors."

Sydney smiles and walks up the steps. Once inside she turns and waves to Thomas. She loves how chivalrous he is.

14
Brunch and a Blog

"We've all ordered. Before we start scanning the Sunday headlines, start spilling Sydney." Michelle says as she and Jordan both place their elbows on the table and lean in towards Sydney.

"I don't know what you are talking about." She says as she picks up the Sunday Globe.

"We're an old married couple over here Sydney. Give us a dose of romance."

She rolls her eyes at Jordan's comment. "I had a lovely time. Both Friday night and Saturday morning."

"WHAT??" Both Jordan and Michelle exclaim.

"No, no. You two are too much. I had a lovely dinner with Thomas on Friday evening. We ate so much that we agreed to MEET Saturday morning and go for a run and work off the dinner."

"Whoa. You ran with someone? You never run with other people." Michelle says.

"I'm not against running with other people. Ben wasn't a runner. I just never had someone to run with."

"I'm sitting right here Syd." Jordan quips.

"Jordan, you run too fast for me and you know it. It was really nice you guys. I have to say. He's so laid back, you know. He just makes everything effortless, like we have been friends for a long time."

"But, you want to be more than friends, right?" Michelle asks.

"I don't know. I don't want to get ahead of myself.

And I did just get out of a serious relationship."

"Syd, you just got out of a boring relationship that lasted well beyond its expiration date."

"Jordan's right Syd. How about not trying to control anything about this, the result or the pace and just let things unfold. How do you feel when you're with him?"

Sydney takes a few moments to consider her friends' comments. "Well, like I said, he makes things feel effortless. On the one hand, I feel as though I'm with an old friend. We get along great and have similar interests. We both love to eat and then run it off. And on the other hand, I'm incredibly attracted to him. He's smart and makes me laugh. Yet, he's not arrogant. He's really a thoughtful and kind man. And…" Sydney pauses. "Never mind that's it."

"And…" Michelle pries.

"It's nothing. It's corny."

"Out with it." Michelle demands.

"It's stupid it's just a quirky thing of mine."

"I know. He has great hands." Jordan says proudly.

"How do you know that?"

"I've heard you comment before. You like strong hands. You don't like chubby hands. It's quirky but no judgment." Jordan says as he sits on his hands.

Michelle rolls her eyes at Jordan. "Babe, you have great hands too. Every girl likes strong hands. It's like this innate thing for women. It's a sign of strength and protection. Not that we need it, but it's nice to know it's there if we do. So how tall is he?"

Sydney gives a warm smile for her friend's understanding and explanation. "He's six four."

"So in summary, he is awesome, hot, tall, and he passes the hand test." Michelle says.

"Yeah." Sydney replies with a soft smile.

"And there's the look. She is done." Jordan proclaims.

"When are you seeing him again?"

"Well, this week is a video week. I film all of my

YouTube videos for the month so it's a hectic week. I told him I wouldn't be free until Saturday. He said that was too long. So we're doing an early few hours at the Museum of Fine Arts on Wednesday evening."

"Wow." Jordan says as he grabs Michelle's hand. "She's head over heels and he can't wait to see her. I think our girl has finally found true romance."

"Stop it." Sydney says as she throws a few home fries at the two of them.

. . .

Sydney heads home after finishing brunch with Michelle and Jordan. She is left feeling excited and uneasy. Yet, she really doesn't have any time to dwell on her emotions, as she has to write her weekly blog and prepare for all of the video shoots. She thinks back to a time when she used to write because she loved to versus having to. She wonders why her weekly blogs are getting to be so difficult. Words used to flow, but now they struggle to appear. Everyone thinks writing is so easy. If it were, everyone would be doing it. Her blog following is where she had always wished it to be, but now she feels pressure and scrutiny, making things much more difficult.

Sydney plops down on her favorite chair and opens up her laptop. She begins to read emails from her blog followers. She smiles as her brain starts to pop with some creative ideas. She has been so busy with events and presentations she lost site of what the blog is for, her readers.

Blog Post # 522: On Line Dating: Are You Done?

So you've matched and harmonized, you've said, "okay to cupid" and swam with plenty of fish, you've tindered and grinded and yet, you are still single. Newsflash: Online dating is a business! A big business!

Do you feel like you are the only single person left in your neighborhood, town, or world? You have friends that met each other in high school, or college, or in their 20's at work, or through friends. However, you have yet to meet anyone. You are not into the bar scene or you feel too "old" for it. You work a lot so you don't have time to meet people; perhaps you live in a suburban area where it seems as though everyone is married.

Of course you turned to online dating, what else would you do? Yet, that doesn't seem to be working either. You have been told there are great results, you have seen the ads, and perhaps you've heard of a friend of a friend who met their perfect mate online. (Those things do happen, I honestly have a good friend who found their perfect match online).

You put your profile up and you go on some dates. You constantly see the same profiles, and you're not getting any interesting connections. Then you get a creepy email from some guy 20 years older than you who lives 2000 miles away, so you hide your profile and you swear off the dating website. You tell everyone you are taking a break; a friend tells you of a really great new dating site you decide to give it a whirl and repeat.

Does any of this sound familiar? First, it's important to note the people who met each other in high school or college or right after college, that typically happened organically. They are people who met through others, at class, or on the job. They had time to get to know each other. They probably shared similar interests or friends. They had some connection other than both being single.

The only connections two people know they have on dating websites, is that at least one of you finds the other attractive and that you are both single (and even that is not always guaranteed). If the attraction is strong enough, we will go on a date ignoring all of the other information that tells us this person is not right for us. If we have a good time we even further ignore all of the things that are wrong because we had fun, we are attracted to them, and they are single. And that my friends, is the recipe for the repeated online dating disasters.

Now, I'm not saying you should completely give up on online dating sites. However, be honest with yourself about what they are: really big picture books that you flip through and occasionally read some of the captions.

If you want to meet someone more organically and whom you share similar interests with; expand your social network. Join a club that focuses on a hobby you like, or try some new meet up groups. "New" is the key word there, if you're already doing some clubs, try some new ones. Expanding your friend circle expands your probability of meeting a potential mate; bring your best business networking game to your dating game.

And remember, there are more single adult Americans than married adult Americans.

To your success in love and life,
    Sydney

Sydney presses, "publish" on her blog site. She closes her laptop and feels a sense of relief for getting the blog done. She looks at the clock and realizes she has exactly thirty minutes before her first coaching call. Her sense of relief is quickly replaced with urgency. She opens her laptop and begins to read her notes from her last session with Rachel. *Oh Rachel, what will you have in store for me today?* Sydney thinks to herself.

Rachel has been an on again off again client of Sydney's. She's really dynamic and has a successful sales career; however, with relationships she tends to go all in full steam and then burn them out before they ever have a chance to get off the ground. She's incredibly independent but when she meets someone it's almost as though she becomes obsessed. She constantly wants their time and bombards them with texts messages. She and Sydney try to work on slowing her down, not an easy task. Sydney suddenly feels a twang of unease. She wonders if she and Thomas are moving too quickly? Sydney takes some deep breaths and stops her negative thoughts. *Remember your number one rule Syd; do not compare your relationship to any other relationship.* Sydney repeats this mantra as she continues her deep breathing.

15
A Mid-Week Rendezvous

Insightful Blogger Headquarters

"Good Morning Benjamin." Harris says as he walks into Ben's office and takes a seat.

"Harris. Perfect timing. We have the blog post for your review. I think you'll be pleased. We worked all weekend and have solid evidence that Ty Kent is one person."

Harris shrugs as he pulls out his phone. "Too late." Harris says and hands his phone over to Ben.

Ben looks at the phone screen and sees a picture of Sydney Graham talking with some women. He reads a bit of the article that is focused on Syd's new book. "I don't get it. This is about Syd."

"Keep reading. This young reporter got Sydney to reveal that she has no evidence that Ty Kent is a group of people she was just randomly throwing the idea out."

Ben keeps reading the article. "But Harris, we have documented why we believe Ty Kent is one person. We wrote a great blog."

Harris shakes his head no. "The story has been told. Let's move on. What else do we know about Ty Kent?"

Ben lets out a sigh. He wants Harris to know how frustrated he is. "Well, we are working on figuring out if Ty Kent is a male or female."

"Great Benjamin. I want that answer by Friday."

"Friday, Harris this is not an easy task."

"I have faith in you Benjamin." Harris says as he

stands up and walks out of Ben's office. "Oh, and one other thing. I don't want anyone else beating us to the scoop. Have one of your teammates keep a close eye on Sydney. I want someone at all of her speaking events."

"Why?"

"It just seems as though wherever Sydney is something about Ty Kent pops up and I want to be on it."

Ben walks into the conference room and shuts the door.

"So, did he love the blog?" Lisa asks excitedly.

"He didn't read it."

"Why?" Alex asks.

"Someone already reported on it. I've emailed all of you the link to the story. I'm sorry. However, we can't let that get us down. We still have great evidence that Ty Kent is one person, which means, we are one step closer to figuring out who Ty Kent is. Let's keep moving forward. Our focus this week is *gender*."

"Ben, I noticed while pouring over the books this weekend that Ty Kent has great detail about the settings for the stories. I think plotting the locations of the stories and time frames may help us. Like Alex and I previously suggested." Samantha suggests.

"Samantha, that seems like a good idea and we will get there eventually. However, this week, our only focus is gender. We need to have a blog written with evidence by Friday."

The team members all groan at once.

"I know. It's a lot to do, but you're some of the smartest journalists I know. We can do this." Ben tries to pump up his team even though he feels exactly as they do. "Oh and I need someone to keep tabs on Sydney Graham."

"You mean like follow her?" Alex asks.

"Well, not in a creepy way no. I just need someone to be at all of her events. You can find the schedule on her publicists website." Ben says as he tosses Maryann's card on to the conference table. "Some of these events are private book club events. And her primary audience is women, so Alex it can't be you. Lisa or Samantha?"

"I'll do it. I have a lot of friends in book clubs so I may be able to find my way into the private events." Lisa says.

"Great. Thank you Lisa."

"No problem. It's kind of exciting. I get to be like a private detective."

"Yeah, well, just stick to the events. I don't want you to stalk her." Ben says feeling a bit apprehensive.

"Got it!" Lisa says enthusiastically.

. . .

"I love this place, Thomas. What a great idea." Sydney says as she and Thomas enter the Museum of Fine Arts.

"Me too. I could spend and entire week here. Did you get a chance to look at the current exhibits?"

"I did. I will view anything here. But I'm curious about the *Art of Influence,* exhibit."

"Really?"

"Yes, but we can see whatever."

"No, that's great. That's the one I really want to see as well. Wait here, I'll go grab us some tickets."

While Sydney waits for Thomas to return she grabs a visitor's guide. She studies the map. It's been a while since she has visited the museum and she has forgotten how large it is. She wonders why she stopped coming here. When did she become so boring and solely focused on work?

"Excuse me. Miss?"

Sydney turns to see a young woman in her twenties trying to get her attention. "Yes."

"Are you Sydney Graham?"

"I am." Sydney says with a smile.

"Oh my gosh, I am such a huge fan. Actually me, all of my friends, we are all huge fans."

"Well thank you very much."

"May I ask to take a selfie with you. My friends are meeting me here and they will never believe me. Oh and I'm Lisa." The young woman says as she extends her hand to Sydney.

Sydney chuckles. "Sure."

They pose for the selfie. Lisa thanks Sydney repeatedly and then bounces off.

"What was that all about?" Thomas asks as he hands Sydney a ticket.

"Thank you. And I have no idea. She said she was a "fan". Whatever that means."

"Well you do have a book coming out Sydney and you've been doing a lot of events lately."

"Maybe, it was just odd. Whatever, let's go see this exhibit."

"Okay. The exhibit is in galleries 169 and 170. Those are both on the first floor and conveniently located just steps away from Taste Café and Wine Bar."

"I'm impressed."

"Shall we?" Thomas says as he offers Sydney his arm.

As Sydney and Thomas head off to see their chosen exhibit, Lisa slyly snaps a few quick shots of the happy couple. *Ben is going to love these.* Lisa thinks to herself.

The exhibit mesmerizes Sydney. It consists of postcards from World War I through Word War II that focus on influencing and persuading people to act, to fight, to be brave and support the cause of various nations. The use of colors and slogans is awe inspiring except for when you consider the purpose, which was war.

The creative is impressive. That is what Sydney focuses on, as the reason behind all of these postcards is unnerving.

Thomas and Sydney had separated when they entered the first room, individually taking in the exhibit at their own pace. Sydney looks at her watch and realizes she has been wondering through the rooms for an hour and forty-five minutes. That certainly speaks to how powerful the exhibit is.

She scans the room and spots Thomas as he gives her a wave and nods his head towards the exit.

The pair head over to the Taste Café and Wine Bar. Sydney grabs a small table while Thomas gets them each a glass of wine. Thomas sits down at the table and slides a glass over to Sydney. "A penny for you thoughts?"

"I wouldn't know where to begin Thomas. I'm still processing everything. But, thank you for this. I can't remember the last time I was here. And now I'm trying to figure out what in the world got in the way of me coming more often."

"First, you're welcome. And thank you for joining me on a school night." Thomas says as he raises his wine glass to toast Sydney. "And secondly, I completely agree. That exhibit was a lot to take in. I feel as if I need to write everything down and organize my thoughts and to be honest, my emotions, before I can even begin to discuss it."

"Exactly. I didn't realize how stimulating it would be. Do you write?"

Thomas takes a thoughtful sip of his wine. "I do. I write quite a bit. Mostly I write papers, reviews, and opinions."

"But, not books?" As the words came out of Sydney's mouth she could see Thomas's face change. "I'm sorry. I just… sorry." Sydney quickly tries to fix her misstep.

"Sydney, don't be sorry. It's a valid question. I'm working on a book or books I should say. I have a lot of starts and half completed novels. Truth is my profession is a blessing and a curse. I know a great deal about literature and like to think I have a vast vocabulary and a solid grasp of the English language, but I compare my work to the great authors. I read it and think would Ernest Hemmingway or Jane Austen ever think this is fit to print. The answer is always no."

"I can understand that. And that is exactly why I wrote a self-help book. The genre isn't exactly overwrought with

Pulitzer Prize winners."

Thomas laughs at Sydney's quick wit. *She really is the trifecta, beauty, brains, and a sense of humor.* He wonders how he got so randomly lucky and yet, hopes he doesn't mess it up. "So tell me, what had you so busy these last three days?"

"I have a YouTube channel."

"You do?"

"Yeah, you really didn't look me up on the Internet?"

"No. Well, I read the blog that my sister sent me and I read your bio. I want to get to know Sydney who is sitting here in front of me, not what the Internet tells me I should know."

"I appreciate that. So, I have a YouTube channel. And I post about two videos per week but we film them ahead of time. We shoot eight to ten videos at a time."

"Wow. And what are you discussing relationship things?"

"Actually, it is more like a lifestyle channel. As a relationship coach it isn't always about someone's relationship with other people. It's often about their relationship with themselves, body image, and their relationship to food, to work, to money. I bring in experts on all of those topics and interview them and do demonstrations. Today we did three cooking segments."

"Sydney, I can't believe how much you do. That's incredible."

"Thank you, the down side, of course, is I don't get to museums as much as I would like to."

"Well, I can help with that." Thomas says as he flashes a big grin.

"I'd like that. You know today, we cooked this really great autumn inspired meal. And if you're not busy Saturday night, I was thinking I could make it for you."

"You cook?"

"Well, a side-effect from doing all of the videos, I've learned how to cook."

"That sounds like a great evening. I would love to, on one condition."

"Which is?"

"I get to be your sous chef."

Sydney can feel her face light up. "That would be awesome!"

16
The Gender Discovery

Sydney rolls over and looks at her alarm clock, which reads five-thirty in the morning. She never actually uses her alarm unless she absolutely has to be up at a certain time. Even in those instances she wakes up before it goes off. She wishes she could be one of those girls who sleeps in. At times, especially on particularly cold winter mornings she tries to roll over and stay snuggled in her bed; but she never lasts more than fifteen minutes.

She pulls herself out of bed and heads upstairs to turn on the coffee. Many highly successful people get out of bed very early, at least that is what she has read. And her routine has worked out for her. However, if she ever had the opportunity to make a wish, or stumbled upon a "genie in a bottle, " she would wish for one day out of seven that she could sleep in, and that day would be Monday. Unlike the rest of the world, weekends tend to be quite busy for Sydney work-wise. Most of her clients want to speak with her on the weekend or occasional weeknights. Her schedule is more like those in the hospitality industry, as Mondays are Sundays.

Her coffee finishes brewing and she pours a cup. She grabs her laptop and phone and curls up in her favorite chair. No sense in worrying about sleep when she is wide-awake. She decides to get a head start on her Sunday blog.

After two hours of reading emails and out lining topic ideas for her blog, Sydney checks her phone and sees a text message from Michelle. *Hey, I'm not going into the office until ten, coffee? 8:30? Usual spot?* Sydney sends an affirmative reply and heads to the shower.

Sydney scans the coffee shop and sees Michelle in the back corner staring at her phone. Of course, that is all anyone is doing. The people in line waiting to order are staring at their phones. The people sitting at tables are staring at their laptops. Sydney wonders how we got here as a society, to the point where we spend more time looking at screens than at each other. She finds it rather sad.

"Good Morning." Sydney says as the sits down with Michelle.

"Hi." Michelle responds without looking up from her phone. "One last sentence. Done." Michelle puts her phone down and gives Sydney a big grin. "I'm so glad you could meet this morning. Here coffee, black, just the way you like it." Michelle pushes a medium cup towards Sydney.

"I know, boring, right?"

"Actually Syd, I think drinking black coffee is kind of daring. I don't know how you stomach the taste without sugar."

"Well, I'll let you in on a little secret, sometimes I'll go rogue and put cinnamon in it."

Michelle laughs. "So, how are things? I feel like I haven't seen you in weeks."

"We had brunch on Sunday Michelle. Things are great."

"Wow, that is quite the smile Sydney. Would that smile have anything to do with a handsome professor?"

"He would have everything to do with it. We went to the MFA Wednesday night and we had a great time."

"We haven't been to the Museum in so long. Why did we stop going?"

"I was thinking the same thing Michelle. We need to start going again."

"So when are you seeing him again?"

"He is coming to my place Saturday night and we are cooking dinner."

"What?" Michelle responds a bit too loudly. "You're having him over to your house? Syd it took you four months before you let Ben come to your house."

"I know. But Thomas is really kind and down to earth. I don't think he will be judgmental or put off. Honestly, I don't think he would even think twice."

"Syd, I think it's great. You shouldn't have to hide your success. You work hard and you have a beautiful home. And you worked really tirelessly to make that home look great."

"Thank you."

"Now, let's talk about your book launch. I'm dying to see the menu."

Sydney excitedly pulls out her phone and the ladies gush over the decadent menu that the chef has outlined. Over the next forty-five minutes, Sydney and Michelle manage to tweak the menu a bit and the décor. Michelle is a designer and has some very thoughtful suggestions.

As Sydney walks home she can't help but feel excited. Michelle had so many great ideas. Yet she wonders if this is too much about her. It's her very first book launch, she can't really help herself; it's super exciting. Her mind drifts to Thomas. She hopes she isn't inviting him in too soon. Michelle did make a good point; there are many reasons why she waits a long time before letting people completely into her life.

Years ago Sydney had fallen for a man named Jake, who was the opposite of who he presented himself to be. He was very handsome and well spoken. He could engage with anyone and had a great sense of humor. They had a lot of fun together.

Then one day Sydney got a phone call from her credit card company. Apparently someone had stolen her card and managed to purchase forty thousand dollars worth of merchandise in less than one hour. The biggest purchase was a thirty thousand dollar diamond ring. And that ring was not for Sydney. Fortunately the jewelry store had many surveillance cameras. The recordings along with the positive identification of Jake, by the security guard and the sales attendant led to his arrest. Everything was eventually resolved and Sydney didn't have to pay for any of the purchases. However, she was left feeling incredibly violated and embarrassed. It took two years of therapy before she even started dating again.

One major thing that Sydney realized with Jake is that he never let her into his life. He never introduced her to friends or family. She tried to find him on social media and via Internet searches, but she had little success. Those were two big red flags that she chose to ignore.

Thomas on the other had has a very public profile. He has been teaching at Harvard for a long time. His picture and biography are publically displayed on their site. And her Internet searches on him typically link to articles he's published and media appearances. Sydney smiles. Yes she is quite confident that Thomas is who he says he is.

Insightful Blogger Headquarters

Ben gathers his team in the conference room. Today is the day they need to reveal, as best they can, Ty Kent's gender. "Okay, let's start with a vote. Who here thinks Ty Kent is a woman?"

Alex and Samantha raise their hands.

"Who thinks Ty Kent is a man?"

Ben and Lisa raise their hands.

"Great." Ben says frustrated with the split vote. "Well, Alex and Samantha, why don't the two of you start by presenting to us why you think Ty Kent is a woman."

For two hours Alex and Samantha present excerpts from various novels that they believe only a woman could write. Lisa and Ben are able to counter argue all but three of the excerpts. The teams switch roles and Ben and Lisa present their case as to why Ty Kent must be a man. In addition to excerpts that they felt were definitely written by a man. They also presented evidence that demonstrated the author to be more familiar with men in general than with women. They even went so far as to point out the author's description of public bathrooms, in particular the bathrooms at Fenway Park.

"Look here." Lisa begins. "This passage is about the couples first meeting. They are both standing in line to use the restroom. Now the female character gives a description of the crowded bathrooms and the conversations going on. The male character does the same. Ben says the male description is spot on. I've gone to a lot of events at Fenway, the description of the women's restrooms is not at all accurate."

Alex and Samantha look at each other and each re-read the passage Lisa is presenting.

"You're right." Samantha says shocked.

"Okay! So are we all in agreement?" Ben asks.

Everyone nods.

"Homestretch here team. Let's get this blog written and submitted to Harris by the end of the day. Nice work everyone!"

17
Cooking for Two

Sydney springs out of bed, runs upstairs to her kitchen and flips on her coffee maker. Her thoughts are racing. She takes a walk around her kitchen, and then through her dinning room. She makes mental notes of what needs to be cleaned. Sydney is a neat freak so not too much needs to be done, just a little dusting and a once over of the kitchen and the bathrooms. She heads up another flight of stairs to her second entertaining area. The large room hosts a big television a large sectional couch and two oversized leather chairs. On the other side of the room, a wet bar covers one wall and Sydney has a large square table with six high back leather chairs. She uses the table to play games with her friends or do jigsaw puzzles. She looks at the half completed puzzle she is currently working on and wonders if she should put it away. She decides to leave it on the table. She loves doing puzzles. She finds it relaxing and one of the few things she doesn't feel she has to immediately complete once she starts it.

On the other side of the table French doors open up to her expansive deck furnished with outdoor couches and chairs and a six-person dining table. In the left corner of the room is a full bathroom, which she will need to clean. As Sydney scans the room she feels a twinge of anxiety. She hopes Thomas isn't put off by her home. She hears Michelle's voice in her head. *Don't feel guilty about your success.* Sydney's eyes look over to the frosted glass door in the back right corner. The door that leads to her mediation room and that is exactly what she needs to do right now.

By one in the afternoon Sydney has coached two clients, her place is completely clean, she has showered, and written her shopping list. Sydney checks her phone before she heads out the door and sees a text message from Thomas.

"Hey Sydney, looking forward to tonight. What may I bring and at what time? Remember, I want to help."

"Hi Thomas, how about six and just bring your culinary skills. Will you be driving over?

"Six is great and yes."

"Great call me when you are out in front of my house, I have an extra parking spot in the back."

"An EXTRA parking spot? I don't think I've ever heard/read those words in this city. See you soon."

Sydney smiles. She is about to put her phone in her purse when she sees that Michelle is calling.

"Hi."

"Hey Syd, are you ready for your big date tonight?"

"I'm getting there. The house is clean and now I am heading to get all of the food."

"Well, I'm sure he will love your cooking! I know I do. I have two quick items. First, you must promise to call me in the morning and tell me all about the date."

Sydney chuckles. "Okay. And second?"

"Did you see the Insightful Blogger today?"

"No. It's certainly not a site a regularly visit."

"Well, brace yourself. They are claiming Ty Kent is a man. As evidence by descriptions of the Fenway bathrooms."

"What?"

"I'm not kidding Syd. They list other examples but they say that Ty Kent's description of the male bathrooms at Fenway is more accurate than the female bathrooms so Ty Kent must have been in the male bathroom; thus their conclusion, Ty Kent is a man."

"Just when you think that site couldn't get anymore ridiculous! Wow, Michelle, that is quite the stretch. I have to run. But, I promise I will call you first thing tomorrow morning."

"Have fun!"

Sydney puts her phone in her purse and heads out the door still shaking her head at the absurdity of the Insightful Blogger.

Insightful Blogger Headquarters

"Benjamin!" Harris shouts from halfway down the hall.

Ben stops and turns around to see Harris waving his hand. "Harris I'm late I really have to get going."

"Of course, I'll only take a second. Do you mind?" Harris says as he points to Ben's office door.

"Five minutes Harris." Ben says firmly as his slides his messenger bag off his shoulder, grabs his keys and unlocks his office door.

"Benjamin, did you see all of the traffic we are getting on the story."

"Yes."

"This is great. I need a follow up for next week."

"What do you mean by follow up?"

"A new piece of information. I don't know maybe and estimation of his age? Perhaps where he might live?"

Ben leans against his desk, crosses his arms and lets out a sigh. "This is not an easy task Harris."

"I know, but look at what you and your team were able to do in one short week. You figured out his gender. You're all amazing."

"Well, the team did see a maturing in the writing over time."

"Doesn't that just happen as you write more?"

"Yes. But the topics and discussions also seem to have matured. I guess we could try and determine a rough estimate of his age by creating a time line of his books and topics discussed."

"Yes!" Harris says as leaps out of the chair.

"There are no guarantees Harris, but we will give it a shot."

"Of course not. Understood. So a blog exposing Ty Kent's age by Friday end of day, and we will post it first thing Saturday morning."

"Harris."

"I know, I know, no guarantees." Harris flicks his hand in the air as he starts to walk out of Ben's office. He then quickly turns around. "Hey, how is Lisa's snooping on Sydney going?"

"I don't know. She hasn't said anything."

"Okay, well follow up on that will you?"

"Sure. Have a great weekend Harris."

"Bye Benjamin." Harris says, already half way down the hall.

Saturday Evening at Sydney's

At precisely six in the evening Thomas calls Sydney to let her know he is in front of her building. Sydney grabs her house keys and races down three flights of stairs. She waves and smiles brightly when she sees Thomas standing outside of his car. He waves and walks around the car to open the passenger side door for her.

"Thank you." She says as she slides into the car.

Thomas gets into the driver's seat. "You look beautiful. And buckle up we have a long drive."

Sydney smiles and does as she's told. "Okay, so we are just looping around and taking the alley to the back of my building."

"Wow!" Thomas says as he sees all of the parking behind the building.

"Just pull up right next to this black car."

"Is that yours?"

"No, it's Michelle and Jordan's car. I don't own a car."

"You have two parking spots and don't have a car?"

"Technically four spots. These are both tandem spots. And I did lease a car but I never used it so it seemed like a waste of money. I just use Michelle and Jordan's if I need to or rent one."

Thomas smiles at Sydney as he exits the car. Sydney tries to open her door but can't. She looks for the button to unlock the door and then Thomas opens her door. "Did you lock me in?"

"A gentleman never tells." Thomas jests as he helps Sydney out of the car and grabs a bag out of the back seat.

"Smooth. Let's go around through the front. What's in the bag?"

"A bottle of red and a bottle of white. I wasn't sure what we were having so I brought both."

Sydney unlocks her condo door and they head up one flight of stairs. "So my place is a bit flip flopped. This level here is the bedroom level."

They walk up another flight of stairs and enter into Sydney's more formal living area.

"Sydney, your place is beautiful." Thomas says as looks around.

"Thank you. It took a very long time to get it to look like this. Here, let's put the wine in the kitchen and I will give you a quick tour."

"How long have you been living here?"

"Since 2009."

"So you lived through renovations, I'm impressed."

Sydney feels a knot in her stomach. She's sick of telling half-truths about her life. If Thomas can't handle this well, he's not the guy for her. "Sort of."

Sydney pulls a large framed collage of pictures from out of a closet and places it on the dining room table. "These are pictures of what the building looked like when I bought it and the progression of the renovation."

Thomas carefully examines each picture. "Syd, this is incredible. And I mean no disrespect when I say this, but this place was a dump! The work you did is truly awe inspiring."

"Well, it wasn't all me. I had a lot of help. And it was a dump. A contractor had bought it just before the market crashed in 2008. He was planning to renovate it and sell it off condo by condo. Unfortunately, he paid top dollar and then when everything went south, he couldn't get a construction loan and eventually the bank foreclosed on the property. I bought it at an auction, but without seeing the inside. When I did my first walk through I cried. And trust me, they weren't tears of joy."

"A tad overwhelmed?"

"Yes. But I fixed up the basement apartment. If you can believe it that one was in the best shape. I lived there as we worked on this one. We then did the first floor apartment and finally we did a real renovation on the basement apartment."

"So do you rent those out now?"

"I did for a few years. But it really got to be more of a headache than it was worth. The apartments would be trashed every time someone moved out. I changed the carpet in the entryway twice. The noise, meeting random strangers in the hallway, it just got to be too much."

"So are they just empty?"

"No. The first floor or parlor level is a nice two bedroom. When friends visit from a distance they stay there. When Michelle or Jordan's parents are in town they will stay there as well. And, I use it to film my YouTube videos. The basement or garden level apartment is now an indoor gym. When I have guest fitness people on my YouTube channel we will film segments down there."

"Sydney, I have to see it all."

"Really?"

"Yes. Not only is the transformation of this building a

huge accomplishment, I watched some of your YouTube videos and they're incredible. I'm excited to see where all of the magic happens."

"Alright." Sydney says as her smile brightens. "Let's go."

"May I take this with us?" Thomas asks about the framed collage.

"I can do one better." Sydney heads back to the closet and pulls out a photo album. "This is a little easier to carry."

Sydney begins the tour at the bottom. Thomas expertly follows along using the album as his guide to what the building once looked like. Sydney is amazed at how much Thomas knows about restoration and how enthralled he is. She feels pride about her house for the first time in a long time. She likes the feeling.

One hour later, Sydney and Thomas arrive back to their starting point, in Sydney's kitchen.

"Are you ready to cook?" She asks.

"Absolutely. What do you need me to do first?"

"Can you chop?"

"I'll have you know, I was a prep cook in high school. Chopping is a highlighted skill on my resume."

"Perfect. How about some music while we cook?"

"Absolutely."

Sydney hits shuffle on her music list and then cringes a bit when Dee-Lite comes on. She loves Dee-Lite but it's not really the best choice for a date. "Oops! This is from my running mix." She says sheepishly.

"I love it." Thomas says as he washes off the lettuce and he sways his hips and sings a long to *Groove is in the Heart*.

They expertly maneuver around each other as Thomas prepares the salad and Sydney the main dish, both shamelessly singing along to the music. Once the chicken is in the oven and the salad almost done, Sydney grabs a frying pan and throws in some sliced almonds and sugar.

"What do we have here?" Thomas asks as he places his

hands on the counter, his arms on either side of Sydney.

She feels a flash of heat run through her body as Thomas leans in a bit closer. She can feel his breath on her neck. "Caramelized almonds." Her voice squeaks.

Thomas leans in closer and presses his cheek to hers. "Smells amazing." He says as he inhales the scent and then heads back to his chopping duties.

Sydney feels flush as she continues to stir the almonds. She can't remember the last time she ever felt this way. She wonders if she has ever felt this way. This is what everyone is speaking about in those romance novels. She certainly felt flutters the first time she met Thomas. And when she thought he blew her off, she may have lost her mind for a bit. And now, him just putting his arms on either side of her, made her feel safe and flustered all at the same time. *Sydney, you know better, these are just passing emotions, and they don't make a relationship. Get your head back in the game!* She scolds herself.

After finishing their meals and returning all of the dishes to the kitchen, Sydney and Thomas retire to the living room, each with a glass of wine in hand.

"Sydney, that meal was amazing. Thank you. Are you sure I can't run in there and clean up?"

"Thomas, I have this very modern machine called a dishwasher! All set. And thank you, but I can't take all of the credit. I have an amazing sous chef. I would be happy to give you his number, for the next time you are planning a party."

Thomas smiles. He hears what Sydney is saying but he is not at all focused. This incredible woman just made him dinner. He can't remember the last time someone other than his mother or grandfather made him a meal. Sydney is so beautiful. She's so funny. All he sees right now are her lips. He just wants to kiss her. He takes her wine glass from her hands and places it on the table. He slides himself across the couch a bit closer to her. He reaches one arm around her shoulder. He places one hand on her face and brushes her cheek with his thumb.

Sydney almost faints as Thomas places his hand on her face and brushes her cheek with his thumb. Her heart pounds as he leans forward and their lips are so close she can feel his breath.

"BEEP." A piercing sound makes Thomas and Sydney jump to their feet.

"What is that?"

"Sorry! It's a warning system that goes off if someone is too close to the cars. If I can find my phone I can see what's going on." Sydney says as she searches for her phone. "Here it is."

Thomas walks over to Sydney. She presses a button on her phone and video of parking area appears. "It looks like just some kids walking through but let me pull up the last five minutes."

"This is some high-tech security Sydney."

Sydney shrugs. "Well, I do live here alone. This is weird. It looks like this person is taking a picture of your car." Sydney hands the phone to Thomas.

Thomas looks at the video. "That is odd. I don't recognize her. It looks like she's taking a picture of my license plate and then runs to catch up with her friends." He feels a sense of anxiety run through his body. He's sure it isn't her but he can't be certain. Thomas restarts the video and pauses it to see if he recognizes the woman's face. He presses play and something catches his eye. Thomas rewinds the video a bit and presses play as he hands the phone back to Sydney. "Keep your eye on the car."

Sydney watches the car and then sees an animal saunter out from under the car. "Is that a cat?"

"A raccoon."

"Oh my gosh." Sydney laughs. "She was taking a picture of the raccoon."

"This sure is one dangerous neighborhood Sydney."

Sydney rolls her eyes and playfully slaps him on the arm.

"Well, it is getting late. I should get going."

"Yes, of course." Sydney says as her heart sinks a bit. "I'll walk you out."

As Thomas and Sydney arrive to the back door of her building. Thomas turns to face her, "I had a great time Sydney. The food was fantastic. I was hoping you might be free on Tuesday evening?"

"I am."

"Great." Thomas smiles. "Some of my students are involved in an improv group in Cambridge and they have a show on Tuesday."

"That sounds like a ton of fun."

"It should be entertaining. The show is at eight in the evening but how about we grab a bite to eat first?"

"Perfect."

"I'll pick you up around six in the evening."

"I look forward to it."

Thomas leans in and gives Sydney a kiss on the cheek before exiting. Sydney waves, closes the door and locks it. She leans against the door and sighs. It was the perfect night and it was about to end with a long awaited kiss. She can't believe that instead of the potentially best kiss ever, she got a peck on the cheek all because of a stupid raccoon. She knows that some day she will find this story funny, but not tonight.

Mandarin Orange Salad with Roasted Almonds

Salad:
1 head of romaine lettuce, washed and chopped
2 celery stalks chopped
2 green onions chopped
1 cup of sliced almonds
2 tablespoons of sugar
1 small can of mandarin oranges drained

Dressing:
Whisk together:
¼ cup vegetable oil
2 Tbsps. sugar
2 Tbsps. red wine vinegar
1 Tbsp. fresh chopped parsley
½ tsp. salt
½ tsp. pepper
2-3 dashes of Tabasco sauce

Over medium heat, roast the almonds and sugar stirring constantly until all the sugar has dissolved. (About 10 minutes). Set aside to cool.

Combine all other ingredients in a bowl. Sprinkle with the roasted almonds and toss with salad dressing.

18
Blogs and Spies

Sydney flips open her laptop and begins to read her emails looking for inspiration for her blog. She finds that she is having a hard time writing her weekly blog. She daydreams more frequently, typically about Thomas. She is swept up in a romance and that is making it difficult for her to offer her usual pragmatic advice.

She begins to read an email with a subject line that reads: PLEASE HELP! The writer is a woman in her forties who has been married for fifteen years. The writer expresses her extreme frustration about the fact that she and her husband argue about the same two things. Their arguments do not start off about the same two things but when they get angry they inevitably re-hash the two, painful old arguments. When they calm down that both say they will stop bringing up the past, but the cycle never seems to stop. The writer states that neither she or her husband want to get divorced but their inability to get passed these two old arguments is wearing them both down.

"Oh boy." Sydney says aloud.

She responds to the writer urging she and her husband to see a couple's counselor. She has numerous experiences with couples that can't let go of past hurt or anger and the results have not been good. She wonders why it is that people tend to want to hold on to the painful memories more strongly than the joyful ones.

Blog Post: #523: Divorce Yourself!

Ok well maybe not your whole self.

Having supported many people through a divorce I don't take the word or the process lightly. I do however feel there is some value in the process. Divorce is final. It takes time. It takes a toll emotionally, physically, and financially. Divorce often has rules and contingencies. And like it or not, when it happens, it changes your world in ways you may have never imagined. I had one client move across the country and changed everything about her life.

Now I'm not suggesting anyone should go out and get divorced, quite the contrary. But what if you could apply that finality of divorce to something you would like to change or get rid of about yourself, your work, or your relationship? And what if, actually committing to it, absolutely and with finality could change your life for the better? For Example:

In a Relationship: How many times have you had the exact same argument with your partner? Years later, even if you are arguing about something completely different, it circles back to the same issue. It takes a toll. What if you could both commit to finally divorcing yourselves from that issue once and for all? What relief would you both be feeling?

Professionally: How many times have you started the new year saying, "this year I will be organized," or, "this year I will no longer procrastinate," or "this year I will…" What if you actually committed to what you said you were going to do? What would your life look like if you made that change?

Personally: How many times have you tried to quit smoking? Tried to lose that extra ten pounds? Tried to start eating healthy and exercising more? Tried to stop being afraid? Tried to move toward what you have always dreamed of? How awesome would you feel if you did?

So how do you do it? Well, it is a process. Start by applying the rules of divorce to whatever you want to get rid of. How? I am glad you asked.

1. Start with careful consideration: Very few people enter a divorce lightly. They have been pondering and considering for quite some time. Most have considered the pros and cons to changing nothing or changing everything. Make your lists.
2. Tell someone. Tell a friend, a partner (especially if it involves them), or a confidant what you are thinking of divorcing yourself from. This makes it a bit more real.
3. List the consequences and the gains for giving up the bad habit or cycle. You may initially think that divorcing yourself from a habit or cycle that you don't like is all gain, but it's not. Not initially anyway. Any negative habit or cycle has some benefit to you, you might not want to admit it; but if you really want to divorce yourself from it you have to. You must be honest. Those "trump card resentments" that you throw at your partner when you need to win an argument, benefit you somehow. (But usually only in the short-term). The consequence to giving up your resentments means you are not always going to win.
4. Brainstorm alternatives for your consequences or negative gains. For example, other stress relievers besides sweets. If you are holding onto resentments in your relationship, how can you let them go?
5. Create a contract, with your partner, friend, or confidant, that outlines **in detail** the penalties you or both of you will suffer if you do not adhere to the contract and the gains you will make if you do. For example: A $5.00 donation in a fun jar for everyday you do exercise; a $10 immediate donation given to someone or a charity for every day you skip planned exercise.
   If either you or your partner brings up the argument you are divorcing yourselves from he/she will a) not be

engaged with; b) the contract will be brought out for them to review; and c) will have to do the housework alone for 2 weeks. For every month we go without having that argument we will celebrate by doing …whatever you chose.
6. Make it official. Sign the contract. Have a witness sign the contract.
7. Celebrate your new beginning, the relief, and the excitement.

Here's to you! Divorce yourselves from the old to make room for the new!

To your success in love and life,
    Sydney

Wednesday Morning Coffee

"Michelle, this is such a mid-week treat, you being able to meet for coffee on a Wednesday. This is like the second time in as many weeks."

"I know, right. My hours are just messed up as I'm working on this overseas project. So, these days I work from eleven in the morning until seven at night. I have to say Syd; I don't mind it at all. I get to work out in the morning, have the place to myself for a bit. And the best part, Jordan is taking over the dinner duties. I come home to a great meal every night, mostly take-out, but still, a great meal."

"Well the new schedule does have some perks."

"So, catch me up on Thomas."

"Michelle, where do I begin? He's great. Things are great. I'm tired. This dating thing is like a whole second job."

"Wait, what? Did you just compare dating Thomas to a job?"

"Oh, no. Well, yes that's what I said, but I don't mean it like that. I just mean it's time consuming."

"He's time consuming?"

"Let me back up. He's not time consuming. I want to spend all of my time with him. My life is time consuming. My work is time consuming and I'm having a little trouble trying to get everything done when I just want to be with him."

"That's better. Have you thought about slowing down a bit? I mean Syd, you have a crazy pace."

"Well, I think mostly it's this book launch. I've never had a book launch before."

"It's your first book Syd, so there's that."

"I know. I just mean it's in addition to everything else I already do. I'm hoping once that's behind me things will naturally slow down a bit."

"So have you kissed him yet?"

"Michelle."

"What? Have you?"

Sydney let's out a sigh and slumps over her coffee. "No. We had the perfect moment and he was just about to kiss me and then a stupid raccoon set off the outside alarm."

Michelle laughs so hard she almost spits out her coffee. "I'm sorry Syd. I don't mean to laugh but that's hysterical."

"No, it's not!"

"Sorry." Michelle says as she tries to stop giggling. "Okay, but you went out last night right?"

"We did, we had a great time. Some of his students are involved in this improv group. It was actually really great. They are talented and funny. And, that takes guts to get up on the stage without any script or plan."

"Syd, you speak in front of groups all of the time."

"Yes, but always with a plan. I know what I'll be discussing. Sure the questions aren't planned but they are still topic related. When your entire objective is to make people laugh, that's intimidating."

"True. So you two had fun, how did the night end? A kiss?"

"Nope. A hug and a peck on the cheek."

"Really?" Michelle cringes. "Are you sure he wasn't going in for a kiss and you turned your cheek?"

"Michelle, you've seen his picture! I wouldn't turn away from that man."

"Good point. Well, are you seeing him again?"

"Yeah. We have a running date at four o'clock this afternoon, so not an ideal situation for anything romantic. And then, Saturday night he's coming over and we are doing a dessert cook off."

"He cooks? A Harvard professor who cooks, Syd, he just keeps getting better. And a dessert cook off, well now, that sounds romantic."

"Yeah, I hope so."

"Who's doing the judging because you know, Jordan and I love your desserts."

"Romantic is two people, not four."

"Right. Would you at least bring some of the leftovers to brunch on Sunday?"

Sydney laughs. "Yes, absolutely!"

. . .

Lisa can't believe her luck. She walks into Starbucks and spots Sydney having coffee with another woman. She quickly hops in line and places her order.

Lisa sits next to Sydney and Michelle and tries to act as causal as she can. Her ear buds are in her ears but she is not listening to anything but their conversation. She opens her laptop and occasionally scrolls down to keep her screen on.

Lisa opens her notebook so it looks as if she is taking notes from a website. Her notes are all about Sydney and her friend. She has learned that Sydney is dating a Harvard professor, perhaps a theater professor as they went to an improv. His name is Thomas. She has his license plate, a few pictures of the two of them from the Museum of Fine Arts, and now knows their next two dates. If she can just gather a few more details and photos, Harris will be very pleased.

Lisa snaps a couple of shots of Sydney and Michelle leaving Starbucks. She quickly begins to search the Harvard website for theater professors. She finds no one by the name of Thomas or anyone who looks like Thomas. She tries to search the website using "Thomas" to no avail. Lisa begins to do what any good investigative reporter would do. She starts to scroll through each and every professor at Harvard in search of Thomas.

After forty-five minutes of searching Lisa finally finds Thomas. Actually she finds Professor Thomas Peters, Ph.D. Lisa begins to read Thomas' bio. He finished his doctorate at Dartmouth. He has an impressive amount of papers that he has authored or co-authored. Lisa is intently reading through his work when her phone vibrates. She looks and sees that it's a text from Ben asking if she was planning on showing up for work today. Lisa looks at the time and realizes she is an hour and a half late. She quickly texts Ben apologizing and lets him know she will be there in five minutes. She closes her laptop, shoves everything in her bag and runs out the door.

Lisa bursts into the conference room at the Insightful Blogger Headquarters, apologizing to everyone.

"Relax Lisa. Where were you?" Ben asks.

"I was at Starbucks doing some research and I just lost track of time."

"Look it's fine. I know we've all been stuck in this room together day after day. I don't have a problem if any of you need to do some of this research elsewhere. Just let me know where you are going to be and when you will be in." Ben pauses. "Now we have about two and a half days left to figure out how old Ty Kent is and write a blog. Does anyone have any progress to report?"

Alex, Lisa, and Samantha uniformly shake their heads no.

"You know Ben, I feel like figuring out Ty Kent's age is

not only incredibly difficult, I don't think it is going to get us any closer to figuring out who he is." Samantha offers her two cents.

"I agree with Samantha. I mean if you think about, it adults write children's books and young adult books all of the time. How are we going to figure out an age?" Alex adds.

Ben understands the frustration his team is feeling. "I hear what you are both saying. But remember, last week we figured out he was a man. That narrowed things down quite a bit. And we are looking for patterns. Ty Kent has written enough books that we should see some patterns. Do his characters or plot details show any progression in maturity. If so can we decipher how old he may be based on the trials and tribulations in his books? Do his later books have single parents dating or characters that are more involved in their careers or their communities? Do they own homes are they more established? Am I making sense?"

The team nods and gets back to their research.

"Oh, Ben, I forgot I have to leave at three forty five this afternoon. I've got a dentist appointment. But I'll do a lot of work from home this evening to make up for it."

"Okay." Ben says even though he doesn't believe Lisa.

The Esplanade

As Sydney heads out to meet Thomas on the Mass Ave Bridge for their running date it occurs to her that she has never had a running partner. She has run with a few people in the past but friends, never a romantic interest. And it's typically not been planned; they just cross paths while running. It's refreshing to find someone who enjoys running as much as she does. She suddenly feels a twinge of anxiety. This is the second time they are running together. She hopes he won't want to run with her all of the time.

Occasionally running with some one is fine. However,

running is Sydney's second form of meditation. She needs her solo runs. She can't be expected to run with him every time she wants to run. Sydney stops walking and tells herself to stop overthinking and getting ahead of the relationship. *This is how people ruin a relationship before it even has a chance to develop Syd.* She scolds herself in her mind. If she keeps this up she is the one who is going to need a relationship coach.

Sydney walks down the ramp to the Esplanade. Just as she sees Thomas stretching on a bench, he looks up and smiles at her. She feels a sense of warmth run through her body and any hint of anxiety just disappear. *Who wouldn't want to run with him every day.*

Thomas gives Sydney a long hug. "So, I was thinking you should set the pace that we run at today. However, I do have a caveat."

Sydney smiles. "And that would be?"

"Well, I'm super excited that you like to run as much as I do. I've never had a girl fr... um I mean I've never dated someone who likes to run."

She smiles. He almost called her his girlfriend. Her inner self is jumping for joy.

"So, my caveat is that you keep the pace slow enough so we can chat. If I'm totally honest running is an excuse to spend more time with you during the week."

"Deal."

Sydney and Thomas start to jog and chat. Sydney asks Thomas to tell her about his family and then purposefully starts to increase the pace. She giggles to herself as she hears his breathing getting heavier as he tries to speak and keep up. Finally Thomas stops and puts his hands on his knees.

"Syd, you're killing me."

Sydney laughs, bends over and tries to catch her breath. "I could barely keep up that pace. I can't believe you could speak the whole time."

Thomas looks over at her. "So you did that on purpose?"

She gives him a sheepish grin. "Maybe."

Sydney tries to run away but Thomas is too quick. He grabs her around the waist, picks her up and playfully spins her around. Laughing, she puts her hands on his shoulders and they look each other in the eye. Thomas stops spinning them around. He begins to loosen his grip around her waist and ease her down to the ground. Suddenly a bump almost knocks them over and snaps them out of their romantic eye lock.

"Oh my gosh I'm so sorry!" Says a girl who is clearly taking a video with her phone. "Oh, oh no, you're Sydney Graham." The girl says still holding the phone up towards Thomas and Sydney.

"Are you recording something?" Sydney asks.

"Sorry. Yes, but not you. I, um, have a blog all about the ins and outs of Boston. I was recording the geese. They are rather famous here along the Esplanade."

"Do I know you?" Sydney asks.

"Yes, well, sort of. I'm Lisa. Lisa Simmons, we met the other night at the MFA. You took a selfie with me. And by the way, thank you. I was the envy of all of my friends."

"Oh right. And what's your blog?"

"What?"

"Your blog, what is the name of it?"

"Oh, yeah it's super new. I'm just starting out. It's called um, The Real Boston."

"Versus a fake Boston?" Thomas asks.

"Ha, funny. Well, no it's just showing the realities of Boston."

"Like the geese?" Sydney asks.

"Yeah, I mean, visitors need to know that you have to not only watch out for the geese but the geese, you know, ah excrement."

Sydney and Thomas laugh, as that is true.

"Well, Lisa, may I offer you a bit of advice as you are just starting out?"

"Please, Sydney, anything."

"You might not want to show people on your videos without their permission. Most people don't like to be unknowingly recorded."

"Yes, of course! I'm just going to show the geese! Okay, well, I'm going to be on my way. Again, really sorry for bumping into you two."

Sydney and Thomas wave as Lisa awkwardly walks away.

"That was odd."

"Very." Sydney replies.

19
A Dessert Bake Off

Insightful Blogger Headquarters

"Well, gang, we are all here on a Saturday morning because of our epic fail at trying to determine Ty Kent's age."

"We knew that from the start Ben." Alex quips.

"We did. But we gave it a valiant effort and thank you. But Harris still needs a post. He needed it for this morning; however, he will not fire all of us if we can put our heads together and get something interesting, remotely related to Ty Kent, by the end of the day today."

"Ben, Alex is right. This is just ridiculous. Why are we wasting our time trying to find a needle in the haystack." Samantha says yawning.

"Well, Samantha, Alex, we care because Harris has $150,000 on the line. I'm guessing that is two full time employee salaries. If he loses and has to pay out that money, I'm quite certain he will make up for it, somehow."

"Are you saying if we don't figure out who Ty Kent is, Harris is going to fire us?"

"What I'm saying is if we don't keep this story going until something else peaks his interest, and he no longer cares about who Ty Kent is, we could be on the line."

Samantha and Alex plop their heads on the conference table in defeat.

"I might have something." Lisa says sheepishly.

"And that would be?" Ben asks.

"Well, it is not totally about Ty Kent. However, it is

about Sydney Graham, who is also someone Harris is very interested in."

Ben's gut churns. "What do you have Lisa?"

"May I?" Lisa points to the projector.

Ben gives her a nod. Lisa hooks her laptop up to the projector screen and dims the lights. She is so excited to show the team what she has. She flashes the first picture on the screen, which is of her and Sydney at the Museum of Fine Arts. Her second picture is of Sydney and Thomas.

"Oh my gosh! Professor Hottie!" Samantha squeals.

Lisa turns to Samantha, frustrated that her presentation is being interrupted. "What?"

"Yeah, that's Professor Peters, AKA, Professor Hottie. I took a few of his classes at Harvard. Go Sydney." Samantha says as she smiles and raises her eyebrows.

"So you gave him the nickname, Professor Hottie?" Ben inquires.

"Oh gosh no. He's had that nickname since he started teaching. I mean seriously, look at him!"

Ben sinks into his chair. "Lisa, your point?"

"Well, look. I have all of these pictures of Sydney and Thomas. They are truly quite a cute couple. What if, ironically…"

"What if what?" Harris says as he barges into the conference room. "Whoa, what do we have here? Is that Sydney Graham? And who is she with? Good looking dude!"

Ben puts his head down on the conference table.

Lisa notices Ben. "I don't have anything just yet, Harris. Just some pictures of Sydney's dating life."

"And who is the gentleman? Oh, wait, I know him."

"He's a professor at Harvard."

"Yeah, I took a few of his classes before I dropped out. This is perfect. Get a blog to me to run for tomorrow. With pictures!"

"But Harris. This has nothing to do with Ty Kent." Ben protests.

"Look it's still provocative and has to do with Sydney. The buzz about Sydney and Ty Kent being polar opposites is still a big discussion. And hey, maybe this Harvard English Professor is Ty Kent. That would be the best story ever!" Harris laughs at his own joke as he walks out of the room.

"No!" Ben says as he looks at his team all raising their eyebrows. "I want nothing to do with this blog. Write it and send it to me for approval and absolutely no mention of Ty Kent!" Ben says as he storms out.

Saturday Evening, Sydney's Home

Thomas walks into Sydney's kitchen carrying two bags.
"Hi there! What's in the bags?"
"Well, one bag has everything I need to win this dessert cook off and the other has a little surprise."
"Well you're rather sure of yourself."
"I was wondering how are we going to judge this little event? I mean, you're going to love what I make and vote for me and I already love what I'm making, so that doesn't seem very fair."
"Ha! Funny you should mention that, my friends Michelle and Jordan offered their taste buds."
"Great, invite them over!"
"Really?"
"Yes, I'd love to meet your friends."
"Alright then." Sydney says as she picks up her phone to text Michelle. As soon as she puts her phone down it vibrates. "Michelle texted 'heck yeah,' what time?"
"Two hours." Thomas suggests.
"All set. I'm excited for you to meet them. They're a fantastic couple."
"Wonderful. Now, since we're going to have company. I should probably give you your surprise now."
Sydney rubs her hands together excitedly as Thomas begins to open one of the bags. He pulls out two black aprons.

One reads, "Team Thomas," and the other reads "Team Sydney".

"They're perfect! Thank you." She says as Thomas holds the two aprons side by side.

Thomas gently places an apron over Sydney's head. His cheek brushes hers as he takes the ties and crisscrosses them behind her back. He brings them around front and ties them in a bow around her waist. Thomas's face remains close to Sydney. She looks up and his eyes are soft. He takes one hand from her waist and places it on her cheek. He gently bushes her cheek with his thumb, his eyes focused on hers. He leans in closer his lips almost touching hers. She closes her eyes. She can feel his breath, his gentle touch on her face, and then ever so lightly his lips brush hers. Sydney feels her heart beat quicken. Thomas places his other hand on her face and his lips gently grab hers. She feels a flicker of his tongue and her body pulses with adrenalin yet relaxes at the same time. Their lips part for a moment. Thomas is still holding her face in his hands and looking deep into her eyes. He kisses her forehead, then her cheek, and then again very softly her lips. Sydney smiles as they separate just a bit.

"Um, you know what, we don't even have to bake anything. You win."

Thomas laughs and moves his hands so they rest gently on Sydney's hips. "Sorry. After my previous attempts to kiss you were hampered by a raccoon and an odd young women video taping geese, I wasn't going to let anything or anyone get in my way."

"Please don't ever apologize for that!" Sydney says as she walks around her kitchen island and sits on a counter stool.

"Are you okay?"

"Never better. Just feeling a little light headed, in a good way."

Thomas laughs. He leans across the kitchen island and motions for Sydney to come closer. He lightly kisses her lips.

"I love your honesty Syd. Everything about you is awesome! Now, are you ready to get to work?"

"One question. What do I get if I win?"

"Another kiss."

"And if I lose?"

Thomas gives Sydney a sly grin. "Another kiss."

"Let's do this!" Sydney bellows as she jumps off the counter stool.

Thomas puts on his apron and Sydney clicks on the music. They move to separate corners of the kitchen and get to work. They try and steal peeks at what the other is cooking. Sydney can't believe how much fun she is having cooking a dessert she has made hundreds of times.

Exactly two hours later, both desserts are completed and the kitchen cleaned, just in time for Michelle and Jordan's arrival. Sydney buzzes her friends in and they enter her apartment raving about how good it smells. They go through the introductions and handshakes, Sydney pours them all some wine and they toast to being together. Michelle notices the flirty glances that Thomas and Sydney are exchanging.

"Hey Syd, before we dive into dessert, may I borrow that blue sweater of yours with the fancy buttons?"

"Sure, it's in my closet."

"Yeah, Syd, your closet is the size our entire apartment." Michelle says as she nods her head towards the stairs.

Sydney shakes her head and walks downstairs with Michelle leaving Jordan and Thomas alone in the kitchen.

Thomas looks at Jordan. "Is she really borrowing a sweater?"

"She could be. Michelle does like to multi-task."

"So she's borrowing a sweater and talking about me?"

"Thomas, I may be the only husband ever who doesn't cringe when his wife says she's going shopping. Michelle's idea of shopping is coming over here and raiding Sydney's closet. She knows every inch of that closet. So more than likely, she doesn't need a sweater, they're just talking about you."

Sydney searches for her blue sweater. She finds it and pulls it out for Michelle. "This one?"

"You kissed him."

"Michelle."

"I can see it. You kissed him!"

"Maybe."

"Spill."

"Is that what this is about? Do you even want this sweater?"

"Yes, I do want the sweater and of course that's what this is about. I want details from start to finish."

"Michelle, we're having brunch tomorrow you can't wait until then."

"No, Jordan's there. You never give as much detail with Jordan around."

Sydney inhales deeply. "Best kiss ever!"

Michelle squeals. "I knew it!"

"Shh, keep your voice down. Okay, quick details and then upstairs."

Sydney and Michelle head back upstairs to find Jordan and Thomas in the kitchen laughing and seemingly getting along well. Sydney quickly sets up the dinning room with some placemats, silverware, napkins and dessert plates. She and Thomas both present their desserts. Thomas has made pumpkin spice cupcakes with an eggnog and cream cheese filling and Sydney made a chocolate raspberry torte with homemade whipped cream.

"Now, I must admit, this torte is one I made this morning because it has to chill for five hours. The one I made with Thomas is still cooling off." Sydney confesses.

"Sydney, this is incredible." Thomas says after taking a few bites of her dessert. "You win."

"I don't know Thomas, the surprise in the middle of your cupcake is stupid good." Sydney looks to Jordan and

Michelle.

"They're both out of this world." Michelle says.

"I think we know what's going on here." Jordan starts in a serious tone. " I mean these desserts are incredible and it looks like we have ourselves a tie. And the only way I know how to settle a tie is with a rematch. I mean, Michelle, am I wrong?"

"Not this time baby. This time you are absolutely correct." She says as she smiles, leans in and rubs her husbands back.

After saying their goodbyes, Michelle and Jordan head out for their quick five-block walk home, goodie bags in hand.

"Okay, I love Thomas! Don't you?"

"No. I don't Michelle."

"What?" She asks shocked as she stops and faces Jordan. "Why not?"

"Why not? Michelle, he is six-foot four. He's dashingly handsome. He's wicked smart, funny, and way too laid back. When you married me, I set a bar for you and Sydney and that bar was right here." Jordan says as he puts his hand level with the top of his nose. "Who does Sydney think she is reaching for the stars?" Jordan let's out an exasperated breath and looks up into the sky. "I love him!"

Sydney and Thomas walk down to the entryway of her building.

"Syd, I had a great time tonight. And Michelle and Jordan are just fantastic."

"Thank you, they are. And I had a great time to."

"So what's this Sunday brunch thing you all do?"

"Oh, well, it's every Sunday. If you'd like to join us tomorrow, we'd love to have you."

"Every Sunday?"

"Yes. Except if Monday is a minor holiday, then we do it on Monday."

"Hmm. Well, I'm actually going to my grandfather's tomorrow to help him with some interior painting. But next

Sunday is a before a minor holiday, correct?"

"Correct."

"Any chance next Sunday you'd like to come out to meet my grandfather? He's amazing and well a big part of my life and.."

"Yes!" Sydney interrupts Thomas before he can finish.

"Great." Thomas says softly as he steps closer to Sydney. He puts his arm around her waist and kisses her. "Sweet dreams."

Thomas leaves. Sydney locks the door behind him. She leans against the door and slides down onto the floor. She thinks she may very well be in love.

Lisa quickly ducks down behind a car as she sees Thomas leave Sydney's place. She waits a few minutes and then looks at the pictures on her phone. She got some great shots of Thomas and Sydney kissing in the well-lit vestibule. She quickly forwards the pictures to Harris for him to add to tomorrow's blog post. Lisa is so pleased. She knows with this kind of work Harris will certainly consider her for a promotion regardless of whether or not they figure out who the heck Ty Kent is.

Chocolate Raspberry Torte

45 chocolate wafers
7 tablespoons unsalted butter at room temperature
½ cup of seedless raspberry jam
8 oz. of semi-sweet chocolate chopped. (I use the mini semi sweet morsels to avoid chopping)
1 cup of heavy cream
Fresh raspberries

 Finely grind the chocolate wafers either via a food processor or in a bag with a rolling pin. Just be sure they are finely ground. In a mixing bowl thoroughly combine the chocolate wafers and butter. Line the chocolate wafer crust into four, 4-inch mini tart pans with a removable bottoms.
 Melt the seedless jam over low heat and stirring constantly. Once melted, using a spoon or a pastry bush, lightly gloss the each chocolate crust with a thin layer of the melted jam. Put into the freezer to cool.
 Over very low heat combine the heave cream and chocolate, stirring constantly. Once all of the chocolate has melted and combined with the cream, pour into the each chocolate crust and chill for 5 hours or up to one day.
Serve with homemade whipped cream and fresh raspberries.

20
A Relationship Exposed

Sydney fell asleep to pleasant thoughts of Thomas dancing around her head. She was not at all prepared for what she woke up to. Sydney leaps out of bed and heads upstairs to her kitchen. She turns on the coffee maker and starts to put away the clean dishes from the evening prior. Sydney is humming and smiling. She can't stop thinking about last night. Actually she can't stop thinking about Thomas kissing her. Sydney pours herself some coffee and realizes she left her phone in her bedroom.

"No!" Sydney shouts after she clicks on a link that Maryann sent her. Sydney races up the stairs and starts pacing from her kitchen through her dining room around her living room and back to the kitchen, all the while staring at her phone.

Sydney sends a text to Michelle asking if she and Jordan would mind coming over to her house versus going out. Sydney is in no mood to be seen in public right now. She goes back to The Insightful Blogger home page and reads the headline: *Sydney Graham and Professor Hottie: Looks Like Your Favorite Relationship Coach has Quite the Hot Relationship.* She scrolls through the pictures. There is one of she and Thomas at the Museum of Fine Arts, another of them embracing on the Charles River, and the most infuriating, she and Thomas kissing in her entry way last night!

"I can't believe this." Sydney mumbles to herself as she continues to pace. Her thoughts switch to Thomas. She feels her emotions flip from anger to angst. She has to call him but she's so afraid. What if he's angry? He would have every right to be angry, she's angry. What if he doesn't want to see her anymore because of this ridiculousness? Who could blame him for that?

This is all her fault. She should have never answered any questions about Ty Kent. Her actions fueled the fire and when you have the media attention you get it from all sides, the good and the gossip. Sydney decides that the best thing to do in this moment is to get her head in the right space before she calls Thomas. She walks upstairs to her meditation room.

After a long meditation and a hot shower, Sydney finds herself sitting at her kitchen counter, staring at her phone and taping her fingers. Although she is calmer she is still very angry. She tries to keep her thoughts focused on where they need to be right now which is on Thomas. She quickly stands up and starts pacing again. She stops after one lap around her dining room and living room and again finds herself in her kitchen staring at her phone.

Sydney takes a deep breath in and lets out a loud exhale. *Sydney, if you don't want to keep feeling this anxiety, make the call. You may not like the answer, but it will be what it will be.* Sydney repeats this out loud two more times and then she picks up her phone. She presses Thomas's number and slowly begins to walk around the kitchen. As she hears the phone ringing she begins to clench her fist as she walks. It keeps ringing and then goes to voicemail. Sydney panics and quickly hits the end button. She let's out a loud groan. She was not ready for voicemail; she had nothing prepared.

Sydney looks at her watch and realizes that Michelle and Jordan will be arriving any minute. She dumps out what is left of the coffee and makes more. She shoves the scoop into the coffee. "I can't believe Ben would do this to me." She says out loud. She shoves harder with every scoop of the coffee. She wonders how they got the pictures. It had to have been Ben. He's the only one who knows where she lives. She taps her fingers on the counter as she waits for the water to fill the coffee pot.

Michelle and Jordan slowly creep up the stairs into Sydney's living room. "Syd, are you alive?"

"In the kitchen."

"Hey." Michelle says as she and Jordan place two brown paper bags on the counter.

"Hey." Sydney says despondently as she fills the coffee maker with water. Sydney puts the pot in its place and turns the coffee on. She spins around to face Jordan and Michelle, the only two people she is able to face at this moment. She notices the bags. "What's all this?"

"Just about everything we could think of that might make you feel better." Michelle says.

"Mostly carbs and sugar." Jordan quips.

"Oh." Sydney hesitates. "I was going to make all of us pancakes."

"We love pancakes!" Michelle says as she gives Jordan a look.

"Your pancakes are the best!" Jordan says as he picks up both of the brown bags and shoves them under the counter.

Sydney remains expressionless as her eyes flit back and forth between Michele and Jordan. "I've clearly lost my mind and my manners. I'm sorry. Thank you both, for changing your plans for me and coming over here with all of this food. Now if you will excuse me for a brief minute, I'm going to go downstairs to put on some big girl pants, and then come back up here acting like one."

Michelle walks over and gives Sydney a hug as Jordan begins to unpack the bags. By the time Sydney comes back upstairs after changing, Jordan and Michelle have the dining room set for three and a huge spread of food.

"Oh my goodness!" Sydney says as she holds her hands over her heart. "This looks amazing. Thanks you two! I'll grab the coffee and let's eat!" Sydney's phone begins to vibrate in her hand. "It's Thomas. I have to take this. Start eating." Sydney says as she runs downstairs to take the call in private.

Ten minutes later, Sydney walks up the stairs and takes a seat next to Michelle.

"That was quick." Jordan says in between bites.

"Is everything okay?"

"Yes. He laughed at me."

"What?" Michelle asks.

"He laughed at the situation. He was incredibly sweet about everything actually. He was more concerned about me. He said he's thrilled to be dating me and doesn't care who knows about it."

"What about the 'Professor Hottie' thing? Was he okay with that?" Michelle asks.

"Apparently, that is a nickname he has had for quite sometime. It wasn't invented by The Insightful Blogger."

"Well, he does live up to his nickname."

Jordan shoots Michelle a look after hearing her comment.

"What? Jordan, you are the sexiest account alive!" Michelle reassures her husband.

"Yeah I am!" Jordan confirms. "Syd, why were you so worked up about this? You didn't write the article."

"I know. But I did get caught up in the Ty Kent stuff and have had the media focus. That was my choice. I was worried that Thomas would be upset with the unsolicited media attention."

"Thomas is a good guy and I see how he looks at you. That guy is head over heals and isn't going to let a stupid gossip blog get in his way." Jordan says as he takes a big bite of hash browns.

"Well, I know that now. And I am so relieved!"

"So, what about the Insightful Blogger? Are you going to speak with Ben?" Michelle asks.

"I don't know. I'm mixed. When I first saw the blog post I was ready to march into his office and rip into him.

And now I wonder if that would just make things worse."

"Syd, I know Michelle and I told you that your relationship with Ben was boring. However, we did get to know Ben well. And yeah, you two weren't exactly the perfect match, but he's still a good guy. I really can't see how Ben could be behind this."

"I know but he's the only one who knows where I live. Wait a second." Sydney says as she heads to the kitchen to grab her phone.

Michelle and Jordan watch Sydney as she frowns at her phone.

"Unbelievable!" Sydney says as she looks up at Michelle and Jordan. She hands her phone to Michelle.

"Who's this?"

"That's Lisa, a staff writer at the Insightful Blogger. That woman came up to me at the Museum of Fine Arts pretending to be a fan. She literally bummed into Thomas and I during our run last week, pretending to be video taping stuff for her blog."

"That woman sounds like a stalker." Michelle says.

"And the plot thickens." Jordan says as he rubs his hands together. "The big question is what are you going to do?"

Sydney looks at Jordan and shakes her head. "Nothing."

"Nothing? Syd, you have to do something."

"Like what Jordan?" Michelle asks confused by what her husband is saying.

"I don't know, but you can't just let them get away with invading your privacy."

"The pictures were all taken in public places Jordan." Sydney shrugs.

"Not the one of you two in your entryway." Jordan stands up from the table and begins to walk around Sydney's living room taping his finger on his chin. "I've got it!" Jordan exclaims as he heads back to the table and takes a seat.

Michelle and Sydney just stare at Jordan with raised eyebrows waiting for his big announcement.

"Reverse stalking."

"What?" Sydney asks as if he's has lost his mind.

"Reverse stalk her."

"That's crazy Jordan." Michelle says.

"No, it's a thing."

"It's not a thing."

"It is Michelle, I saw it in a movie. Sydney can reverse stalk Lisa. You could wait outside The Insightful Blogger and snap photos of her. You have a huge following on your blog you could post the photos. It would be fun and you get your point across."

Sydney shakes her head and smiles. "Although, Jordan, I do think your idea is humorous, I'm not going to reverse stalk anyone. Look if Harris thinks this blog post is bothering me in the slightest, he will just keep up his antics."

"You're probably right." Jordan says as he hangs his head. Jordan quickly picks his head back up. "Okay, last idea. At least if you and Thomas see this Lisa person around, have a little fun and pose for the pictures."

Michelle and Sydney both burst out in laughter.

"That's an idea I can get behind!"

· · ·

Thomas hangs up the phone. He is relieved that Sydney is okay. He is happy and doesn't care about the gossip blog. What he is more concerned about is who took the pictures. He really hopes his ex-girlfriend Marie is not involved. This is just the sort of thing she would do. Yet, he pays attention, he watches for any sign of her. He is quite certain she is still living in Chicago. Maybe he should call her brother to find out for certain. Yet, he hasn't had any sign of her. If she's not around, he doesn't want to insight her old stalking behavior by calling her brother and having him let her know he called. Thomas is not completely trusting of her brother to keep things confidential. The last thing he needs is Marie in the picture. *It can't be Marie. This is all Harris. It has to be all Harris.* Thomas hopes.

· · ·

After saying goodbye to Jordan and Michelle, Sydney begins to clean up all of the dishes. She chuckles to herself when she thinks of Jordan's reverse stalking idea. He can come up with some good ones. Sydney looks at her phone and feels a twinge of panic when she realizes she only has two hours before her first client and needs to get a blog post up.

Sydney sits down at her desk and begins to read through emails for inspiration. After reading about one hundred subject lines that read things like, "way to go Syd!" and "Professor Hottie is right," she sees a subject line that piques her interest, *Divorced and wondering when to start dating!*

Dear Sydney,

I'm newly divorced. We signed the papers last week. I don't have any children and am in my mid-thirties. Everyone seems to have an opinion about when I should start dating again. I was wondering what your thoughts were on how soon to date after a divorce?

Blog Post #524: When Should I Start Dating After a Divorce? You're Asking the Wrong Question.

"When should I start dating after a divorce (or a major breakup)?" I'm frequently asked this question. Unfortunately, that's the wrong question to be asking. You may start dating whenever you feel like it. What feels okay to me, may not feel okay to you. When you start dating is quite frankly a decision only you can make.

There are some obvious and less obvious things to

consider before you jump back into the dating scene. How much time are you willing to devote to dating? Do you have the time? If you have children, how are you going to address your dating with them? Are you going to use online dating? If so, which one is best for you? Are you up to date on all of the "dating lingo"? For example do you know what "ghosting" means? What about finances, do you have the means to start dating again?

I believe there are two important questions to ask yourself before you start dating. The first, "am I emotionally ready to start dating?" After a divorce or major break up, our egos may be a bit weaker than usual. It would be in our best interest to consider not just the fun things about dating, but the pitfalls too. You may want to ask yourself if you are ready for a rejection or how you will feel if you think a date went really well and then you were "ghosted." Divorces and major break-ups can be emotionally charged. Are you truly over any guilt, shame, anger or resentment?

The second question to ask yourself is, "how is my relationship with myself?" Look, after being in a long-term relationship we have to learn how to be by ourselves again. We have to learn what it's like to not to be able to call the person, who probably knows us best. The person we call when something goes wrong at work.

We have to learn how to embrace a quiet house, for long periods of time. We have to learn how to do things on our own, go out to dinner or the movies by ourselves. When you can do all of that, and you can confidently say: "No, I'm not dating to replace my former partner or fill a void. I love my life and I feel so comfortable in my own skin, and I want to share that with someone." Then maybe, you are ready to start dating.

To your success in love and life,
    Sydney

Ben's Apartment

It's seven o'clock in the evening and Ben has not so much as showered. He sits on the couch with his laptop open, scrolling the blog and the pictures of Sydney and Thomas. He finds a tiny bit of humor in the fact that he broke up with Sydney to find passion and romance and her passion and romance is staring him straight in the face. He has to admit he's never seen her look so happy and charged with energy. Not that Sydney wasn't always full of energy, she was. It just wasn't passionate, not towards him anyway.

Ben can't decide whether to feel angry or full of guilt and shame. His company exposed her like this. His company invaded her privacy. He is quite certain he will have a visit from Sydney tomorrow and he needs to be able to face that. If she is angry, which he's sure she will be, she has every right to be. But he's angry too.

He wonders why she was never like this with him. Was it his fault? Did he not bring out the best in her? Does any of it even matter now? He and Syd were perfect in every way as far as practicality in a relationship. They were just missing the romance and the passion.

Perhaps Ben could try and get that with Syd. Why wouldn't he try? He knows they are great together in every other way. He just failed at the passion and romance. Ben sits up. He's going to try and get Sydney back. He takes another look at the picture of Sydney and Thomas in an embrace on the Esplanade. He lets out a loud groan as he realizes he doesn't have the slightest chance at getting Sydney back.

21
Flowers and a Thank You

Monday Morning, Insightful Blogger Headquarters

"Good Morning Benjamin!" Harris shouts from across the room filled with cubicles.

Ben just nods and raises his metal coffee cup in the air. He pulls his keys out of his pocket and unlocks his door.

"Great Monday Benjamin!"

Ben drops his keys. "Geez Harris, how'd you get here so fast? What did you leap frog over all of the cubicles?"

Harris winks at Ben. "I'm just lightening fast Benjamin. You dropped your keys. Let me tell you what fuels me Benjamin." Harris says he walks past Ben, into Ben's office and sits down in a chair across from his desk. "What fuels me is our consistently viral content. Did you see our numbers from the Sydney Graham story?"

"I did Harris." Ben says soberly as he plops his messenger bag on his desk.

"Then why are you so glum?"

"Are you prepared to deal with Sydney's wrath?"

"Benjamin, please. I run a gossip blog, all I do is deal with wrath. Wrath, wrath, wrath, all day long."

"Okay, well when she shows up here today, and she will, you deal with her."

"No problem Benjamin. I've got you covered. Now, what is the angle this week? We need to figure out this Ty Kent thing."

"I don't know Harris. I meet with the team at nine-thirty this morning."

"Good, well, let me know the angle by nine-forty."

Ben glares at Harris.

"I'm kidding! You have to lighten up Benjamin." Harris says as he walks out of Ben's office.

Ben shuts his office door behind Harris and leans against it. "Why am I here?"

Ben walks into the conference room promptly at nine-thirty. Lisa is sitting at the conference room table and Samantha and Alex are standing on either side of a large map pinned to the wall.

"What do we have here?"

"It's a map!" Samantha says excitedly as she claps her hands and grins from ear to ear.

"I can see that it's a map Samantha, I too graduated from college." Ben sees as all of the joy and excitement instantly drain from Samantha's face. He puts his hands on the table, bows his head and takes a deep breath. "Samantha, I apologize. That was a very bad attempt at sarcasm. I'm actually excited and so relieved that you and Alex have an idea to present so please forgive me and tell me what you have."

Samantha hesitates for a second but she can't contain her enthusiasm. "Okay, so as Alex and I have pointed out in the past, we really think that Ty Kent has been to all of the locations that he writes about. Each book is set in a different location. The details are so intimate there is no way he wrote what he wrote just by doing Internet research. Alex and I are suggesting we map out all of the locations and label each location with the title of the book and year it was published. We ask ourselves, are there any back-to-back books in the same region? If so, what can we garner from that? What were the topics, what age might he have been?"

Ben remains silent, as he considers all that Samantha is saying. He thinks she has the forethought and tenacity to be a great investigative reporter if she can ever extricate herself out of this gossipy blog.

"I like it. Nice work you two. Now, I know we can analyze the locations that we all know or have been to. How do we do it for the places we haven't? He's written twenty-four books."

"I've thought about that Ben." Alex chimes in. "Look between all of us and our social networks we can find someone who has been to a location we are unfamiliar with. We pull out some of the detailed location descriptions from his books and have the person who has lived there or spent some solid time there give us their opinion about the accuracy."

"We can even use Harris." Lisa says as she finally looks up from her phone. "He's been to all of the locations in the books I've read thus far."

Alex, Samantha, and Ben stare at each other without even blinking.

"No!!" Alex shouts breaking the silence. "He would have had to have been publishing at age twelve."

"Although, greatest publicity stunt ever!" Samantha says with her eyebrows raised.

"No. No way. We have no idea who Ty Kent is. That much we know. Now, I love the focus Alex and Samantha have presented so let's get to it!"

The team begins to put pushpins labeled with book titles and years published across the map. They then divide the books and locations amongst the team members for further review. Lisa's phone vibrates during the discussion. She looks to see that it's a text message from Harris. She waits until everyone has his or her assignments before excusing herself to use the restroom.

Lisa heads past all of the cubicles and exits out a back door to a stairwell.

"Lisa." Harris whispers from a corner.

"What's going on?"

"I'm assigning you a very top secret project."

Lisa begins to smile. "Sure."

"I'm serious Lisa. This is very top secret, you can't tell anyone."

"You can trust me Harris."

"Okay. I need you to be my mole. I want a report on every detail that happens in that conference room each day."

Lisa nods.

"I mean every detail Lisa, every conversation, no matter how irrelevant you may think it is."

"Got it."

"Good. I'm counting on you."

Lisa exits the back staircase feeling as if she was just assigned the biggest case of her life. "Special agent Lisa at your service." She mumbles to herself.

At one in the afternoon, Ben notices his team doing a lot of yawning and eye rubbing. "Okay, team, we need a break. And by a break, I don't mean ordering in. We need some fresh air, food, coffee and just a general recharge. Let's go, it's on me."

The team members gratefully stand up and grab their things to head out. As they are about to all exit the conference room they are blocked by two delivery people walking by the conference room door carrying huge flower arrangements.

"Wow!" Alex says. "Someone sure is loved!"

Sydney's Home

"Thanks for coming over and meeting me here Maryann. Even though I've had a ton of positive feedback from the Insightful Blogger's ridiculous post, I'm still not totally ready to be out and about."

"Of course. Sydney, it's not like coming here is any kind of punishment. Besides, we can get a lot more accomplished in this quiet space versus any busy coffee shop. Now tell me, how did Thomas take everything?" Maryann asks with a grimace.

"He was great. He had absolutely no problem with it at all. I will be honest I had a lot of angst before I spoke with him, but he remained his remarkably cool and charming self."

"Good! Now, I did hear you say you are feeling a bit anxious about being out and about. We have just a few more events before your book launch, one of which is tomorrow. Are you going to be okay?"

"Yes. It's more the random public that I'm fearful of. Or, I should say, the random public who just happen to take pictures of me without my knowledge."

"Great. We are on the homestretch Sydney. We have a book club luncheon tomorrow in Hartford, Connecticut. I'll have the car here by nine-thirty in the morning. And then Thursday, your last book club event, is just down the street in Wellesley. You have two more interviews next Tuesday. One with a radio station and one with a local television station that will be airing the interview the night before your book launch."

"Wow. Maryann, we are almost there!"

"Well, we're almost to your book launch. You don't even want me to tell you your schedule after the launch."

"Just tell me I will have a few days to sleep before it gets really crazy!"

"You will have exactly three days." Maryann says with a grin. "Okay, I have to get going. Are you all set for tomorrow?"

"I'm all set. I will be downstairs and ready to go at nine-thirty in the morning."

"Great." Maryann says as she grabs her trench coat. "Oh, I almost forgot. I did you a huge favor today!"

"Which was?" Sydney says as she grabs their empty coffee mugs and brings them to the sink.

"I sent Harris two huge, I mean ridiculously huge flower bouquets and I signed the card 'thanks for the uptick in sales Sydney Graham.' You're welcome."

Sydney spins around. "You did WHAT?"

Sydney begins to rapidly pace around the kitchen, dining room and living room. Every time Maryann tries to say something, Sydney just puts her hand in the air letting her know she is not ready. This cycle continues for ten minutes.

Sydney finally stops pacing. She rests her elbows on the counter and puts her head in her hands. She rubs her eyes and takes a deep breath. She looks up at Maryann and calmly asks, "you did what now?"

"I'm not sure what the problem is Sydney." Maryann says timidly. "After his post you had another 2,000 pre-sales of your book! Do you know how incredible that is? Sure I was being a bit sarcastic with the flowers, but all in good fun. I was thinking this would lighten things up, am I wrong?"

"I'm sorry. In any other situation Maryann, you would be right. However, in this one, I think you may be terribly wrong."

"I don't understand Syd. I've done this stuff with reporters thousands of times. They always find it funny. And quite honestly, I know most of them so well I send them stuff they truly love. I just don't know Harris yet, so I thought I would start with a joke and get to know him from there."

"There's a reason you don't know Harris, Maryann. Harris is all about Harris. He doesn't care about anyone else. My fear is how Harris operates. If he feels as though his latest stunt has backfired, then he will do everything he can to fix it."

Maryann's face turns expressionless. She begins to pace the room as if she is Sydney. She returns to the kitchen and looks at Sydney. "So you're telling me I've turned your book sales into something very bad."

Sydney nods.

"Oh my gosh Sydney! I can fix this. I just have to think. I'm so sorry. How did this happen?"

"Maryann, calm down. I'm not sure you can fix this. Harris is a particular person. What I mean by that is he's very egocentric. You just wounded his ego. The point of the blog was to some how get more energy around his main focus of finding out who Ty Kent is. I'm quite certain, because of all of the media around me he thought if he posted my life on line he could get more people tied up into the Insightful Blogger 'mission of the day.' But, instead, you just told him how many books he sold for me."

"So I've wounded his ego with my sarcastic gifts and there is going to be a price to pay. Meaning, he's going to go after your personal life even more. Does that sum it up Syd?"

"Yes it does. But, I think we can figure out a way to be a few steps ahead of him. Maryann, we are two very smart women. We're not going to let him publicly embarrass me right before my book launch."

"Not if I have anything to do with it! Besides Syd, what could he do? He's already exposed your relationship. Every one loved the story and are happy for you and Thomas. I know you were worried about Thomas but he's not bothered by the exposure. You don't have any crazy secrets from your past, right?"

Sydney just keeps her head down and stares at the counter watching her own fingers tap rapidly against the granite.

"Syd, do you have secrets?"

"Um, ah, no. I mean none that I can think of."

"Then we are all set. What can Harris do?"

"He could lie. He could insinuate things."

"Yes, he could do those things. If he does, we take him head on. You will post on your YouTube channel, your blog, I will get you in front of every media outlet, and we call him out on his lies. It's that simple."

Sydney smiles and nods her head. She wishes it were that simple.

Part 3:
A Word from Ty Kent

22
Everyone is Scheming

Tuesday Morning, Insightful Blogger Headquarters

"Good morning my band of detectives!" Harris says as he bursts into the conference room. He walks over to the map on the wall. "What do we have here?"

Samantha eagerly jumps to her feet to explain to Harris the details of this week's project of mapping out all of the locations and publishing dates of Ty Kent's books.

"You see Harris, his descriptions of the locations where his stories take place are so accurate that we believe he has not only been to all of these places but spent quite a bit of time in each location.

"At the very least Harris we'll have a blog that details all of the locations and time frames of when we suspect Ty Kent was in each of these cities or towns. We're hoping that will trigger some phone calls. Someone may read the blog and suddenly realize that their brother or good friend has been to all of these locations within the same time frames." Ben clarifies.

Harris cups his chin with his hand and carefully examines the map. "This is interesting. This could really lead us to determining who Ty Kent is." Harris stops speaking and focuses on the map.

"Is there a problem Harris?" Ben asks.

"Well, there could be." Harris turns away from the map and looks at the team. "We only get one guess. We call Green Publishing with who we think Ty Kent is and if we're wrong, it's game over, right?" Harris says looking at Ben for clarification.

"No. Green Publishing will only confirm the identity of Ty Kent if someone guesses who he is and signs an agreement to keep it confidential, at which point it would be game over. Green Publishing will never give us any confirmation about Ty Kent's identity."

"Right, that's what I meant." Harris says.

"Wait a second." Alex says with frustration in his voice. "You're telling us that we're doing all of this work and we will never actually know who Ty Kent is? This is all just a fabricated story to get people talking and searching for an answer, which will never be confirmed? What a waste of time!"

"Alex, first of all, we are a gossip blog. Creating curiosity and hype is our purpose. Second, this is hardly a waste of time. Have you seen the amount of visitors we have had since we started this whole thing? Have you seen the amount of media attention our blog is getting? Do you understand how we operate? The more visitors we have the more advertisers we have. Who pays for all of your salaries? Advertisers!" Harris says.

Alex leans back in his chair and rubs his eyes.

"Look Alex, here's the thing. If we are right and we publish a guess as to who Ty Kent is with a solid list of why we think this, it will generate a ton of media attention. There will be so much pressure that Ty Kent will have to reveal himself."

Ben watches as disappointment washes over everyone's face. "You know what, I think it's time for a coffee break. Why don't you all head over to Starbucks and I'll be there in a few."

The team members grab their things and head out the door. Ben stands up and shuts the door before Harris can make an exit.

"What are you doing Harris?"

"What? Have they not figured out that they all work for a gossip blog?" Harris says with sarcasm.

"No, I mean this." Ben pauses to contain his anger. "This wild goose chase."

"Look Benjamin, I didn't create the curiosity regarding Ty Kent's real identity. Some book blogger posed the question to her readers and it became a thing. All I did was up the ante by throwing some money at it and then it became a bigger thing." Harris says as he shrugs his shoulders.

"But what if we get it wrong Harris. You said it yourself, who ever we put out there as Ty Kent, that person is going to be engulfed by media frenzy. And what if we are wrong? We could really de-rail someone."

"If we're wrong Benjamin, then all that happens is someone gets their fifteen minutes of fame. And if it seems to be really negative well maybe that will prompt the real Ty Kent to reveal himself."

Ben shakes his head and grabs his messenger bag off of the conference room table. "You sure are good at spinning things Harris." Ben says as he walks out of the room.

"You say that like it's a bad thing Benjamin!" Harris shouts.

Tuesday Evening, Sydney's Home

"Hi!" Thomas says with a big grin on his face as Sydney opens her door. "You look beautiful."

Sydney tilts her head and smiles brightly as she sees Thomas standing in front of her with a bouquet of lilies and a take out bag. "Thank you. Come in."

"Thomas these flowers are beautiful and they smell even better." Sydney says as she arranges the lilies in a vase and places them on the dining room table.

Thomas smiles. "Good. Now, I figured you were in the car most of the day and probably had nothing but a banana, coffee, and water."

Sydney nods. "Guilty as charged."

"I brought us both salads with grilled chicken."

"Thank you!"

Sydney and Thomas sit down to enjoy their meals. Sydney is a bit anxious about asking Thomas how things were going at work, but she has to know that everything is truly okay. Of course it is. If it wasn't he would be here let alone bring her flowers and dinner.

"How was Hartford?"

"It was good. A small group, only about thirty people."

"Really. Maryann brought you all the way to Hartford for thirty people?"

"That was my initial reaction as well. They are a small core group but they have a huge online following and a podcast. Their podcast has thirty thousand subscribers."

"Wow. Did you do the podcast?"

"No, but they did ask if they could interview me for the podcast once the book is released and their followers have had an opportunity to read it. I also got a few comments and questions about you."

"Did you." Thomas says smiling.

"I did. You got rave reviews, mostly related to, what was it that one woman said, oh yes your, 'dashing good looks'. Speaking of which, any backlash from the blog post?"

"Not really. Well, I did get called to the President's office."

"What?" Sydney says as she drops her fork and puts her hand over her mouth. "Thomas, I'm so sorry!"

"Syd." Thomas says as he reaches across the table and grabs Sydney's hand. "I'm joking. Everything is just fine. I did get a couple of whistles as I walked around campus. And I few of my colleagues got creative and texted some rather humorous memes. Like I said on the phone, the nickname has been around for years and I'm proud to be seen with you. I want to be seen with you."

"I know. I just hate that you're involved in this stupid drama. I mean, I don't care what they write about me but I do feel as though they overstepped when they wrote about us. And I feel a bit responsible."

"For what? You didn't write the article."

"I know but if I hadn't of said anything about Ty Kent or offered up my opinion to reporters I wouldn't even be on Harris' radar."

"Syd, I was there, remember. You didn't have a choice but to say something. They were bombarding you with questions about Ty Kent, which you handled beautifully. I don't understand why this is upsetting you so much, it doesn't seem like the rational Sydney I know."

Sydney feels herself getting warm. She let's out a big sigh. "I don't know. I think, maybe, everything is just starting to get to me. Perhaps I'm more nervous about next week, than I care to admit. I was absolutely freaked out by the fact we had our pictures taken without knowing it. And knowing that someone was outside my house taking pictures is unnerving. I feel like things are getting away from me. Am I even making sense?"

"You are actually. When people do things without your consent or knowledge it can make you feel as though your losing control. You're completely in control of everything in your life, so I get how this would make you uncomfortable."

"But you don't seem rattled by it."

"No one was parked outside of my house. I don't have a huge event coming up. I don't have my first book coming out. I get it. The problem is, that's exactly what Harris wants. He wants to make you feel uneasy. He likes embarrassing people whenever he can. He justifies it by saying that if they're in the public eye then they're fair game."

"Exactly! How do you know so much about Harris?"

"He took a few of my classes. He's really not as complicated as he would like everyone to believe."

Sydney laughs.

"As a matter of fact." Thomas begins as he stands up and walks into the kitchen. He stands there for a bit with his hands on his hips.

"Is everything okay?"

He saunters back into the dining room with a big grin on his face. He sits down next to Sydney and slides her chair so she is facing him. "I have an idea. Now it's a little out there, it will take some work and we will have to move quickly. However, I think it's just what you need to shift the power back to you."

Wednesday Morning, Insightful Blogger Headquarters

"What's all this?" Ben asks as he walks into the conference room.

"Well, I'm a very visual person. I know everyone loves the map but I needed to visualize the cities and towns. Seeing some pictures of Paris or London seems so much more energizing than just reading the word, Paris." Lisa continues. "And, you all still have your map, this is just in addition to it."

"I like it." Alex says nodding his head.

"I know that the pictures represent the more obvious places, the Eifel Tower, Big Ben, the Hollywood sign; however it's all I could find on the Internet. Speaking of which, I did try to find some of the random locations Ty Kent writes about. I found the streets, neighborhoods, and even some of the restaurants he talks about but the information was sparse. Which, of course, further substantiates our hypothesis that he actually spent time in all of these locations."

"I think it's great Lisa. I like the pictures." Ben says.

Lisa gets a bit worried as she watches Samantha who is standing in the back corner of the room, staring at the pictures with her arms crossed and her head tilted. "Samantha, if you don't like these I will totally take them down."

Samantha puts her hand up and shakes her head. She continues to stare without saying a word.

Ben, Alex, and Lisa keep their eyes fixated on Samantha as she continues to stare at the pictures. They don't dare interrupt her in case she is on to something.

"Ugh!" Samantha says as she waves her hands around her head. "I can't figure it out."

"Can't figure what out?" Alex asks.

"This." Samantha says as she walks to the front of the room and waves her arm around all of the pictures. "This is so familiar to me. I feel as though I have seen all of these pictures just like this and I can't remember where."

"Seriously!" Lisa squeals.

"Seriously. But it's driving me crazy!"

"Samantha, this is great. I think I can help you. First, let's seat you over here so your back is to the pictures. If you keep staring, it's never going to come to you. Second, let's give you some repetitive tasks to do to keep your mind occupied and not thinking about the pictures. I've always found that if I'm busy and focused on other things whatever I was trying to remember just pops into my head at some point." Ben turns to Lisa and Alex. "What do we have for Samantha to take her mind elsewhere?"

"Well, we need more information on Boring." Alex says.

"What?" Ben asks.

"Boring, Oregon. That's where Ty Kent's book, <u>A Not So Boring Affair,</u> was set."

"There's a town named Boring? And why does that sound familiar?" Ben asks.

"Okay." Alex says as he sees his boss get the same blank look Samantha had. "Samantha, I want you to focus on Boring. Boss, I'm going to have you sit over here with your back to the wall of pictures. I know you've spent a good deal of time in London so how about you confirm the details in <u>My</u>

London Love."

Just as everyone begins to focus on the work in front of them, Harris walks into the conference room.

"How's my favorite team?"

"You mean your only…"

"You mean your only team working this hard." Ben says as he jumps up and interrupts Alex to prevent him from finishing his sentence and being fired on the spot. Ben shoots Alex a look of warning.

"Oh, what's this?" Harris asks as he makes his way over to the wall of pictures.

"That's mine." Lisa says proudly as she stands up and walks over to Harris to explain her thought process.

"This is great!" Harris says. "I've been there, and there, and there. Yep, I've been to all of theses places."

"You have?" Alex asks.

"Yeah, my dad basically opened a bank in all of these locations."

"Your dad opened a bank in Boring, Oregon?" Ben challenges.

"Oh, no. Not there. I did however go through a phase in high school and I got really into mountain biking. We were living in Los Angeles at the time so I convinced my parents to let me go to Boring and bike for the summer."

The entire team looks at Ben with wide eyes. Ben quickly shakes his head and returns his focus to Harris. "So you've been to every single one of these locations."

"Yep!" Harris says as he turns to face Ben. "Again, maybe I'm Ty Kent!" Harris laughs at his own joke as he walks out of the room.

Ben shuts the conference room door behind Harris. He turns to his team and says, "No. No way."

"But you just heard him Ben, not only has he been to all of these locations he has lived in the majority of them." Alex protests.

"Again, he would have had to start writing novels, full

length, good novels, at the age of twelve. And besides, <u>Paper Cuts</u> was set in Quebec, when has Harris been to Canada?"

"He's goes to the Quebec City Summer Fest every year." Samantha says.

"How do you know this?"

"We went to college together. I've known Harris since he was eighteen."

"So he's been going to the Quebec City Summer Fest for five years?"

"Yes." Samantha confirms.

"Again, he would have been twelve. And we all know Harris can't string two sentences together which is why we all work here."

"Or can he?" Alex asks provoking more curiosity among his team members.

"Oh my gosh! That's it! Ben you're a genius!" Samantha shouts as she springs to her feet and runs over to the pictures on the wall.

The team watches as Samantha looks at the pictures while mumbling to herself. She grabs a marker off of the table and begins to list out the locations and puts an X next to most of them.

Boston (2)	X
Nantucket	
Martha's Vineyard	X
Plum Island	X
Portland, Maine	X
Stowe, Vermont	X
Newport, Rhode Island	X
Paris	X
London	X
Los Angeles	X
Austin, Texas	X

New York City	X
Scottsdale, Arizona	X
Boulder, Colorado	
Seattle, Washington	X
Boring, Oregon	
Vail, Colorado	
Miami	
Amsterdam	X
New Canaan, Connecticut	
Dublin, Ireland	X
York, Maine	
Quebec City	

Samantha spins around and faces the team. She lets out a deep breath. "Okay, Ben when you said 'string two sentences together,' I remembered what was familiar about these pictures. I have seen postcards of these places strung together. I put an "X" next to the ones I know I've seen a post card of. The ones that are blank I'm not sure of."

"More importantly Samantha, where have you seen these?" Ben asks.

"They are strung up on a wall in my old professors office. Professor Thomas Peters."

"Professor Hottie!" Alex blurts out.

"Yes. I mean think about it. He's an English professor. He travels and he has the time to write novels, and he's in his late thirties."

"Wow! Professor Hottie is Ty Kent!" Alex says as he puts his hands on top of his head. "My mind is blown."

"Whoa. Let's slow down. We still have a great deal to figure out. First off, we need to determine if Samantha's memory is correct. We need to know for certain that he has been to all of the destinations on the list. And we need time frames. I mean what if he did all of this travel as a child." Ben says.

"Ben, can we please just take a little bit of pleasure in

this. I mean this is the closest we've come to even having a guess." Alex protests.

"Yes, of course. Samantha, this is great. Now are you sure he went to those places and the postcards were not sent to him from friends?"

"Yes. I am sure. I asked him about it. I remember because he said that some people collect ornaments or coffee mugs when they travel but that his travels light so he collects postcards."

"Great. We still have to be as certain as we can and need to check the facts and the holes that still exist. And Harris is not to know any of this!"

"Why?" Lisa asks.

"Because Harris will get overly excited and want to print something tomorrow. If we don't have all of our facts checked, it would be really easy for Thomas to dispute and we end up looking like idiots." Ben explains.

The team agrees to keep their findings from Harris for the time being. They begin to explore ways in which they can find out if Thomas has actually been to all of the locations and if so, when.

23
The Power Shift

Thursday evening, Sydney's home

"Okay, I just got a text. They're all set up downstairs. Are you ready?" Sydney asks Thomas.

"Almost."

"Are you nervous?"

Thomas shakes his head as he walks closer to Sydney. He stares straight into her eyes. He cradles her face in both of his hands. He leans down and gently kisses her lips. He pulls away from her, let's his hands drop and walks away towards the stairs. "Now, I'm ready."

Sydney hangs her head and chuckles. "You better be running down those stairs Thomas!"

"What? I can't hear you I'm already half way down the stairs." Thomas says as he leaps down the stairs two steps at a time.

Thomas waits for Sydney in front of the door to her first floor apartment.

"That was mean."

"No, it was for good luck." He says as he gives her a wink. "I'm really excited about this."

"Me too. This is a great idea and thank you!"

Sydney and Thomas walk into the first floor apartment and make their way down a short hallway to the large open concept kitchen and living room. They are greeted by Sydney's videographer Rob, her video editor Justin, Maryann, Jordan, and Michelle. Sydney heads over to check in with her friends while Rob and Justin immediately lead Thomas to the kitchen to explain to him how the filming works. They let Thomas know that there will always be two cameras rolling. One will be stationary in the front of the kitchen island and the other will be moving to capture the angles as they use different areas of the kitchen.

"This is such a great idea Syd." Michelle says.

"I'm excited."

"What if it comes out poorly?"

"Jordan!" Michelle scolds her husband by smacking his arm.

"If it comes out poorly then we don't post it. That's the beauty of not doing it live!"

"This is going to be great. I've already called a few of my close and trustworthy media friends just to give them the slight edge." Maryann says.

"Wait, wouldn't you tell everyone?" Michelle asks.

"We will, and I have that email blast ready to go right as we post this to Sydney's YouTube channel. However, we don't want Harris to catch wind of it before we can post it."

Rob walks over to Sydney. "Okay, we're ready to get going. Let's get you mic'd up."

Sydney and Thomas give each other a warm smile as they take their places behind the kitchen island.

"Ready when you are Syd." Rob says.

"Hi Everyone! I would like to welcome you all to this very special edition of Living Life with Sydney. For many of us here in Massachusetts and around the country, this weekend is a wonderful three day holiday weekend. That also means that I will not be doing my usual Sunday blog. However, we are going to give you this bonus YouTube video to kick start your weekend. Many of you saw the article about me and the man I'm currently dating that was posted on a gossip blog that I shall not name. I thank you all for the wonderful comments and emails. They were greatly appreciated.

If I'm truly honest with all of you I was mortified when I saw the article. I had a hard time believing that someone would take pictures of me without my knowing. I felt, well, scared, that someone parked themselves outside of my home and took pictures. I wondered what kind of person feels so entitled to do such a thing and then post them on line for the world to see. My biggest concern; however, was Thomas. I know I'm in the public eye. But just because he and I are dating doesn't mean his life has to be as well.

I was very relieved when Thomas told me that he didn't care. With that said, let me introduce you to our guest, Mr. Thomas Peters, aka, Professor Hottie!"

Thomas leans in and gives Sydney a kiss on the cheek. "Thank you Sydney for having me today. I also want to thank the gossip blog that shall continue to go unnamed for giving me not only my fifteen minutes of fame, but now, the opportunity to show off my culinary skills on Living Life with Sydney!"

"Oh my gosh he's incredible." Maryann whispers to Michelle.

"So what are we cooking today Thomas?"

"Well, Sydney. We are cooking a simple yet flexible and flavorful dish. This is a dish that you can use as an appetizer for a crowd if you're heading to a football party or use as a nice dinner for two. Today we are making caramelized onion, black bean, and cheddar cheese quesadillas. And, I want to let the audience know that these are baked not fried, so they are a healthier version of a great comfort food. Speaking of which let's pre-heat the oven to 425 degrees."

"He's beyond incredible!" Michelle whispers to Maryann.

"Thomas they sound delicious. Where do we start?"

"Let's go." Thomas says as he rubs his hands together. "First of all I do want all of your viewers to know that this recipe can be changed to meet your individual tastes. You can add peppers, broccoli, or corn, but the key is the first part, caramelizing the onions. So here we have two medium onions cut in half and then sliced. Now if you prefer your onions chopped, be my guest and chop them up. Personally, onions really make my eyes water so the less chopping the better."

Jordan rolls his eyes as he watches Michelle and Maryann gush over Thomas. He's secretly hoping the food tastes awful.

"Sydney your audience should also know, I'm a guy, so I'm a bit of a lazy cook, I don't measure things. We are going to coat a frying pan with olive oil and start cooking these onions over medium heat, stirring occasionally until they become translucent. This should take about ten to fifteen minutes."

Thomas has Sydney cook the onions while he rinses out the black beans and lays four tortilla shells on two separate cookie sheets.

"The onions look to be done Thomas."

"Great. This is the best part. We need oregano, cumin and about one tablespoon of freshly squeezed lime juice. Now thoroughly coat your onions with the cumin." Thomas says as he holds his hand six inches above the onions and starts to sprinkle the cumin and then adds about a tablespoon of oregano. "Stir this up and continue to cook for about a minute and then turn off the heat and stir in the lime juice."

"This smells so good."

Thomas and Sydney assemble the quesadillas and place them in the oven. While they wait for the food to cook, Sydney asks Thomas some questions about himself so the audience can get to know him a bit. She asks about his favorite things to do in Boston and his hobbies. She has him describe what it was like to get his Ph.D.

"Okay so here is something I do with every guest we have on the show Thomas. It's the speed round of questions. I'm going to fire off the questions and you just say the first thing that comes to your mind. Are you ready?"

"Go for it."

"Food you could never live without?"

"Pizza."

"Sport you've always wanted to try?"

"Surfing."

"A place you've never been to but have always wanted to go?"

"Nantucket at Christmas. Well, technically I've been to Nantucket, just not at Christmas"

"A place you've never been to and never want to go?"

"Ah, prison."

Sydney tries to hold in her laughter. "Okay last one, what do women do that drives you crazy?"

"Well, I don't know about women but your smile drives me insane." Thomas says softly while staring into Sydney's eyes.

Sydney smiles sheepishly. She can feel her face getting flush.

"See right there, that smile." He says as he grabs a towel to take out the quesadillas.

"You got to admit that was kind of cheesy." Jordan whispers to Michelle.

"Are you kidding? That was so sweet."

"Well, your smile drives me insane." He whispers.

Michelle rolls her eyes and gives Jordan a nudge with her shoulder.

Thomas pulls the quesadillas out of the oven and expertly cuts one into six pieces. Using a fork he cuts a bite of one piece and feeds it to Sydney.

Sydney finishes chewing and turns toward the camera. "That's amazing! Well folks there you have it. You all now know a bit more about Professor Hottie. And trust me, he can cook. Thank you so much Thomas for being on the show with me today. Please viewers, we would love to hear your thoughts about today's show. Perhaps if we get enough feedback maybe we can convince Thomas to come on the show again. Enjoy your weekend and to your success in love and life!"

The cameras turn off and Sydney turns to Thomas. "You were incredible!"

"Well thank you. So were you. I had so much fun doing that."

Rob and Justin come over to congratulate Sydney and Thomas on a great show. "Dude you're a natural." Rob says.

"So when do you think the edit will be done?" Maryann asks Justin.

"Well since these two made so few errors, there's not a lot to do, just the captioning. I can probably have it to you by midnight."

"Lucky for me, my editor is a night owl! What do you think Maryann, post it first thing tomorrow morning?"

"Yes. That's great!"

Sydney turns to Thomas. "Don't worry I will not post anything until you watch it and approve it."

"I'm not worried. I am worried, however, about this food going to waste. Let's dig in shall we? We have avocado, salsa and sour cream here as well."

Everyone grabs plates and starts to eat. They groan with delight as they take bite after bite. While Sydney and Maryann go over the posting details, Thomas walks over to check in with Michelle and Jordan.

"Thomas, you were fantastic and this food is so good."

"Thanks Michelle."

"So, you can't surf?" Jordan asks.

"I've never tried but I want to. It looks like so much fun. Do you surf?"

"Well, I have a few times but not really."

"When have you surfed?" Michelle asks her husband.

"Remember when we went to the Jersey shore a few summers ago? I tried it then."

"Jordan, that was a video game at the beach arcade."

"Yeah, but it was the same idea. You still had to stand

on the board and make the right moves so you didn't wipe out."

Thomas laughs. "Well, maybe you and I should take a lesson together?"

Jordan sighs. "Yeah, that's probably never going to happen."

"Why?"

"He's afraid of sharks." Michelle pipes in.

"That does sound like an obstacle for surfing."

Jordan shrugs. "What can I say? I've always been more of a pool kind of guy."

"So what are you two doing this weekend?" Michelle asks.

"We are heading to my grandfather's place, just for Saturday night. I know Syd has a big week ahead of her."

"That sounds lovely."

"And on our way home on Sunday, Thomas is taking me apple picking. So, I was wondering if perhaps you two would like to come to my house on Monday for an apple-themed brunch?"

"We're in." Michelle and Jordon say in unison.

"But really, that sounds like a great trip. Where does your grandfather live?" Michelle asks.

"Northampton."

"That's your favorite town Syd!" Michelle says.

"It's perfect. And my grandfather is absolutely over the moon to see his former.. ah." Thomas stops himself mid-sentence.

Sydney gives Thomas a curious look. "Did you say former? Former what?"

"I meant famous YouTube star."

"No, you said 'his former' and then you stopped."

"Thanks Jordan. Ugh, I'm ruining the surprise." Thomas says in frustration.

"Syd hates surprises."

"Jordan, no I don't!"

"Okay, well, I do. What's the surprise?"

"No. Thomas don't say another word. I love surprises and I can't wait to meet your grandfather."

Caramelized Onion and Black Bean Quesadillas

2 medium onions sliced
1 can of reduced sodium black beans rinsed and drained
4 cups of sharp cheddar cheese, shredded. (Or shredded Mexican cheese)
1 tablespoon of oregano
1 tablespoon of fresh lime juice
Olive oil
Cumin
8 tortillas

Preheat oven to 425. Over medium heat sauté the onions in olive oil until they are translucent. (About 10 to 15 minutes).

Add oregano and thoroughly coat the onions with cumin. Cook for one minute. Remove from heat and add lime juice.

Lay out four tortillas on two cookie sheets. (Two to a sheet).

Spread the onions evenly around each tortilla. Add a layer of black beans. Add one cup of cheese. Be sure to spread the cheese to the edges of the tortilla. Place a second tortilla on top of the cheese.

Bake for 8 minutes. Check the tortillas after about 5 minutes. If the edges are getting too brown, cover with foil and continue to cook.

Cut into quarters and serve warm. Serve with salsa, avocado, and sour cream if desired.

24
One Step Closer

Friday Morning, Insightful Blogger Headquarters

Ben walks into the conference room to see Harris sitting by himself at the table. "Good Morning."

"Benjamin, where is everyone?"

"Relax Harris. We were here until nine last night. I told everyone they could come in at ten this morning."

"Oh. Did you see the post?"

"When you say post, I'm assuming you mean Sydney's video not the Washington Post."

Harris just gives Ben a confused look.

"Yes, Harris I saw her video."

"She's clever, Benjamin. That was well played. Did you see the amount of response she has received from it? Everyone loves those two and most are slamming us. She's stealing my thunder Benjamin."

"You did strike first Harris."

"No, Benjamin, we struck first. We did. We're in this together. I need a outstanding Ty Kent post for this weekend!" Harris says as he walks out of the conference room.

Ben flops down on a chair and let's out a big sigh. When Harris repeatedly used the term "we" it was like turning a knife into Ben's stomach. He is left asking himself the same question he's asked for over a year. *Why is he working for this blog?*

Ben broke up with Sydney so he could find passion and

romance. It's hard to find that when you are so passion-less about your own life. He's been on a few dates but finds the 'what do you do for a living' question to be incredibly daunting.

Watching the video of Sydney and Thomas was painful. She seemed so bright and happy. She was playful. He can't believe she did a show with someone she's dating. She never would have had Ben on the show. Of course he understands why she did it. It was a brilliant kick in the pants to the Insightful Blogger. He thought for sure she would just lose her temper and come to headquarters threatening a lawsuit. Ben wonders if he actually really knew Sydney at all.

"Oh my gosh!" Samantha says as she bursts into the conference room with Alex and Lisa following closely behind. "Did you see Sydney Graham's post?"

"Yes."

"And Professor Hottie was so dreamy!" Samantha says as she twirls around.

"Samantha, come on, that's Ben's ex-girlfriend." Lisa scolds.

"Yeah, but Ben broke up with Sydney, right Ben?" Alex says.

"I did."

"You did?" Samantha asks with questioning look on her face.

"I did."

Lisa is scrolling through her phone. "The positive comments she's getting are incredible. I mean they just keep being posted. And no one likes us. I'm sort of annoyed that everyone keeps referring to us as that 'gossip blog'."

"That's what we are Lisa." Alex says.

"We're an entertainment blog." Lisa corrects him and then goes back to her phone.

Listening to his team's conversation is simply reiterating to Ben that he needs a change and he needs it very soon. Ben watches as the team begins to organize themselves and review the findings thus far. They are the real reason Ben is still here. Or are they? Ben wonders if that is just the excuse he's been using because he's scared to actually go for a real writing job or better yet, write a book. Alex has the leadership skills and Samantha's writing has really grown. Even Lisa, minus her stalking behavior, has a great sense of what people want to read. Ben realizes he has absolutely been using them as a poor excuse to not make a change.

"What do you think Ben?"

"I'm sorry?"

Alex frowns. "What do you think about what Thomas said in the video, about Nantucket?"

"He wants to go to Nantucket at Christmas time." Ben says.

"Yes, but he said he has been just not at Christmas time. So do you think we can put an "X" next to Nantucket."

"Yeah. Sounds good."

"Yes!" Samantha says as she jumps out of her seat. "She got it!"

"Got what?" Alex asks.

"Okay so I have a friend who is still at Harvard and taking Professor Peters class. She saw him this morning and she got this!" Samantha shows her phone to the team.

"Nice! So she got a picture of the postcard string? Send that to me Samantha, I will blow it up and put it on the big screen in here." Alex says.

The team examines the postcards that have been blown up onto the conference room screen. They originally had eight towns that they were not certain Thomas had visited. They checked off Nantucket as he said he had been there in Sydney's YouTube video.

Alex recognizes a postcard that pictures the Flat Irons in Boulder so they put an "X" next to Boulder. They see another postcard that is clearly labeled "Vail" so they check off that city. They see a postcard of a famous taffy shop in York, Maine, so they check off York. They are now left with

Boring, Oregon; Miami, Florida; New Canaan, Connecticut; and Quebec City, Canada.

"We're so close!" Lisa says. "What's that picture of? It's like some sort of mural. We should be able to find that on the Internet somewhere."

"Look, I realize that we have narrowed things down a great deal. We still have four places to check in on. However, all of the locations of Ty Kent's books are not uncommon travel destinations, except perhaps Boring, Oregon and New Canaan, Connecticut. We need more. We need time frames here. And how are we going to do that?" Ben asks.

"Well, Ben, I don't agree. There are a lot of locations in New England, ten to be exact. That's almost half of his books. And, the other locations, all very easily accessed from Boston. I'm quite certain Ty Kent is located somewhere in New England. Yes, we need time frames. But I don't think we are too far off." Alex says.

Friday Evening

Sydney walks into Stephanie's on Newbury and sees Jordan and Michelle sitting in a booth in the bar area.

"Hi!" Sydney says as she scoots into the booth next to Michelle. "I'm so sorry, but I only have time for one drink. I have three hundred books to sign for the book launch and I'm doing it in small doses. This is technically my 'signing break'."

"No worries. It's Friday. We're all exhausted on a Friday. Although what's not exhausted is your YouTube video! Syd, that got so much love!" Michelle congratulates her friend.

"I know. I can't believe it. That's not true, I can believe it. Thomas was fantastic. What I love the most is how supportive everyone was about being unsupportive of the Insightful Blogger."

"That's not surprising it's such a trashy gossip site."

Michelle adds.

"Perhaps but they have a huge following. It's like everyone's guilty pleasure. And for advertisers it's all about the number of people visiting the site. I'm worried though. Harris doesn't like things turned around on him. Who knows what he's conjuring up now."

"Yeah but Syd, you didn't do anything wrong. You and Thomas just had fun with it."

"Yes however, we called his site a gossip blog in the video. Harris considers his site to be an entertainment blog. And, earlier in the week Maryann sent him two huge bouquets of flowers with a note that thanked him for bumping up my pre-sales."

"Ooh." Michelle says.

"Have you talked to Ben at all?"

"No Jordan. I haven't heard a word from him. You know he broke up with me to find passion and romance. Now he's doing is a story on my romance. For all I know, he is angry too and helping Harris conjure something up."

"I don't know Syd. I mean, no you two were not great together, however I don't see Ben as a vindictive guy."

"But he does work for the Insightful Blogger." Michelle says. "Let's not worry about what Harris may or may not do. Let's talk about this weekend! Are you excited?"

"I am. I can't wait to meet his grandfather he sounds like a great man. Thomas has been helping him restore this old Victorian. Having been through a massive renovation myself, I'm really excited to see it."

"Seriously, is there anything this guy can't do?"

"You heard him Jordan, he can't surf."

"No, he said he's never surfed Syd. I'm certain this guy can do anything he puts his mind to. And for the record, I'm now back to not liking him."

Sydney laughs at Jordan. "Well, do me a favor and pretend to like him on Monday. Speaking of which, I'm going to feed you really well and then put you to work. My top floor is covered with gift bags all waiting for a signed copy of my book."

"Then those better be darn good pancakes!"

"Jordan!" Michelle says as she reaches across the table and gives him a playful slap. "And, yeah, he's right, they better be good! Speaking of good, what do you think the surprise is?"

"I have no idea and it's killing me. Jordan, you were absolutely right, I hate surprises. I mean seriously, I've set my life up to purposely avoid surprises."

"Thomas was a surprise. And if I'm honest Syd, I really like who you are these days."

"What's that suppose to mean Michelle?"

"It's not bad. You've been my best friend for ten years. I love everything about you. I just mean, lately, well, you've been lighter, more whimsical, and very happy. And let me finish." Michelle says as she puts her hands up to signal Sydney not to interrupt. "You have had every second of every day, of every year planned out. And it has been great. You've had tremendous success because of your planning, focus, and hard work. I also know you experienced the worst surprise anyone could. To lose your parents in a car accident must have been horrific. But Thomas has been a great surprise. And you are experiencing life, not just work. I love seeing you this happy. As for Thomas, well, he's head over heals. I don't think he would give you anything but pleasant surprises."

"She's right Syd, that man is done."

"How do you know?"

"Because he looks at you the way I look at Michelle."

"Awe!" Michelle says as she grabs her husband's hand!

"Alright, break it up you two. I hear you Michelle and I will try my hardest to embrace surprises. But now I must go, and sign books until my hand hurts. I'll see you both Monday!" Sydney gives each of her friends a kiss on the cheek before she heads out the door.

As Sydney walks home she considers what Michelle said. Sydney knows she is controlling. She used to love surprises but ever since her parents' death she's hated them. She's structured her life so that she's in control of everything. And everything is just as it should be. Her parents' left her some money and she did not want to be frivolous with it. She wanted to make them proud by using the money to grow versus carelessly spending it. She has built a great business that she thinks they would be proud of. And she did this in their honor. Them being proud of her is all she's ever wanted.

She does recognize that since she's met Thomas, she's let go a bit. She also realizes how much that scares her. At the same time, Michelle is absolutely right, she's happier than she's ever been. And, she has a huge event coming up and all the while concerned about what Harris will do next. Being whimsical can also create problems, and she prays the problems will not be too big.

25
Surprises

Saturday Arrival, Thomas's Grandfather's Home

Sydney's mouth opens wide as Thomas turns into the driveway. The driveway is long and either side is lined with perfectly symmetric tall pine trees. You can tell by their height and girth that not only are they well-taken care of, they have guarded this driveway for a long time. The driveway ends in a big round circle that sits in front of a gorgeous and giant Victorian.

The home is all white and on either side of the home sits two large maple trees that are covered in bright orange leaves. The wide staircase leading up to the wrap-around-porch is tastefully decorated with pumpkins and large pots of mums in just about every color.

"Thomas, this house is spectacular!"

"Wait until you see the 'before' pictures. It originally looked like a house straight out of a horror film."

Sydney grabs Thomas's arm. "It's not haunted is it?"

Thomas smiles. "No, it's not haunted."

"You sure?"

"Fairly certain." He says as he grabs their bags and heads up the stairs.

Sydney cautiously follows Thomas up to the house. She is afraid of ghosts. She never watches horror films, as she won't sleep for weeks. There is a note on the front door from Thomas's grandfather letting them know he just went to the bakery and to make themselves at home.

Thomas opens the door and motions for Sydney to enter first. She is in awe as she walks into the foyer. The wide-pine floors are perfectly refurbished. Sydney thinks the two-level staircase that climbs up the left wall coupled with the high ceilings are just begging for a bride to walk down them. Thomas puts their suitcases down in the corner.

"Would you like a tour?"

"Would I ever!"

Thomas and Sydney tour the home. Sydney feels each room is more spectacular than the last. The old woodwork that Thomas and his grandfather painstakingly restored contrasts beautifully with the modern features found in the kitchen and bathrooms. As they begin to head up the stairs Thomas points out a picture of the house when his grandfather purchased it. He was right, it looked like it was straight out of a horror movie.

"I can't believe how much work you two have done. How long did this take you?"

"Well, we still are working on the third floor. But thus far, it's been about two years." He says as he grabs their bags and starts to make his way up the staircase.

"And your grandfather lives here alone? This is such a huge house."

"Well, he's is considering opening it up as a bed and breakfast."

"Oh, this would be perfect for a bed and breakfast!"

"Yes, but he's getting older and what concerns me is him doing it alone. It would be a lot of work."

"True."

Thomas walks into a corner bedroom that hosts a queen sized four-post bed. Sydney follows him wide-eyed. The room is huge and has a small seating area in front of a fireplace. Sydney's eyes move to the corner of the room, she sees a wooden desk and an old black typewriter. Sydney makes a beeline for it. She runs her hands over the keys and then presses down just to hear the "click."

"Wow!"

Thomas smiles. "I thought you might like that. That was one of my grandfather's old typewriters."

"Is this his room?"

"No, this is where you'll be staying. I'll be in the room to the left and my sister will be in the room to the right. That way we can protect you from any unwanted ghosts."

"Ha, ha. Wait, your sister is coming?"

"Oh, yeah, is that okay? She's dying to meet you."

"That's great! Did you just blow my surprise?"

"Nope. You actually hate surprises."

"No, Thomas, I love surprises."

Thomas cocks his head to one side signaling to Sydney he doesn't believe her.

Sydney covers her face with her hands. "Okay, I hate them!"

"Well, I think you're really going to like this one. Trust me."

Thomas reaches for Sydney's hand, he brings it up to his mouth and gently kisses it. He smiles and then leads her out of her temporary bedroom to continue the tour. She instantaneously forgets why she hates surprises.

Sydney and Thomas sit in the kitchen as they wait for his grandfather to return. Thomas makes a pot of coffee while Sydney flips through a photo album documenting the progression of the restoration.

"Hello, hello, hello." Thomas's grandfather calls out as they hear the front door close.

"Stay here." Thomas says to Sydney.

She does just that but jumps off the counter stool so she is standing to greet his grandfather.

"Is the famous Sydney Graham, actually in my house?"

Sydney recognizes the voice she hears, but she can't quite place it. Thomas and his grandfather walk into the kitchen.

"Sydney!" He says with his arms outstretched.

Sydney gasps and covers her mouth with her hands and then slowly moves her hands down to her heart. "Professor Kent!"

Saturday Afternoon, Insightful Blogger Headquarters

"Why not just throw it out there? We think Thomas Peters is Ty Kent and see what happens?" Samantha asks.

"Because we only have one shot at this. If we do that and he's not Ty Kent, game over." Alex says while never taking his eyes off his laptop.

"This is so frustrating! Who agreed to these stupid rules?"

"Harris." Ben and Alex say in unison.

Samantha paces back and forth in the front of the conference room. "Ugh! We are so close. Lisa, do you have anything?"

"I might."

Ben and Alex pick their heads up from their laptops.

"You might what?" Samantha says almost in a whisper.

"Just give me five minutes." Lisa says.

Samantha goes back to pacing and Ben and Alex focus their attention back to their laptops. After what feels like an hour to Samantha, Lisa finally asks Alex to dim the lights.

"This is so exciting!" Lisa says as she hooks her laptop up to the projector. She rubs her hands together. "Are you ready?"

"Yes!" They all say at once.

Lisa hits a button on her laptop and a photo splashes across the conference room screen.

"What are we looking at?" Alex asks.

"This is a photo of Thomas Peters at his graduation, after completing his Ph.D."

"And this means what?" Ben pries.

"Here." Lisa says as she taps a button on her laptop a

few times to zoom in. "Read the names."

"Kimberly Peters, Thomas Peters, Suzanne Peters, and…" Samantha stops.

"Theodore Kent." Alex finishes the listing of names.

"Theodore Kent!" Lisa shouts as jumps up and down. "Okay wait, there's more." Lisa fiddles with her laptop and puts up a picture with a biography. "May I introduce you to a retired English professor, formerly with the University of Massachusetts, Professor Theodore Young Kent! Aka the grandfather of Thomas Peters!"

The team sits in silence.

"What are you proposing here Lisa?" Ben asks.

"What do you mean?"

"Are you saying Thomas Peters is Ty Kent or that his grandfather, Theodore Young Kent is Ty Kent?" Ben asks.

Lisa stares at the screen. "I'm not really sure. I just thought this was the affirmation we needed that Thomas Peters is Ty Kent. I didn't consider the grandfather."

"Really, you never considered Theodore Young Kent as potentially being Ty Kent?"

"Samantha!" Ben scolds in an attempt to stop her from making further sarcastic comments.

"That would be too obvious, using your own name as a pen name." Alex says.

"Or would it be the most obvious name that he knew everyone would overlook and dismiss." Samantha challenges.

"What do you all have for me?" Harris says as he walks into the conference room. "We have a major Sunday blog to post. Let me have it!"

Alex quickly turns off the projector.

"We don't have anything yet Harris." Ben says.

"You must have something because Alex shut that projector off in a hurry."

"We are working on an hypothesis but there are still a lot of holes."

"And we have another potential glitch." Samantha

adds to Ben's comment.

"What are they?"

"Okay, Harris here's what we have. We can place Thomas Peters at the majority of places where Ty Kent's books take place. However, we have yet to compare the timing of his visits against the publication dates of the novels. We don't know how to get that information. And we are still unsure about whether or not he has been to all of the locations. Secondly, Lisa just discovered that Thomas Peters' grandfather is a retired English professor and his name happens to be Theodore Young Kent. Harris keep in mind, we just learned this information and that's all we know." Ben cautions.

"Alex, turn on the projector." Harris says.

The team watches as Harris carefully reads and re-reads Theodore Kent's biography. He examines the graduation photo and then asks Alex to go back to the biography. Harris begins to pace around the room. Samantha's frustration reaches her limit.

"Harris, why can't we take more than one guess?"

Harris turns and looks at Samantha. "Well, if I get the one guess wrong, they will confirm that I got it wrong by the way. If I, sorry, if we guess wrong then I'm obliged to donate the $150,000 to a charity of Ty Kent's choice."

"And what if someone guesses right, but wants to keep his name anonymous?" Alex asks.

"Well, then, I'm still out $150,000. In that scenario, I again have to donate the money to the charity of his choosing. The only way I'm not out of money is if we guess right."

"But I thought you said Green Publishing will never confirm you are right." Lisa says.

"That's my confirmation. If I don't have to donate, I, sorry, we got it right."

"Wait a second." Alex says, as he is completely confused. "So, if you get it wrong, you donate money. If someone gets it right, but keeps Ty Kent's identity anonymous, you donate money. If someone guess's right and exposes Ty Kent's identity, you give them the money. The only way you keep the money is for us to correctly identify Ty Kent, which will never publically be confirmed, but you'll know because you won't have to donate. And you can't say anything about being right, but you don't lose any money?"

"Exactly!" Harris says with pride.

"That is so mes…"

"Interesting!" Ben interrupts Alex before he can finish his sentence.

"Yeah, interesting." Alex mumbles.

"Wait, so we are doing all of this work and we don't even get to tell people that we figured it out?" Lisa asks.

"Well, we will tell people, we just can't confirm that it's accurate." Harris responds.

"Then what's the point?"

"What's the point? First of all, I'm not out $150,000. And secondly, winning. Winning is always the point, Samantha." Harris says as he continues to pace. "So what your telling me is that you have an inclination, without any proof?"

"Yes." Ben replies.

"Great, send me the information you have, the graduation picture and the biography on Theodore Kent. I'll write the blog post."

"Harris, what are you going to write?"

"I'm just going to write something that may perhaps lead people to make their own conclusions."

"Harris, I'm your editor, nothing gets posted unless I see it."

"That's true Benjamin, unless of course the owner is writing it." Harris says as he exits the conference room.

Ben was about to follow Harris and then decides against it. He turns around and sees his team just staring blankly at him.

"Listen, I know we all joke about Harris's poor writing

skills, but let's remember he did attend Harvard. He's a smart guy."

"Doesn't mean he can write." Alex quips.

"What do you suggest I do Alex? He's right, it's his blog, his company."

Alex shrugs.

"You know, there is a silver lining to all of this. It's Saturday and since Harris is going to write the blog, we all get to go home. And better yet, go home, turn off your phones, unplug, whatever, don't even think about Ty Kent or the Insightful Blogger."

Without speaking, the team members somberly pack up their things and exit the conference room. Ben leans back in a chair and sighs. He knows this is just one more sign telling him to get out. He wonders whom he could reach out to about job prospects. His thoughts switch to Sydney. He should do the right thing and at least give her a heads up that something might be coming out. On the other hand if he does warn her, all she'll do is worry about it. He doesn't know what Harris is going to write. He doesn't have that much to tell her. Except of course he could tell her everything they know.

"Ben."

Ben looks up to see Alex and Samantha standing in the doorway.

"Do you have a second?"

"Of course."

"Ben, we both really like working with you, and because of that we thought we should be completely honest with you." Alex says.

"Okay. What's going on?"

"Nothing yet. However, both Alex and I are actively looking for different jobs." Samantha adds.

Ben nods his head.

"And again, we love working with you Ben."

Ben puts up his hand to stop Samantha. "I don't need

an explanation. I get it. And please, let me know if I can help in any way. I'll give you both excellent recommendations and if I hear of anything that might be suitable for either of you, I'll be sure to let you know."

"Thanks Ben." They both say.

"Of course! Now get out of here and go enjoy your weekend!"

Ben was not surprised at all by the fact that Samantha and Alex are looking for new jobs. It was unexpected that they told him. He appreciates their honesty, but he was not surprised. Ben turns around and looks at the map on the wall. He can't tell Sydney what Harris will be writing but he can tell her everything he knows. One thing Ben is sure of is that Sydney Graham hates surprises. At the very least he can prevent her from being completely caught off guard.

Theodore Kent's Home

Sydney walks straight into Theodore Kent's outstretched arms. "I can't believe this."

Theodore hugs her tightly. "It's so very good to see you Sydney."

"Wow. Professor Kent this is crazy."

"Please, Sydney, call me Teddy."

"How about some coffee? You two have a lot of catching up to do and I probably have a bit of explaining to do." Thomas says.

The trio sits down at the kitchen table. Sydney gushes over the beautifully restored Victorian that is Teddy's home. Thomas explains that last weekend when the photos came out he showed the pictures to his grandfather and the connections were made.

"At that point, my grandfather demanded that I bring his all time favorite student to see him."

"It was more like a firm request." Teddy jests. "I have to say, I loved the little show you two did together."

"Wait, you saw the YouTube video?"

"I watch all of your videos Sydney. And I read all of your blogs as well. And books!"

"Books?" Thomas asks as he looks at Sydney.

"Well, book so far, I'm assuming you won't be a one hit wonder." Teddy says.

Sydney laughs. "Wait, how did you get my book?"

"I may have some very good friends in the publishing world."

"What, Grandpa, why didn't you tell me? I haven't even read Sydney's book yet."

Teddy shrugs his shoulders and gives Sydney a wink. Sydney smiles. She is so grateful to be sitting here with Thomas who she has adored for a few weeks and with Professor Kent, who she's adored for nearly two decades.

"Well, now your sister is going to be here in about an hour so we should get to work on dinner Thomas."

"Yes sir."

"May I help?"

"Of course! There's nothing more fun than cooking together. How about you start with chopping the carrots Sydney and we'll make Thomas chop the onions."

"I know what you're trying to do Grandpa."

Teddy smiles, leans over to Sydney and whispers. "He cries like a baby when he cuts onions."

After finishing Teddy's famous vegetarian chili and cleaning up, Sydney realizes it's been a few hours since she has checked her phone. She excuses herself and heads to her room to search for her phone. Although she has taken the weekend off and doesn't have any scheduled appointments, her clients know they can text her if they are really struggling. Sydney finds her phone and it's completely dead. She figures the universe is making sure she actually takes time off. She plugs it in and hears some voices coming from the driveway.

Sydney peers out the window and sees Thomas and Teddy greeting Kimberly with long hugs. They are all so happy to see each other. Sydney smiles. She feels joy, a bit of envy, and some sadness as she watches their reunion. She always wished she had a sibling, especially after her parents passed. Sydney turns from the window as the rush of sadness washes over her. She takes a deep breath and reminds herself to stay present and be grateful. *"Don't let the past spoil your beautiful present."* She thinks to herself.

"Sydney! Sydney!" She hears Teddy yelling her name from outside.

She heads to the window to see Teddy pointing at the back of Kimberly's car. He waves his leg underneath the bumper and the hatchback opens. He looks up to the window with a look of pure astonishment. He waves his leg under the car and the hatchback closes. He shakes his head in disbelief. And there you have Professor Kent. This brilliant man who has always found pure joy in the simplest things. That was always his gift, opening your eyes to things you take for granted and showing you just how incredible those things truly are. He's a true lover of life and wonder.

26
Fair Warning

Michelle and Jordan's Apartment

Michelle walks into the living room with her phone in her hand. "That was Ben. He's on his way over." Michelle stops as she hears their buzzer beep. "He's here now."

"Why?"

"I don't know he just said it was really important." Michelle says as she presses the button to unlock the front door.

Michelle opens her apartment door and gives Ben a hug. "Come in, please."

Jordan is standing behind Michelle and gives Ben a firm handshake. "May I get you anything? A beer?"

"Actually, Jordan, I'd love one. Thanks. And I'm really sorry to barge in on you two like this. I just, ah, well, I need some assistance."

"Let's have a seat in the living room." Michelle suggests.

"Have you both heard about this Ty Kent thing?"

"Yes.

"Well myself and three others were tasked with finding out Ty Kent's identity."

Jordan shakes his head. "So basically, you go to work everyday, look at the haystack and say, 'look out needle, here I come'?"

"Jordan!" Michelle scolds.

"No, he's right Michelle. And Jordan, I'd probably

have an easier time finding a needle. We did however come up with a lead. We were gathering evidence and then we found some more interesting information. But it is all conjecture, we don't have proof of anything."

"So what's the problem?" Michelle asks.

"Well, Harris took all of the information and is going to write what he thinks is a tantalizing post but in actuality it will be misleading and unsubstantiated."

"So, it will be like every thing else you all write."

"Jordan! Seriously, stop!" Michelle says as she shakes her head.

"I'm sorry Ben. I have a problem. When someone throws me softballs, I have to swing."

Ben laughs. "I get it."

"So who was the lead you were all following up on?" Michelle asks.

Ben goes on to explain all of the details leading up to today. He let's Jordan and Michelle know that Thomas Peters was their focus and that through the research they found out that his grandfather is Theodore Young Kent, a retired English Professor.

"Ben, that's actually intriguing." Jordan says.

"Yes, but we don't have any facts to back it up. And now Harris is going to write something that will probably suggest the possibility that either Thomas or his grandfather is Ty Kent. That could really disrupt their lives, albeit briefly."

"And Syd will be furious!" Michelle adds.

"I know and that's why I'm here. I'm wondering if you two know where she may be. I've tried to call her but her phone goes right to voicemail. I've texted but I haven't heard back from her."

"Are you planning on giving her a heads up?" Michelle asks.

"I plan on telling her everything."

"Aren't you worried that Harris might find out? I mean that could put your job in jeopardy." Jordan says.

"Well, if I had a job. I left my keys and my resignation letter on my desk. What used to be my desk. I can't do this anymore."

Michelle stands up and heads to the kitchen. She returns with her phone pressed against her ear. "Syd, this is Michelle. Call me as soon as possible. No one's hurt or anything but call me."

Michelle shrugs her shoulders. "I'll send her a text and then I guess we just wait. Maybe the reception is bad there."

"Where is she?" Ben asks.

"She's with Thomas, at his grandfather's place in Northampton."

"Oh my gosh! They must be at Theodore Kent's house. He was an English professor at the University of Massachusetts."

Teddy Kent's Home

Everyone sits down to eat Teddy's famous homemade vegetarian chili and cornbread. Teddy passes a basket of the cornbread. "Sydney, you have to try this it's homemade."

"Thank you." Sydney takes a bite and moans. "This is incredible! You made this?"

"No. But it's made at the home of the bakers. Good right?" Teddy says as he giggles.

"Grandpa, you crack yourself up." Kimberly jests. "Sydney, I have to say. I'm a super fan. I read and watch everything. So, if I get annoying with my questions, and I have a lot of them, please just tell me to stop at anytime."

"Fire away."

"What's your degree in? I can't find that anywhere and I'm just curious how you got started."

"Well, I have a degree in psychology and a minor in economics."

"Of course, your pragmatic approach to everything. That makes perfect sense." Kimberly says excitedly.

"I was very close to having minor in English. I had a very influential creative writing professor."

"Wait, you took Grandpa's class?"

"I took six of his classes. He really pushed me out of my comfort zone. I attribute a lot of my success to him." Sydney says as she looks at Teddy and he gives her a wink.

Teddy and Thomas share the post dinner clean up. Kimberly and Sydney sit at the kitchen table and Kimberly continues with her interrogation. Thomas and Sydney occasionally exchange smiles and adoring looks. Sydney could not be happier. This is what family is all about and she feels like she may have hit the jackpot.

When the kitchen is clean, they all retire to the family room for what Sydney learns is the official post meal activity, charades. Much to Kimberly's chagrin, Thomas places himself on the couch next to Sydney. He puts his hand on her knee and gives her a smile. Teddy enters the living room with pens, small pieces of paper, a hat, and an egg timer. Everything they need to get the game going.

"Okay, what are the teams going to look like?" Teddy asks.

"Guys against the girls!" Kimberly swiftly responds.

"Are you okay with that?" Thomas whispers to Sydney.

"Perfectly okay." She says with a smile.

Thomas and his grandfather have clearly been partners in this game before. Surprisingly though, new partners Sydney and Kimberly are keeping up. Sydney laughs every time someone guesses the correct answer, mostly because no matter which team got it write, Teddy is jumping up and down with excitement. This is family. This is called fun and this is what Sydney needs more of in her life.

"It's eight to eight everyone! We're down to the wire. Who needs a quick ten minute break?" Teddy asks.

"Oh, I do!" Sydney says as she realizes she plugged her phone in hours ago and forgot about it. It's been great not having her phone but she should just be sure she doesn't have any calls.

Sydney heads to her room and picks up her phone. She sees she has fourteen missed calls and ten text messages. They are all from Michelle and Ben. She immediately calls Michelle.

"Sydney! Are you okay?"

"I'm fine Michelle. Bigger question are you and Jordan okay? I have so many calls from you and Ben. I called you first!"

"Jordan's fine. We are all fine. Why haven't you been answering your phone?"

"It died. I plugged it in and forgot about it. What's going on?"

"Well Ben is here."

"Ben? Why is he at your house?"

"Um, perhaps I should let him explain that. May I put you on speaker phone?"

"Yes. Of course." Sydney says as she feels herself become more annoyed. If Ben is involved, it means the Insightful Blogger is involved. She's quite certain she's not going to like what she hears.

After hearing Ben's explanation of everything that has been going on at the Insightful Blogger and what Ben' thinks Harris may post, Sydney remains silent.

"Syd, are you okay?" Michelle asks.

"It's just ridiculous. I mean this family is so kind and wonderful. Why does Harris have to pick on them? And it's my fault. I'm the one who dove head first into this Ty Kent thing."

"Harris created this Syd, not you." Ben says.

"But if I had kept my mouth shut, Harris wouldn't care what I was doing and certainly wouldn't be trying to expose Thomas as someone he's not."

"That's not entirely true Syd. Samantha had Thomas as a professor. She's the one who suggested this hypothesis."

"I appreciate that Ben. However, right now I have to go

downstairs and tell this amazing family that they will probably have lies printed about them tomorrow.

Sydney takes a moment to center herself before she goes downstairs to deliver the news. She feels incredible guilty. She knows that Thomas was okay with the last stunt Harris pulled, but this could involve his grandfather. She's not sure he'll be so forgiving. And how will Teddy react to being thrown into the middle of this circus act? She looks out the window. It's a clear evening and the stars look like sparkling sequins spread out across the black sky. *Too bad wishing isn't an actual solution.* She thinks to herself.

Sydney walks into the living room to find Thomas, Kimberly, and Teddy laughing about something. Thomas looks up and sees her first. He stands up and slowly makes his way over to her. She can feel her eyes well up with tears as he makes his way closer.

"Sydney, what's wrong?" He asks as he wraps his arms around her and pulls her into him.

She feels so safe in his embrace that it makes her cry more. She's not used to being this vulnerable. She's also not used to having anyone hug her when she feels this way. Sydney pulls away in order to not lose her focus. Thomas reluctantly let's her go and Kimberly hands her a box of tissues.

"Let's sit." Kimberly suggests.

Sydney takes a seat on the couch next to Thomas. Kimberly and Teddy sit opposite them in big leather chairs. Teddy sits up and moves to the edge of his chair.

"What's this Harris fellow up to now, Sydney?" Teddy asks in the only serious tone he's used all day.

Sydney clears her throat. "Well, the team was exploring the possibility of Ty Kent actually being Thomas."

Kimberly bursts into laughter while Teddy tries to hide his smile.

"Wait, why are you two laughing? I'm an English Professor and I travel. It could be me." Thomas says in his own defense.

Teddy shakes his head. "Thomas, I think you're one of the most gifted writers. I've read your work, and I love it. I can safely say a romance novelist, you are not."

"Why are they focusing on Thomas?" Kimberly asks.

"For the reasons Thomas just pointed out. Apparently one of the team members took a number of your classes. They were analyzing all of the locations where Ty Kent's novels take place. She remembered you had some sort of wall of postcards or something."

"Yes, in my office I have postcards from everywhere I've traveled."

"So somehow they got a picture of your office and were trying to place you in all of the locations that would make sense with the timing of each book being published."

"That's actually clever." Teddy says.

"But one of Ty Kent's best selling books of all time took place in London and Thomas has never been to London. I would think that would have ruled him out right away." Kimberly adds.

"How do you know his books?" Thomas asks.

"I've read most of them. Sorry Sydney. I love the romance novels, but then everything you do keeps me grounded."

"That's actually why I do what I do Kimberly. I've read Ty Kent's books as well. There's more though." Sydney says as she looks up at Teddy. "While they were doing research on Thomas they discovered that Thomas's grandfather is the one and only Theodore Young Kent."

"Oh my gosh his initials! I never made that connection." Kimberly says as she flops back in the chair.

"Wait." Teddy says as she leaps out of his chair. "Are you saying I'm going to be a part of this scandal? That's so exciting!"

Sydney looks at Thomas confused. He just shrugs and smiles.

"So you all seem to be taking this well. Even though we don't know exactly what Harris is going to write, he's probably going to suggest that one of you is Ty Kent."

"It's so exciting. Someone may suggest that I'm Ty Kent. One of the most notable romance novelists of the last decade and a half." Teddy says.

"But, you are a romance novelist Grandpa." Kimberly adds.

"Not really. I wrote historical fiction that usually contained a love affair. My stories were not at all as romantic as Ty Kent's."

"You've read Ty Kent's books?" Thomas asks.

"Oh yes, every one of them. But Sydney, why does this upset you so much? This isn't your doing."

"I'm the one who got involved with all of this Ty Kent stuff and used it to sell more books. If Harris was just focusing on me and trying to make stuff up about me, I wouldn't care. I don't want this hurting any of you."

"Syd, how could a gossip blog hurt us?" Thomas asks.

"Well, it's a gossip blog with millions of viewers! What about your career?"

"My career is fine, Syd. And yes, he has millions of viewers, mostly because people need a break from the real news that's always depressing. The majority of people don't believe half the stuff they read online these days."

"Syd, you can't get caught up in other people's drama, just like you can't let your drama stir things up. You have to stick to the facts and make rational decisions from there."

"Are you quoting me Kimberly?"

Kimberly shrugs. "What can I say, I've learned from the best. Don't let your emotional mind make your decisions."

Sydney's phone buzzes. She sees an email from Ben. "So the person I know who works at, well used to work at the Insightful Blogger, just sent me all of the details that Harris has to work with."

"This is truly exciting." Teddy says.

Sydney scrolls through the email and then focuses in on something. "Wait, Thomas, Kimberly said you have never been to London. Yet look at this. Why is there a picture of London you your wall?"

Insightful Blogger Headquarters

Harris picks up his phone and sees nothing. He can't understand it. He has texted and called Ben, Lisa, Samantha, and Alex at least three times each. He looks at the clock that reads eight-thirty in the evening. It's Saturday and he did tell them that he was taking responsibility for writing the most waited upon Sunday blog post. The problem is he doesn't know what to write. Actually, he knows what to write he just doesn't know how to do it as enticingly as the team does. And he needs Ben to write the headline. He picks up his phone and sends a fourth group text message asking for some assistance.

Harris decides to take a walk around the office building to see if he can create a good headline. He thinks that if he starts with the headline that will encourage his writing and give it direction. He always hated writing, which is why he has a team of writers. Harris hears something in the distance. It sounds like a phone ringing. He follows the sound right to Ben's office.

Harris turns the handle but the office is locked. He digs out he's keys and opens the door. Harris flips on the light and sees a phone, a letter, and a set of keys.

He opens the envelope and reads:

Harris,

I quit.

Ben

Harris laughs. Ben does have a quirky, yet, sarcastic side to him. He understands Ben's point. Harris shouldn't have dismissed him as quickly as he did. He just didn't think Ben would have the guts to expose his ex-girlfriend's current boyfriend in the way that the Insightful Blogger likes to expose things. He'll iron it out with Ben on Monday. Perhaps he'll give Ben a raise. He deserves one after this rather humorous prank.

Harris is still chuckling about Ben's letter as he walks back to his office. He thinks about the points that Ben was pushing back about. One major issuing was timing and the second was that they couldn't place Thomas Peters in all of the locations. Harris quickly pulls out his phone.

"Harris, you've got to be kidding me?"

"John, my friend! How are you?"

"I'm great! Harris! How's life online?"

"Yeah, well, I little different than biking in the woods. Are you still in Boring."

"Sure am. Why would I ever leave these trails?"

"So, are you still in charge of maintaining the trail guest list?"

"You bet!"

"Any chance you could tell me if a Thomas Peters or Theodore Kent are in there anywhere?

"Sure I can. Just give me a second. I just came back from a ride."

"Oh, I'm so sorry. You can get back to me."

"No, stop it Harris. It's all right here on my laptop. Our famous guest book is now online. Well, you still sign in, but we put it all online. Okay, so Thomas Peters and Theodore. Yes, Thomas Peters, it looks like he was here back in 2000. Now, I don't have anything for Theodore."

"2000. John you are a life saver! Thank you my

friend."

"Sure thing Harris, and hey, we haven't seen you in forever. Come out for a ride!"

"Will do John! Take care."

Harris ends the call with John feeling more confident but knows he doesn't have all of the facts. His phone vibrates and he sees it's a text from Lisa. Harris reads the text and can't believe his eyes. He jumps in the air and then runs back to his office.

Teddy Kent's Home

"Well, I was on my way back from Paris and I had an eight-hour layover in London. I jumped in a cab and had the driver show me as many of the big sights as possible. When I got back to the airport, I grabbed a postcard of Big Ben because technically I did see it with my own eyes." Thomas confesses.

"It totally counts." Sydney says feeling a bit lighter after experiencing how little any of this seems to bother everyone. "Okay well they can't seem to place you in Boring, Oregon; New Canaan, Connecticut, Miami, Florida; or Quebec City, Canada. Have you been to any of those places?"

"I've been to Boring, Oregon and Quebec City. That's interesting they did not place me in Quebec. I have a post card of a rather famous mural from the old city."

"You've been to Boring, Oregon?" Sydney asks surprised.

"I was really into mountain biking in my younger years. One of my college roommates actually grew up there. I took a week one summer and went out there. It's truly beautiful. And really close to Portland."

"I know, that just so crazy."

"Wait, you've been there?" Kimberly asks.

"Yeah. I was taking a three-day advanced coaching course and it was held in Portland and I spent an extra few days out there. I wanted to go to Happy Valley, because I thought the name was so cool and then I realized right down the road was Boring. I wanted to be in both places on the same day. I know totally weird."

"Not weird at all, that sounds exactly like something Grandpa would do." Thomas says as he gives his grandfather a smile.

"I would absolutely want to do that. So much so that I've done exactly that!" Teddy says excitedly.

"So I'm the only one here who hasn't been to Boring?" Kimberly says a bit disappointed.

"When were you in Boring?" Thomas asks.

"Remember, right after I retired I was asked to teach for a semester for the graduate program at the University of Portland. When you are there you want to explore."

"Okay, back to the task at hand. So Thomas, you've never been to Miami or New Canaan?"

"Correct." Thomas says.

"Perfect. Then we have evidence to disprove their theory."

"What about Grandpa?" Kimberly asks. "He's been everywhere."

"Actually, I haven't been to Vail or Boulder."

Sydney looks at Ben's email. "How did you know those were on the list?"

"I'm a super fan of Ty Kent. I know all of the locations of every book."

Sydney feels a rush of emotion come over her. She didn't think her adoration of Professor Kent could be any stronger, until now.

"So we are all set. Whatever the Insightful Blogger posts we can disprove." Kimberly says.

"Yes. However, I'm always leery of Harris." Sydney replies.

"We got this Syd." Thomas says as he grabs a hold of her hand.

"How about some tea before we all go to bed?" Teddy asks.

Vegetarian Chili

1 medium onion chopped
2 cups of chopped carrots
2 green peppers chopped
Olive oil
4 tablespoons of chili powder
2 teaspoons of cayenne pepper
2 cans of diced tomatoes (I use unsalted)
2 jars of chili sauce
16 oz. of kidney beans, rinsed and drained
8 oz. black beans, rinsed and drained
8 oz. of chickpeas, rinsed and drained
2 ½ cups of frozen corn
Hot sauce

Lightly coat the bottom of a large stockpot with olive oil. Over medium heat sauté onions, about 5 minutes. Add carrots and green pepper and continue to cook for another 3 minutes. Add chili powder and cayenne pepper and continue to cook for 2 minutes.

Add tomatoes, beans, chili sauce and frozen corn. Add two teaspoons of hot sauce and bring to a boil, stirring occasionally. Reduce heat and simmer for about 30 minutes, stirring occasionally. If desired, add more hot sauce for a "hotter" chili.

Sprinkle with cheese and serve with corn bread or tortilla chips.

27
A Picture Does Not Lie

Teddy Kent's Home

Sydney wakes up and looks at the time. It's eight in the morning. She can't believe she slept in. The bed is magic. She is going to ask Teddy about the mattress and covers so she can replicate this in her own home. She picks up her phone and frowns at the amount of text messages she has. It's Sunday and she is quite certain she smells pancakes. Sydney really doesn't want to start her morning by sorting through all of these text messages. And then she sees one from Michelle that catches her eye.

Syd, are you okay? I'm so sorry. Call me!

She reads a second text from Maryann.

I'm sending a car to pick you up it will be there at eight-fifteen. Just please text me that you're okay. Harris is not a nice person!

Sydney's heart sinks as she reads Maryann's text. It must be bad if she sent a car. She hesitates for a second before going to the Insightful Blogger website. She closes her eyes and takes a deep breath. "You can handle whatever Harris throws at you." She says to herself. She opens her eyes. She inhales sharply. She stares at her phone. She was wrong. She can't handle it. Sydney walks over to a corner in the room, she sits on the floor and cries.

After about ten minutes of sobbing, Sydney hears a car pull up to the house. She slowly stands up and sees a black SUV sitting in the driveway. She smiles for a brief second as she knows that was Maryann's way of sending her some strength. Sydney heads to the bathroom washes her face and brushes her teeth. She changes into a pair of jeans and a sweater and shoves everything into her small suitcase. She takes one last look in the mirror and reminds herself that she needs to make a gracious exit.

Sydney quietly makes her way down the staircase and leaves her bag at the front door. She hears everyone in the kitchen. She takes a few deep breaths before continuing on.

"Well good morning sleepy girl." Thomas says as he stands up and begins to make his way towards Sydney.

Sydney quickly puts her hand up to signal him to stop.

"Syd, are you okay?" Kimberly asks.

"Yeah, fine." Sydney says with a forced smile. "Unfortunately, something has come up and I have to get back right away. Maryann, my publicist, has sent a car and it's here."

"I'll bring you back Syd." Thomas says.

"No. It's all set. You stay."

Sydney makes her way over to Teddy. "I can't thank you enough for absolutely everything." She gives Teddy a smile and a big hug.

"Kimberly, it was such a pleasure to get to know you." Sydney says as she gives her a hug.

"Thomas." Sydney says as she turns and walks towards the door.

Kimberly and Teddy give Thomas a confused look, as Thomas stands motionless.

"Go!" Kimberly firmly whispers.

As Thomas runs after Sydney, Kimberly pulls out her phone. "This has to be about the Insightful Blogger post." She says to her grandfather.

Kimberly pulls up the Insightful Blogger website. She gasps. She zooms in on the picture and then shows her phone to her grandfather.

"Oh dear!" Teddy says and then goes back to flipping

pancakes.

"Syd! Wait! Why are you leaving? What's going on?" Thomas asks as he stops her in the driveway.

"You tell me Thomas. Do you have anything you need to get off your chest?"

"What? No. What's this about?"

"So you have nothing to tell me?"

"No. Sydney?"

She reaches for her phone and pulls up the Insightful Blogger website. She hands the phone to Thomas. "Still nothing?"

Thomas takes the phone hesitantly, never looking away from Sydney. He looks at the picture. "Syd, I can explain, this is not what you think."

"A timed-stamped and dated photo of you kissing another woman, merely hours before you came to my house to do a video, is not what I think? You're right. It's what I see and evidently true."

"Syd, I can explain."

"Here's the thing Thomas, I don't need an explanation about why you kissed another woman. I should never have to have that explained to me, because it should never happen!"

Thomas feels his frustration growing. "Syd, I didn't kiss her."

Sydney swipes her phone from Thomas's hand. 'Really? Looks like kissing to me!" She yells as she hands her bags to the driver.

"Let me get this straight." Thomas begins with a louder tone. "You can get me and my entire family wrapped up in this Ty Kent mess. You have the time to explain everything and we understand. But you will not give me one second to say anything?"

"I never had to explain me kissing anyone!"

"No, Syd, you did not. However, other things had to be explained and many things were ignored."

"What exactly was ignored?"

"Oh, I don't know Syd, perhaps the fact that your ex-boyfriend is the editor of the Insightful Blogger. And isn't that kind of a coincidence that once we start dating, not only am I a person of interest but my grandfather is a person of interest as possibly being the elusive Ty Kent. How did they really come up with that connection Syd? My grandfather was your professor in college. You expect me to believe you that you didn't feed them any information?"

"Are you serious? That's your defense for kissing another woman?"

"I'm not defending anything. You won't listen to me. But we all listened to you. We all rallied around you last night. How did you know what Harris might have posted today?"

"You're joking?"

"No, I'm not."

"Ben quit his job and wanted to help. Unfortunately he can't help with the fact that you kissed another woman."

"This is absurd! Harris creates random stuff and now you are believing it." Thomas's frustration continues to grow.

"Harris does create random stuff, but he doesn't' create actual pictures Thomas. And I would have easily put a stop to anything regarding Ty Kent. But what I can't put a stop to is you kissing a girl!"

Thomas is so frustrated he doesn't even hear half of what Sydney is saying. "And how exactly would you put a stop to things Syd?"

"By telling the truth, Thomas." Sydney pauses. She's so angry and hurt she can't even think.

"What truth is that?"

Sydney stares at Thomas for a minute. She feels an odd sense of calm wash over her. "I am Ty Kent." She says quietly. She turns away and gets into the car.

28
A Quest for Redemption

Ben's Apartment

Ben sits on his couch with his laptop open resting on the coffee table. He can't believe his eyes. He did everything he could to prevent Sydney from being caught off guard. He's quite certain she's completely caught off guard. He had no idea Harris had a picture like this. Ben zooms in on the picture to see if he can detect any signs that the photo has been edited. He knows Harris will stop at nothing if he's going to get a good story out of it. Ben wonders how Harris even got this picture. "Lisa!" Ben says aloud.

Ben immediately picks up his phone to call Lisa. She doesn't answer so Ben leaves her a voicemail to meet him at the café in The Book Bag in one hour. He then sends her a text saying the same thing. He's hoping she's feeling guilty enough to show up.

Ben orders a coffee and then grabs a table by the window. He can't believe he ever had anything to do with the Insightful Blogger. It's anything but insightful. He hopes the fact that he worked there doesn't impede his chances at getting a real journalist job.

"Hi." Lisa says as she sits down.

"Hi."

"Ben before you say anything there's something I need to tell you." Lisa says as she slides an envelope across the table.

"What's this?"

"It's my resignation letter."

"Why?"

"I can't do this. I feel horrible."

"So you took the picture that Harris posted?"

"Yes, well, not exactly. I sent him this." Lisa says as she hands her phone to Ben. "He had me following Thomas and Sydney but I was just walking when I saw this."

"Lisa, come on. You live in Southie. You just happened to being going for a walk in Cambridge on the Harvard campus?"

Lisa shakes her head. "I'm taking two graduate classes at Harvard." She pulls out her student identification card to prove her honesty.

"Sorry."

"I deserve it."

"So this is what you sent Harris and then he clipped and printed that one photo."

"Yeah. But I took it and I sent it to Harris and I completely regret it."

"Will you text it to me please. And I can't accept your resignation."

"What? Why not."

"I quit yesterday."

"What about Samantha and Alex?"

"I'm going to meet with them later today. First I need to try and get in touch with Sydney."

"Ugh. I feel so awful. She must be devastated. I'm sorry Ben."

"I'm not the one you should apologize to."

Teddy Kent's Home

Thomas stands motionless as he watches the car drive away. He just wishes Sydney had listened to his explanation. He scolds himself for losing his temper and making matters worse. And how on earth could Sydney be Ty Kent?

Thomas shoves his hands in his pockets and slowly walks back into the house.

"She left?" Kimberly asks as Thomas enters the kitchen. Thomas nods.

Kimberly looks at her grandfather and he gives her a wink and motions his head towards the stairs. "Okay, I, um, think I'm going to go take a shower."

"I wasn't prepared for any of this. I don't even know what to do. Did you see the picture?" Thomas asks.

"I did."

"It's not the whole story Grandpa, I would never hurt Sydney like that."

"I know."

"She's an ex-girlfriend who I broke up with over a year ago. You remember Marie?"

Teddy nods.

"She used to follow me everywhere. She saw the pictures online of Sydney and me and I don't know. I guess she got jealous or thought we could get back together. I ran into her on campus and she started saying all this crazy stuff like how much she missed me and how much she has changed and then she just kissed me. What that photo doesn't show is me pushing her away." Thomas sits at a stool and puts his head down on the counter.

"Did you tell that to Sydney?"

"She wouldn't let me. Even if I did how can I prove it to her."

"She's hurt."

"She wouldn't even listen to me. I can't believe she wouldn't give me the opportunity to explain."

"Ha. If you saw a picture of Sydney kissing another man, how would you feel?"

"Ah, I don't know. I would be upset, but I have to think that I would let her explain."

"Perhaps. Do you think you'd believe her explanation when faced with a picture like that? She was too shocked and hurt to listen. She'll calm down."

"I don't know about that. I lost my cool. I said some things I shouldn't have said. And you know what, that's not the craziest thing that happened today."

Teddy nods his head. "She told you who she is?"

"Wait, you know?"

"That Sydney is Ty Kent, yes."

"How?"

"She was my student. And she was, or is, and exceptional writer. When her parents died, I watched Sydney go from being the smiling, energetic, young woman who lit up any room, to being ghost like. She was flat and lost all of her drive. She was in one of my creative writing classes at the time. It was small and very individualized. Each week I gave her an assignment that focused on finding joy, even in unlikely areas. She was seeing a therapist obviously, but I wanted to try and help her find her joy again."

Thomas is dumb-founded. "I had no idea you two were so close."

"Oh yes, she was one of my favorite students. She didn't have any other family, at least no one on this side of the country. We all rallied around her and she needed us to. And she is so strong. To pull herself out from under her grief, must have been very difficult." Teddy pours some more coffee for he and Thomas. "One day, at the end of her junior year, she handed me a short story. It was one of the most captivating love stories I had ever read. I've always thought that perhaps it was her version of her parents' love story."

"That's how she started writing romance novels."

"Yes I suppose. When school started back up I gave her my feedback and encouraged her to challenge herself and write a novel. What a book she wrote. She was afraid to seek publication as most authors are. However, she was also afraid that no one would take her work seriously if they knew it was written by a twenty-one year old girl."

"Hence the pen name." Thomas says. "Did you offer

her to use your name?"

"Oh no. I merely suggested the idea of using a pen name. Her first book came out a year after she graduated. Incredible."

"So, you don't mind that she's using your name?"

"Mind? I think it's the best compliment a writing teacher could ever get."

Thomas considers what his grandfather is telling him. He can't believe Sydney is Ty Kent. "Grandpa, did you put the money up to keep Ty Kent's identity a secret?"

Teddy's eyes light up and large grin spreads across his face. "I did!"

Thomas can't help but chuckle as he sees his grandfather's face light up. "Why though?"

"Well, first of all this Harris person seems quite mean to me and clearly I'm correct. Second, this is Sydney's first actual book launch, even though she has written twenty-four best selling books. I wanted her to be able to experience everything that goes along with that. I wanted her to do the book tour and media interviews and have a fabulous party. I wanted to try and help her do this as Sydney Graham, not Sydney Graham who everyone just found out is Ty Kent."

"Why do you think Sydney is a relationship coach and does all of these other things when she's done so well with her books?"

Teddy shrugs. "Only Sydney can answer that."

"I don't know if I can fix things with Sydney."

"Do you love her?"

Thomas considers his grandfather's question. "Yes, I do. In a very maddening sort of way."

Teddy laughs. "Then you will find a way to fix this.

Sydney's Home

Sydney walks into her home at eleven in the morning. She did nothing on the car ride home but stare out the window and hold back her tears. Her phone has been vibrating constantly. Other than texting Michelle and Maryann that she was okay and just wanted to be alone, she hasn't looked at her phone.

She drops her bags in her bedroom and heads up the stairs. She sits at her counter waiting for her coffee to brew. She keeps going over the events of the morning. She woke up so happy. As much as she tries, she can't seem to get the picture of Thomas kissing the woman out of her head. She wonders why he would do this. It really doesn't seem like him.

Sydney shakes her head a she pours some coffee. She thinks about how many times she has heard that line. How many of her clients have cried to her and said, "He just didn't seem like the type of guy who would do this." Not that it's always the man's fault. It just very much feels that way for Sydney right now. It's not even Harris's fault. If there wasn't a kiss, there wouldn't be a picture.

She feels the pressure in her chest and the tears beginning to form. She walks downstairs, crawls into bed, and cries.

Monday Morning

Sydney lies awake in bed. It's five o'clock in the morning. Except for a few trips to get water and use the bathroom she's been in her bed for nearly eighteen hours. She wills herself out of bed and looks in the mirror. Her eyes are puffy and blood shot from crying.

She continues to stare at her rather drab reflection. This is her week. The book launch and party are finally here. She puts her head down. She's been waiting for this day for so long. She can't let a man she's known for barely a month ruin this. She needs to focus, smile, and get on with her work and her life. She picks her head up and looks in the mirror and sees the same drab reflection. Clearly she's going to need to do more than just give herself a pep talk.

Sydney waits for her coffee to finish brewing. She knows she needs to run but it's too early and too dark to run outside. She pours a cup of coffee and decides to sign fifty books and then she'll head down to her gym and run on the treadmill. This is how she is going to have to operate for the time being. Just giving herself small achievable goals to accomplish.

Michelle and Jordan are shocked by the amazing scents they smell as they walk into Sydney's home.

"Has she been cooking?" Jordan whispers to Michelle as they walk up the stairs.

Michelle just shrugs her shoulders.

"Hey there!" Sydney says as she walks over to greet her friends.

"Hey Sydney. You seem in much better spirits than I expected." Michelle says a bit concerned by Sydney's cheerfulness.

"Well, I can't change what happened but I can change my attitude about it. Believe me, I cried all day and night. This morning I decided to put one foot in front of the other. I signed some books. I went for a long run and meditated."

"And cooked?" Jordan asks.

"Yes, I cooked. I have cinnamon apple pancakes warming in the oven. The bacon is all done, the coffee is hot, there is fruit salad on the table, and I even made home fries."

Jordan's eyes widen listening to all that Sydney has prepared. "What time did you get up?"

"Early. Let's eat while the food is still warm."

After eating too much and finishing the clean up, Jordan, Michelle, and Sydney fill up their coffee mugs and head upstairs to Sydney's entertainment area.

"Wow!" Jordan says as he sees the stacks of books and the gift bags lining the floor.

"I know, why do you think I made so much food? It was a total bribe."

"We can do this." Michelle says.

"It's not that bad. The signed books are on the couch and every bag needs a book, all three hundred of them."

Michelle's phone vibrates. Her face scrunches up as she reads a text message. "Syd, have you checked your phone?"

"No, it's plugged in downstairs why?"

"I think you should go get it. Ben says he's been trying to get a hold of you since last night and he has something really important for you."

"I don't think I want to know."

"Syd, as you know Ben was at our house on Saturday night. He just wants to do the right thing." Jordan adds.

Reluctantly Sydney gets up and heads down two flights of stairs to get her phone. She takes a deep breath before she unlocks the screen. She sees notifications for eighty-seven text messages, thirty missed calls, and fifteen voicemails. Sydney notices a text message from a number she doesn't recognize but the line that is showing catches her attention. It reads: "This is Teddy."

Sydney pauses. She is unsure if she wants to read the message. She's doing so well with her one foot in front of the other routine. She doesn't want to derail her progress and end up back in bed with a tear-stained pillow. But this is from Professor Kent. Where would she be if it were not for his guidance and faith? She opens the text message and reads:

"Sydney, have faith. What today feels like may be the exact opposite of what tomorrow brings! I'm so proud of you and can't wait to see you Thursday! Teddy."

Sydney sits on the side of her bed and looks up at the ceiling trying to keep the tears from flowing down. It's not just Thomas she is going to miss; it's his family too. Sydney reminds herself that she is here for a purpose. She needs to stay focused on one task at a time. Right now her task is finding out what Ben wants.

Ben left her three voicemails, each sounding more

desperate than the previous one. She reads his text messages that say nothing more than his voicemails did. "Please call me. Are you okay? I have something really important to show you." Not once does he mention what that "something is." She texts Ben that she is sorry for being absent and if he wants to come by now he is more than welcome.

Sydney heads back upstairs to sign books. She didn't even bother to look at any of the other texts or listen to any other voicemails. She's not ready to completely face reality. Sydney signs about seven books and the doorbell rings to her phone. She see's that it's Ben and lets him in.

"I should probably go downstairs and at least get him some coffee." Sydney says.

"I'll do it." Jordan says.

"Too late." Ben says as he reaches the top level of Sydney's home.

"How'd you get here so fast?" Sydney asks.

"Oh, I was at the coffee shop up the street."

"Do you need a warm up?" Sydney asks.

"All set. What's all this?"

"Signed books for the launch party."

"Well, may I at least get a copy? I mean, I was dating you while you wrote it."

Sydney smiles. Ben was very supportive of her work. "Of course. So what is this important thing you need to show me?"

Ben takes a seat in a chair in front of Sydney. "I hope you know I knew nothing about that picture. If I had, I would have told you and somehow I would've figured out a way to stop Harris. I'm embarrassed I ever worked there and I'm sorry."

"Thanks Ben. I know you would never do something like that."

Ben takes a deep breath. "I spent all of yesterday morning staring at that picture trying to figure out how Harris got the picture and if he had edited it in someway. And then I reached out to Lisa, the girl who snapped all of the photos of you and Thomas."

Sydney stands up. "She took that picture!"

Ben stands up and puts his hands in the air signaling Sydney to calm down. "No, she took a video." He reaches for his phone.

Sydney quickly shakes her head. "No, I don't want to see a video!"

"Syd, trust me. You want to see this." He says as he gently places his phone on the desk.

She covers her face with her hands and takes a few deep breaths. She hears Ben and trusts Ben, but she also knows that she will see Thomas kissing another woman. She only looked at the picture once and it is engraved in her brain.

"Syd." Ben says softly. "I know what you don't want to see, but I also know what you will want to see.

She reaches for his phone and watches the video. She watches it three more times before handing the phone to Michelle.

Jordan peers over Michelle's shoulder as she presses play. "What? This is great!" Michelle screams and jumps up and down. "He pushed her away Syd! He clearly wanted nothing to do with her."

"Yeah he looks pretty angry." Jordan adds.

"Why aren't you jumping for joy?" Michelle asks.

"I don't know. I mean, Ben, thank you. I'm very grateful for this. It's just been such a difficult emotional ride. Honestly, I don't know if I want to get back on."

"Syd, most of the craziness has been caused by Harris. That coupled with your first book coming out, sure there have been some bumps but..." Michelle is unsure of what to say next.

"Syd, I've seen all of the pictures and I've never seen you look so happy. And he's clearly crazy about you. That video of you two cooking together, your chemistry was electric. And mind you, this is coming from your ex-boyfriend. When I first saw the pictures of the two of you, I felt insanely jealous. And to be honest, I was jealous because I want to look at someone the way you look at him and have that person look at me with half as much adoration that Thomas has in his eyes when he looks at you."

Sydney feels her eyes welling up. "Stop Ben, you're going to make me cry and my eyes just got back to their normal size!"

Michelle, Jordan, and Ben all wrap their arms around Sydney. It's exactly what she needs. They may not be relatives, but they are her family, even Ben.

Teddy Kent's Home

Thomas brings his bag and Kimberly's bag out to their cars. Kimberly and Teddy are walking arm and arm close behind.

"There you go kid. All packed up." Thomas says.

"So when I get my Ph.D. like the two of you, is it then that you will stop calling me 'kid'?"

"Afraid not."

Kimberly gives her grandfather a hug. "Thanks Grandpa! I'm not sure if I can get back up here before Christmas."

"Wait, aren't you coming to Boston for Syd's launch?"

"Well, I was, but are we still invited?"

"Kimberly, I told you she doesn't know the whole story and I will fix this."

"How Thomas? It's going to take a bit more than just flowers. And Grandpa, are you still going?"

"Sydney is not mad at me. I wouldn't miss it!"

"I guess she's not mad at me since she gave me a hug good-bye. I'll be your date."

"How can I lose? Walking into Sydney's book launch with the most beautiful woman by my side." Teddy says as he kisses his granddaughter on the cheek.

"Again, I will fix this. We will all be there together to support Sydney. Is 'hope' a strategy?"

"No!" Teddy and Kimberly say in unison.

"Hope is not a strategy and flowers are cliché, perhaps now is the time when you should utilize your true talent, writing!" Teddy says.

"Talent! Grandpa you are a genius! I got this. I will see you both at the book launch." Thomas says as he hugs his grandfather and sister goodbye.

Insightful Blogger Headquarters

Harris walks into the conference room to find Lisa, Samantha, and Alex taking down everything they had hung on the walls.

"Good Morning! What's going on?"

"We're just cleaning up." Samantha says.

"Where's Ben?"

The trio just looks at Harris confused.

"Is he coming in?" Harris asks.

"He quit. He said he told you." Alex says.

"Really? I thought it was just a joke. Hmm. Well, I guess I need a new editor. How about you Alex, you up for the job?"

"Have you read your email today Harris?" Alex asks.

"No, why?"

"I resigned."

"Oh. Okay. How about you Samantha? Editor? I will give you a good raise."

Lisa feels the anger rising inside of her. She can't believe what an idiot she's been. She thought that if she did Harris's dirty work, it would actually pay off. But here he is offering the job to everyone but her. Samantha reaches over and squeezes Lisa's hand under the table.

"I resigned as well Harris."

"I guess I should read my email. I guess I need to post

a position."

"What about me Harris?" Lisa asks.

"Lisa, you are way too valuable. You are my number one investigative reporter. I need you in that position."

"Well, I guess you should read your email Harris, because I've resigned too."

"What? What's going on here?"

"Were done with destroying lives Harris." Alex says.

"That's not what we do. We make people happy by printing funny things."

"Goodbye Harris." Samantha says.

"Well, good luck trying to get a job when the only job you've ever had will not give you a recommendation!" Harris shouts at the trio as they leave the conference room.

Sydney's Home

"Okay that's it!" Sydney says as she closes the cover to the final book she had to sign.

"Yay!" Michelle says. "I know exactly what we need." Michelle heads downstairs.

A few minutes later Michelle comes up the stairs with a bottle of champagne and a tray of cheese and crackers.

"Where did this come from?" Syd asks.

"We brought it and I snuck in your refrigerator when you weren't looking. We need to celebrate. You've worked so hard for this and it's finally coming to fruition."

"Thank you!" She says clapping her hands.

"Oh, excuse me for one second everyone. I need to take this." Ben says as he puts his phone to his ear and walks downstairs.

"Do we need to wait?" Michelle asks.

"Yes!" Syd says firmly.

"So what are you going to do about Thomas?" Michelle asks.

"I don't know. He was upset when I refused to give

him the opportunity to explain. I was perhaps too firm about that."

"Syd, you just saw a picture that was devastating. I'm sure he'll understand why you were unable to hear an explanation at that moment."

"I don't know."

"How do you feel when you're around him?"

"I feel pure joy and everything good. I can't really explain it."

"Love?"

Sydney gives Michelle a smile.

Ben walks up the stairs apologizing. Michelle gives him a look and he stops talking.

"Let's all raise our glasses to Sydney, my best friend, and the most talented and generous woman on the planet. Congratulations!"

They all take a sip and then start gorging on the cheese and cracker plate.

"So what was the call about?" Sydney asks between bites.

"It was Alex. They all resigned today and it didn't go so well."

"Wait, all? Your whole team resigned?" Sydney asks.

"Yeah. Well technically, Lisa resigned first when I met with her yesterday. Then I had dinner with Alex and Samantha and they told me the same. Unfortunately, since I had already resigned they had to go in to give back their keys and laptops."

"Wow, that is quite an exodus." Jordan says.

"Yes, and Harris of course said they will never get a job and he will never give them a recommendation. So they are a bit panicked to say the least as this is the only job they have had since graduating from college."

"So Lisa resigned first?" Syd asks.

"Well, yes, after me. Look, I know she has caused you some trouble. But she was devastated when she saw what

Harris printed. She's truly remorseful. And I get it if you can't understand that. However, you know how manipulative Harris is. She's twenty-two and got sucked in."

"Syd, you know how bad bosses at a young age can make you do things you wouldn't normally do. Me being a case and point." Michelle says.

"Yeah, I remember. So you really think she's remorseful?"

"I do." Ben says.

Sydney sits back in her chair and thinks for a moment. "I have an idea Ben. May I meet with you and your team tomorrow for lunch?"

"Sure." Ben says not knowing where any of this is going but always knowing when Syd has an idea it usually works.

29
A Book Launch Party

"I can't believe this day is finally here." Sydney squeals as she walks up the steps of the Boston Public Library.

"Wait until you see the room. It's divine." Michelle says.

"Thanks so much for helping with the decorating."

"Of course. Now, before we head inside, have you spoken with Thomas?"

"Not exactly. I sent him a text asking him to come tonight. I also apologized for my behavior. He said he wanted to give me my space, but that he'll try to make it."

"He'll be here."

"I hope so. I really want him here."

"Hey, nothing deters from this moment okay." Michelle says as she squeezes Sydney's hand.

Sydney and Michelle enter the Guastavino Room and Michelle was absolutely correct. The room is breathtaking. The high round tabletops are covered in white linen. The centerpieces constructed of silver vases and pink tea roses are simple but give the right amount of color. Next to the columns that run down the middle of the room are large vases of pink roses and white lilies.

"Sydney! Maryann calls from across the room.

"Maryann, this is perfect. I'm so grateful for this and everything you've done."

Maryann takes a proud look around the room. "It came out great. I mean the room is gorgeous on its own. It's a great canvass to work with. And look at you Sydney, you look stunning."

"Thank you. Linda and everyone are all set with the numbers doubling?"

"Yes, that was quite the jump going from seventy-five to one hundred and fifty, but it has all come together."

"Wait, one hundred and fifty? Why did we fill three hundred bags?" Michelle asks.

"Trust me, they will all be gone. People always ask for an extra bag."

"So, now what? Just standing here is making me very nervous." Sydney says.

"The doors will open in about ten minutes so you will be doing a lot of hand shaking. The speeches will begin at six-thirty. I've planned for an hour as you requested. After that we just have some light mingling and we wrap up promptly at eight o'clock this evening."

"You make it sound so easy Maryann. Hey did Harris confirm?"

"He sure did."

"You're the best. Thank you!"

Sydney stands next to Maryann inside the room and about ten feet from the door. Maryann directed her to this spot in order to keep people flowing through the doorway and preventing a line from forming. After about twenty minutes of shaking hands and smiling with a number of people she does not know, Sydney sees Teddy and Kimberly. She's thrilled to see the two of them but her heart sinks a bit when she doesn't see Thomas with them.

"Sydney, you look divine." Teddy says as he wraps his arms around her.

"Simply beautiful." Kimberly says as she gives Sydney a kiss on the cheek.

"I'm so happy you are both here. Thank you." She wants to ask about Thomas but she knows now is not the time or the place.

"Syd." Maryann says as she points at her watch and

nods her head to the front of the room.

"Will you both excuse me, it looks like it's game time. I'll catch up after."

"Go get 'em Sydney. This is so exciting." Teddy says.

Sydney searches for Ben. Once she finds him she asks him to gather Alex, Samantha and Lisa and bring them to the front of the room. Sydney stands to the side of the stage while Maryann does the welcome speech. She scans the room and was not exactly happy, but more like satisfied to see that Harris has arrived.

A representative from Green Publishing takes the stand. Sydney can hear her speaking about books sales and how hard publishing is these days. She says some lovely things about Sydney, which Sydney doesn't pay much attention to. She's still focused on finding one person that she can't seem to find. And then Sydney hears her call. "Ladies and Gentlemen a big round of applause for Sydney Graham."

Sydney walks on to the stage smiling and waving. She gives the representative from Green Publishing a big hug and steps up to the microphone.

"Thank you. Thank you all so much for being here tonight it means the world to me. I would like to thank Green Publishing for without them, well, you all wouldn't be drinking free champagne." The room fills with laughter.

"I would also like to thank from the bottom of my heart, my publicist. You know this woman works tirelessly to make things happen. All of the pre-sale numbers are because of her efforts. I mean if you want to sell anything, well, you can't have her but I suggest you find someone just like her. A round of applause for Maryann Hannigan!" Sydney steps away from the podium and motions for Maryann to step on the stage and take a bow.

Sydney steps back up to the microphone. "I'm often asked why I decided to write this book. That answer is very simple. Not everyone can afford a coach and I wanted to provide the same kind of guidance that I give my clients at a more affordable price. Another question I am often asked is why I became a relationship coach in the first place. That one is a little more difficult answer.

I started to get numerous letters and emails from people who were quite frustrated with dating and their relationships. I quickly realized they were comparing their realities to fictional love stories. That was a problem. I felt a tremendous amount of guilt because my passion is writing love stories." Sydney pauses as she hears mumbling in the room.

"Yes, you heard me correctly. I took a bunch of courses and became a certified relationship coach. That was my solution and I love every minute of it. I can still write my love stories and I can help people have more grounded expectations about love. You see the letters and emails I was receiving were addressed to Ty Kent. I am Sydney Graham, relationship coach and I am Ty Kent, romance novelist."

The room goes silent after a universal gasp. Sydney doesn't start speaking again until she hears the people in the room beginning to whisper.

"I'm sure you all have some questions. I'm happy to answer them. But first let me explain why I used a pen name and why I used the one I did. I started writing because I had the most incredible creative writing professor. He pushed me and he encouraged me. I was scared that being twenty-one years of age, no one would take me seriously. However, my professor, triple dog-dared me to submit my first novel. By the way, I didn't even know what that meant but it sounded like a big challenge and what can I say I was twenty-one, I said yes." The room fills with laughter.

"What I didn't know at the time was that my professor, Theodore Kent, had a middle name which is Young. I chose my pen name as a tribute to the man who believed in me more than I believed in myself. Ty Kent stands for Thank you Kent. Ladies and gentlemen, a round of applause for Professor Kent." Sydney says as she motions her hand in Teddy's direction.

Everyone in the room turns towards Teddy as they clap, whistle, and cheer.

"I have one more item I would like to address." Sydney begins. "I'm sure most of you are aware of the interesting little competition that was started. Apparently, someone named Harris really wanted to know who I was. It's my understanding that if I identified myself before anyone guessed my identity, then Harris would have to donate $150,000 to the charity of my choice. Is that correct Harris?"

Harris stands stunned in the back of the room and nods.

"Great. Then I choose Unsung. This is a brand new start-up. It's a non-profit blog that focuses on doing beautiful pieces about agencies that are helping others. They will focus on the unsung companies and people whose mission and lives revolve around helping others. This will be a very exciting blog and if you have any questions about it, the team is here to answer them." Sydney signals for the team to come on the stage. "Please let me introduce you to the Unsung team, Ben, Samantha, Alex, and Lisa."

The room offers a powerful round of applause.

"In addition to Harris's generous donation, Green Publishing along with six other major companies have signed on for a year of advertising."

Again, loud cheers come from the audience.

"Thank you all for coming tonight. Enjoy the free champagne and enjoy the rest of the evening. To your success in love and life."

Sydney exited the stage to a huge round of applause. She went right to Maryann first and gave her a long hug. "I can't thank you enough Maryann."

"You did a great job Syd. I can't think of a better ending. Now stay with me for about five minutes. Let some of this crowd thin out or you will never get out of here."

After a few minutes, Sydney makes a beeline for

Kimberly and Teddy. Teddy greeted her with an even bigger hug than before.

"I'm so proud of you Sydney!"

"I couldn't have done any of this without you. Thank you for being the best teacher, motivator, and inspiration."

Kimberly joins in on their hugs. Reporters and bloggers surround the trio asking questions and wanting photographs. Sydney leans over to Teddy. "You know your going to be in the paper right?"

"Well I should hope so!"

At about five minutes to eight, Michelle and Jordan attempt to help Sydney out of the room. They exit the room and are greeted by the new Unsung team.

"Hey Syd." Ben says. "We're not going to keep you but we all just want to thank you for everything."

"Seriously? The thanks go to all of you. Together, we just gave Harris a good dose of his own medicine! Congratulations, and truly I can't wait to read the first story!" Sydney says as they share in a group hug.

As Sydney walks down the hall she hears her name called. She stops and turns to see Lisa running after her.

"Sydney. I'm sorry I know you're on your way out. I just want to say again how truly grateful I am for this opportunity. And how very sorry I am for everything I did."

"It's fine Lisa. Thank you. Listen bad bosses are a dime a dozen, but a good boss, well, when you find one, you pay attention. Ben's a great boss!"

Lisa smiles. "I know."

Sydney, Michelle, and Jordan finally make there way out of the library. Sydney begins to walk towards home and she realizes Michelle and Jordan are not by her side.

"Are you two coming?"

Michelle and Jordan smile as a limousine pulls up beside them.

"Seriously! We are four blocks from my house."

"This is your special night Syd!" Michelle says with a

smile.

"Wow! Thanks you two!"

They all climb into the car and Jordan pulls out a bottle of champagne. "I told the driver to take us on a little drive. We need to have at least one glass in the car."

"Why do you look sad Syd?" Michelle asks.

"I'm not. Or, I'm trying to not be. Thomas didn't show up. That's a bummer. I understand. We haven't had a chance to speak and person, so maybe the thought of showing up felt awkward."

"No, Syd. This is your night. If that guy can't figure out a way to get here, then, he's not your guy." Jordan says firmly.

"Jordan."

"No he's right Michelle. He's not my guy."

"A toast to you Syd, way to be so very brave." Jordan says.

"Thank you!"

"Now, on to another issue to discuss." Jordan says as he looks at his wife. "I was right."

"You were."

"No, you need to say it!"

"Jordan, you were right."

"Oh wait are you talking about the time when Jordan almost figured out I was Ty Kent?"

"Michelle, you told Syd?" Jordan says as he watches the looks that Michelle and Sydney exchange. "You knew! How long have you known?"

"About eight years." Michelle says.

"You've know Sydney was Ty Kent for eight years?"

"Sounds about right." Sydney says.

"Do you two know everything?"

"Pretty much." They say in unison.

The Limousine pulls up to Sydney's place and all three get out. Sydney suddenly feels an overwhelming emptiness.

"You two are coming up right?" Syd asks.

"Of course." Michelle says.

Sydney opens the door to her place and she notices something red.

"What's this?"

"No idea." Michelle says.

"Is this a red carpet?" Sydney asks as the trio makes their way up the stairs to Sydney's main floor. The red carpet then splits. It continues up the next flight of stairs and it also veers off into her formal living room.

"We're just going to go this way." Michelle says.

Sydney follows the carpet into her living room. She inhales sharply when she sees Thomas standing in her living room dressed in a tux. She feels the emotions of the evening and those of the present moment start to overwhelm her. She puts her hand over her mouth and begins to tear up. Thomas smiles.

Sydney gets a hold of her emotions. "What is this?"

"Let's wait and see. Shall we?" Thomas asks as he extends his hand to her.

They walk up the staircase to Sydney's third floor. The staircase is not only lined with red carpet, either side is lined with enlarged photos of her book covers. When they get to the top of the stairs she is greeted with, "Surprise!"

The room is full with her closest friends and colleagues, each holding a book. There are vases of red roses throughout the room and an entire team of people carrying trays of food and champagne. Lining the back of the room are more enlarged photos of her book covers. Sydney is overwhelmed.

"Will you all excuse me for one moment." Sydney says as she makes a beeline for her meditation room.

Thomas is worried that he has done the absolutely wrong thing. He knows Sydney hates surprises. He tries to go after her but Jordan stops him.

"Thomas, just give her a minute."

The room has become quiet and the guests just look at each other not knowing what to do. After ten uncomfortable minutes, Sydney opens the door and steps out of her meditation room.

"I apologize everyone. This is just a lot to take in." Sydney looks at Thomas. "And it is the most thoughtful thing anyone has ever done for me. Thank you Thomas. And thank you all so very much."

Teddy approaches Sydney with a book in hand, entitled <u>Love in the Berkshires</u>. The first book she ever wrote. "Will you do me the honor Syd, of signing my book?"

Sydney wipes away her tears and nods as she signs Teddy's book. Then one after another, in order of the publication dates, her friends continue to ask her to sign all of the books she's ever written, except for her last. Sydney hugs, kisses and thanks every person in the room. She scans the room for Thomas.

"I think he maybe out on the deck." Kimberly whispers.

Sydney heads out onto the deck to find Thomas, holding a book.

"Would you be so kind as to sign my book?"

"How did you do this?"

"I had a lot of help."

"Thank you. I missed you tonight."

"I was there!"

"You were?"

"Well, Kimberly face-timed me so I could see everything while I did all of this. You were incredible!"

"Thank you Thomas! But in this particular moment I think you are the incredible one."

"You know, I'm sorry Sydney, but, I've grown to like these fairy tales."

"Really? And what book do you have there?"

"Well, this is my favorite, <u>Paper Cuts</u>."

"Wow, who do you know? That hasn't even been released yet."

"I pulled some strings."

"So you like Ty Kent's work?"

Thomas steps closer and wraps one hand around Sydney's waist. He puts down the book and gently rubs her cheek. "Some may call me a super fan."

"What exactly does that mean?"

"This." Thomas says as puts both hands on her face and gently kisses her lips. He breaks away for a moment and looks directly in her eyes. "This, from now on." And then he kisses her with such passion she feels herself melting into him.

This is worth everything. Sydney thinks as she wraps her arms around Thomas.

#

In loving memory of John Hanlon and Thomas Stewart

Made in the USA
Middletown, DE
28 April 2019